WORKING THE ANGLES

by Max Willi Fischer

www.historiumpress.com

www.thehistoricalfictioncompany.com/hp-authors

www.maxwilli.weebly.com

Cover design by White Rabbit Arts at
The Historical Fiction Company

EBOOK ISBN: 978-1-964700-81-6
PAPERBACK ISBN: 978-1-964700-82-3

Published by Historium Press 2026
USA / UK

"Not everything that is faced can be changed, but nothing can be changed until it is faced." – James Baldwin, American writer and Civil Rights activist

TABLE OF CONTENTS

Introduction

In February of 1933, about a month before the inauguration of Franklin Delano Roosevelt as President of the United States, my great uncle Willi, who had emigrated to Akron, Ohio, from Germany in 1930, wrote a letter to my father. My father was eighteen at the time and still in Germany. It was the height of the Great Depression, the worst economic disaster this nation has ever experienced. A portion of that letter read as follows:

> *I've been reading the newspapers, and it seems that Germany is doing poorly, and there seems to be no chance of improvement; on the contrary, Hitler wants war again and the whole world seems to be screaming for it. Hopefully, you'll be spared that, and Hitler will break his neck soon, otherwise he'll bring to fruition that which we all don't want. Here in America, there is trouble brewing, everywhere riots because unemployment just keeps getting worse and there's no support system. Every day, you read about unrest in the cities; murders and homicides are part of everyday life. It's not a good sign. It seems as if a revolution could erupt any day now. I am glad that I moved out of the big city of Akron,*

Big changes were on the way, and there was a palpable fear of the rise of communism. Although Roosevelt had initiated various government-sponsored work programs and the safety net of Social Security by the middle of the decade, there were those Americans who viewed FDR as a communist because of those programs. The United States simmered with conflicting political ideologies in the 1930's—fascism, communism, nationalism, unionism. Even as Roosevelt won reelection by a landslide, as of 1937 some Americans, led by Charles Lindbergh, had a favorable view of Adolph Hitler. Fascism, dictatorial rule promising efficient government at the cost of individual freedoms, was advocated by those who held white nationalist beliefs of racial superiority. Meanwhile, Father Charles Coughlin, a Roman Catholic radio priest, was the most listened to personality of the decade. He railed against capitalism and socialism while blaming Jews and communists for all of America's problems. While not illegal at the time, communism was endeared by some as a chance at leveling the economic playing field for all while being despised by many for the excesses of violence and oppression in Bolshevik Russia.

Working the Angles tells the story of the late 30's in Akron through the lens of recent high school graduate, Deet Jenkins. While still not completely out of the grips of the depression, Akron's rubber industry flourished enough at that time to keep a fair portion of its workers employed as the majority of the nation's tire and rubber goods production was located there. The stench of the rubber factories proclaimed *the smell of money*. Rubber factories worked round the clock, and the city virtually didn't sleep while crime never took a holiday. A December 19, 1936, edition of *The New Yorker* featured an unflattering expose about Akron—*Uneasy City*. In it, a former mayor was quoted as saying federal agents, who came to town to "arrest everyone in sight", called the Rubber Capital of the World America's toughest city.

The characters in W*orking the Angles* are completely fictitious, but the backdrop of the times and the social issues people like Deet Jenkins, Theo Dixon, and Lacey Frazier faced, as well as many of the episodes, are based upon the historical record.

Chapter 1

Akron, Ohio

June 1937

Only ten minutes into factory life, lanky eighteen-year-old Dietrich, *Deet*, Jenkins' ears were ringing from a clatter that rattled his brain as if he'd been knocked on his ass during a football game. The boy felt like Jonah in the belly of a mechanized whale. Under a roof greater than several football fields in either direction, with numerous milling machines producing wide belts of rubber ply for tires, snaking down several hundred feet conveyors, talking to a co-worker in Plant One was accomplished by yelling.

"You fill the bucket with the rubber." The Negro, introduced to Deet only as Dixon, shouted as he took small bundles of raw rubber, about the size of a small sofa pillow, from a holding rack and filled the rolling dumping cart to its rim before pulling it along a bed of steel rollers. Sweat poured off his face like the beads of water on a brown beer bottle upon its removal from the ice box on a hot summer's day. "Now listen, Traveler, this is important."

Deet wanted to interrupt but didn't.

"When your cart rolls down to the scale, it's got to be within a half-pound of the marked weight, or it'll throw off the mixture of carbon black and oil that's already been preset." He raised his voice to another octave. "If you forget to weigh your cart, or if your cart isn't weighed correctly, you'll be warned. A second time, you're gone." He made a fist with an outstretched thumb and pointed it behind him.

Dixon grabbed Deet's shoulder. "You might get fired, but I'll get docked for not training you right, Traveler." The Black man's eyes narrowed. "So don't screw it up!"

Deet had known a couple Negroes at Central, and they'd been good joes. This tall Black man with a wide nose seemed unreasonably irritable. "Why do you keep calling me *Traveler*? My name's Deet. If you don't like the sound of that, call me Jenkins."

"Listen, in the past nine years, I've trained and shipped out dozens of white boys—wet behind the ears, right out of high school, more muscle than brains, but still getting paid more than my fifty cents an hour—just like you from this mill room to the house of royalty upstairs where they became tire makers. I'm supposed to be grateful that I'm not stuck outside as a yard worker, digging up frozen water lines in January or swabbing out vulcanizer heater pits in August. Compared to my sentence, you won't be here long. That's why I call you Traveler . . . the name I've called every trainee for the past seven years."

"Hey, boy!" Harley Kershaw, the burly line inspector who paired Deet with Dixon fifteen minutes earlier, interrupted the two.

"Yes, sir." Deet snapped to attention.

"No, not you kid." Kershaw shook his near bald head with a smirk that puffed one cheek.

"Dixon, you've been here long enough to know it's not a bullshitting session . . . unless you got a hankerin' for yard work." The sly half-smile deflated one cheek while it edged itself towards the other.

Dixon's eyes dropped to the black powder covering the floor. "No, sir, I don't. Just getting young Jenkins—"

"Mister Dixon was making a point to me about getting the weight of each cart just right so's not to mess up the compound. I wouldn't want to get fired on my first day on the job, Mister Kershaw."

"Mister Dixon, huh?" Kershaw's fleshy face fell a bit and the bristles on top of his head popped up before he coughed out a chuckle. "Try to make the point with less words and more work."

"Yes, sir." Dixon stood erect and spoke with eyes still cast downward.

After Kershaw continued on with his rounds of the other machine crews, the Black millworker headed back to the scale. "Jenkins," he called out with a stern face, "look at your cart. What's wrong with it?"

The teen wiped his hands on his old undershirt, already blackened by the carbon black dust spewing out of his machine. "It's over by two pounds. I guess I need to take some out."

"Here." The experienced worker reached behind him and took a small machete off a table. "For small adjustments, we cut a chunk off one of the bundles until the weight is good."

With little effort, Deet sliced a healthy corner off one of the cubed pieces of rubber. The scale registered its approval, and he pushed the cart down the line toward the mixer infusing the carbon black and oil into the rubber.

"Just because you had my back with Kershaw," Dixon faced the mixer as he raised his voice above the roar of the machines, "don't make us buddy-buddy. Understand?"

"Yeah, I get it," Deet yelled back.

"It does get you a piece of advice. There's a good number of paid snitches in this plant. Be careful what you say and to who you say it. Consolidated has big ears."

"Thanks, I'll remem—"

"Ah-e-e-e-e!" A hideous scream pierced the screeching wheels of the carts and the rumblings of the compound mixers. The mill next to them—the rolling conveyor that kneaded the compounded rubber like bread dough into a taffy-like consistency—sat in silence, replaced by the agonizing torment of a worker.

"What'd I do? What'd I do?" Another man of the south, whose voice gave away his origin, stood in a panic while his partner lay up to his right forearm in between the steel rollers, blood spurting out, flooding the black crumbles of rubber still stuck to them.

"Shit!" Dixon shouted as he pushed the alarm button near the machine, activating an incessant, high-pitched bell ringing. "Jenkins grab that spud bar!" The Black man pointed to a six-foot iron bar with a flattened end propped up against a tool table. From another location, the veteran gum miner got another bar. "Stick the flat end between the rollers on your side while I do the same on this side. Carver," he spoke to the injured man's co-worker, "pull Simpkins out gently once the rollers separate."

"Somebody get a clean rag or shirt, something that can be torn easily." Dixon jammed the bar's end in between the rollers as Deet did likewise. "Ready, Jenkins? Now!"

Carver pulled the unconscious man from the machine with the skin torn off his hand, mangled half-way up his wrist, with blood draining from the fingertips.

At the sight of the injury, Carver lost his lunch just as Kershaw and another supervisor arrived on the scene, spewing what looked to be a partially digested hot dog onto the foreman's black boots. "What the hel-l-l?" the hillbilly boss cried out.

Deet turned away from the sight of the gruesome injury but somehow managed to keep his stomach anchored.

"Give me that shirt." Focused on Simpkins, Dixon took a clean white undershirt from a worker, ripped it apart at the seam, and tied it around the upper arm of the injured man as a tourniquet. He put the man in a sitting position on the floor with his mashed limb strapped to a table leg above his head. "He must have tried to pull his hand out at the last second, and it made it worse."

"Who put you in charge, boy?" Kershaw wiped the vomit off his boot with a greasy rag. "Negra, you think you're a doctor or what?" With a wide grin, he elbowed the supervisor next to him.

"No, sir. I've just seen it happen too often down here in the years I've been here. Call it *on-the-job training*."

"Oh yeah, well, if Simpkins here doesn't pull through, we'll know who to blame."

Within minutes an ambulance crew came by and placed Simpkins on a stretcher to carry him out, but not before the lead attendant spoke to Kershaw with words everyone in the area could hear since the mills were still down. "Whoever put the tourniquet on that man's arm and strapped it in that upward position should be commended. He kept the man from bleeding out."

"That would be Mister Dixon I take it, Kershaw." The other supervisor sucked in his cheeks as he loosened his dark blue tie from its white collar, as he continued talking to the foreman. "Go get a couple Squad members to take over on this machine."

Turning towards Dixon and the teen, the geometry of his face shifted into a broad smile. "Mister Dixon, I'm Nate Benson, Plant One's night shift manager, and for Consolidated and myself, I want to thank you for what you did in saving Mister Simpkins' life." He held out his hand.

Deet watched as Dixon hesitated before extending his own hand. "The boy helped me get him out of the rollers," he said with a nod of his head.

Benson shot out his hand to Deet in turn. "And your name, young man?"

"Deet . . . Deet Jenkins." The boy's fingers felt decades of calluses on Benson's hand, reddened just like his father's from years of tire building.

"By any chance, Arch's boy?" Benson's arms were akimbo, and his face beamed.

"Yes, sir."

Benson patted Deet's shoulder. "You're going to make a great living inside these brick walls. Again, thank you, both."

"Oh, yeah," Dixon muttered as the two headed back to their machine. "You be a *Traveler* alright."

****

Deet hesitated as he breathed the rain-cooled air with a hint of his mother's roses from the dining room window. Rarely had he appreciated their delicate scent, let alone any floral fragrance. After a week's work at Consolidated, he treasured any smell that took his mind off his job. Since it was Sunday, the city's burnt rubber stink— as if a good portion of Summit County lay smack dab in the cavity of a gigantic smoldering tire—had subsided enough to allow space for natural aromas.

"Dietrich," his mother called from the adjacent kitchen. "Would you bring me the cake platter?" She named her eldest after her father, but everyone else in his life knew the teen as *Deet*—his preference.

"Alright! I'm coming." He lowered the sash of the window as if it were a guillotine, almost breaking the glass when it hit the sill. Less than two weeks after graduation from Central High, and he already missed it.

All ten of his fingers clutched the cut-glass cake platter as he strode into the kitchen. A crackling voice seeped out of the table radio on the far counter near the ice box. The broadcaster's speech reminded him of his grade school principal. With machine-like precision, the school leader's lips always ejected every word with perfect diction, even when he held his dreaded, perforated *board of education*. While his ears reddened as he seethed within because of Deet's foolishness, the schoolmaster would cock his head a bit as his compressed lips forced a grimaced smile. For a few fleeting moments, Deet's school days raced through his mind—from a kindergarten train ride to the paddling for splashing mud on Sally Newton's dress to his game- winning homerun against South, which won the city championship. The innocent times were over, and real work had begun a week earlier . . . the first of a lifelong sentence of drudgery at Consolidated.

"Hey, Deet." His father popped up from behind the basement door. "Come join me and Louie for a Burger on the porch." Arch Jenkins detoured his path long enough to grab his wife, Trudi, by her shoulders and kiss the nape of her neck, which was hidden by a gathered bun of her dark brown hair.

"Sure," the teen said as he gave the chocolate crumb-covered platter to his mother, who ignored her husband's advances.

"Thank you, Dietrich." Having emigrated to this country as a child at the turn of century, she still kept a slight German accent. She tilted an ear towards the voice of the determined presenter coming out of the wooden Motorola.

And in the meantime, the epidemic of sit-down strikeism has gone over America. Residents are silenced . . . congresses are silenced . . . while this industrial revolution bids fair to cause a constellation of evil to the most level-minded man. Where will it end? No one knows.

"Bullshit, Father Coughlin." Arch spoke from within the ice box as he poked around for three bottles of Burger beer.

"Archie, Father Coughlin is good people." Trudi's face soured as she cocked her head and waited until he backed out of the ice box. "You should listen to him."

"No, thanks." Arch walked into the foyer on his way to the enclosed front porch. "The good father should talk about godly religion and keep his nose out of politics, labor relations, and everything else about which *he knows nothing.*"

"Why should I be surprised?" Trudi threw her dish rag into the sink, water splashing out wetting her apron as her anger flared. "Since when do you listen to anyone but yourself!"

The kitchen became quite cold at that moment. The radio preacher's words evaporated into nothingness as Trudi stormed ahead of her son and up the stairs while Deet followed behind his father, who was already on the porch. The boy stopped in the front doorway, as Jimmy Dorsey's clarinet music danced down from his brother's second floor bedroom, blending with his mother's stomping up the creaky stairway. He hated to see his mother upset, and he knew someone other than Father Coughlin stirred this pot.

"Ricky, either clean this pigsty you call a room today, or tomorrow I will put most of this *Schies* out with the trash." A slammed door punctuated his mother's order.

His father, a man with a medium, but rugged build, shrugged his shoulders and smiled at Louie, his brother, who sat on a dilapidated sleeper sofa on the enclosed front porch. Deet's eyes caught the neck of a small liquor bottle popping out of his uncle's back trouser pocket just as Arch plopped down next to his brother.

"Did you get your URW card at the union hall like I told you?" Arch took a swig of beer. "I don't want someone coming up to me during second shift telling me about how you got thrown out on your ass for some piddly infraction and you having no backup."

Deet took a few steps and looked out the glass-paned porch door and onto Laird Street across the narrow tree lawn just below. With light but steady rain falling, the hum of a gray Ford Deluxe coupe's tires over the brick surface of the road accompanied the occasional splash and *thump* in the street's sunken divots. The sound of rolling tires, an everyday occurrence, took on added significance in the past week.

"Well, did ya?" An annoyed Arch asked.

"What?"

"Wake up, boy!" This time Arch covered his frustration with a laugh. "Old Jenkokov would have boxed our ears with his cuffed hand if either one of us would have been so daft." Arch smiled at Louie as he referred to his father, Ivan Jenkokov, who'd emigrated to Akron in the 1880's. "Did you join the United Rubber Workers union *after your first pay* like I told you?"

"Oh, yeah I did." Deet fished out his smudged card to show his father. Aware of the Jenkokov name, he never paid much attention to the family history of people who only existed in old photographs.

"Good. That could save your ass someday." Arch handed the card back to his son.

"No game today, Deet?" Louie asked as he took a sip of beer from the brown bottle. He was five years younger than his brother, but intermittent streaks of gray already highlighted his combed back brown hair.

Deet turned away from his father and uncle and stared at the darkened water flowing into a storm drain across the street. The first rain in a week cleansed the accumulated soot from everything that stood above ground.

"Hey, Deet," Arch barked. "Louie asked you a question."

"Oh, sorry, Uncle Louie." Still standing by the screen door, the boy's eyes widened as if he just regained consciousness. "I was daydreaming. Mind repeating it?"

"No game today?"

The curly-haired teen shook his head as he downed a mouthful of the weak beer. The state only allowed minors the privilege of 3.2 alcohol, but it still tasted good, even if it just signified a mile marker of age toward adulthood. "Coach Simmons called right before you came and said all the Legion games in the city had been called because of the rain."

"Tell 'em 'bout that call, Deet." Squirming back and forth on the sun-bleached, flowery pattern of the sofa, his father cracked up. "Old lady Dingus, geez!"

Louie gave a weak smile, which barely stretched the heavy stubble on his face, and looked toward his nephew.

"Oh," Deet smirked. "Just as Simmons started to talk, Missus Dingus picked up on her phone." He mimicked the old woman, holding his left fist with thumb and pinkie finger extended. *Hello, is this Keller's Pharmacy?* Both Coach and me are trying to explain to her that the call wasn't for her, but she kept yakin' about some suppositories she needed. Simmons gave up, told me about the cancellation and hung up. What a screwball."

Louie bobbed his head once and cracked a smile, allowing a look at his dingy yellow teeth. "Damn party lines. Everybody gets into everyone else's business." He reached behind him and dug out the liquor before taking a swig. "I got four other houses on mine." He took another nip. "Makes running a business a pain in the ass."

"We got three other parties on ours." Arch grabbed the neck of his bottle with his gnarled fingers to take another sip. "You got a phone in your shop and your house don't you, Louie?"

"Yep, one phone in each building but the same line and the same number of other folks meddling in my business. Wasn't as bad when Betty . . . was around." The puffy bags under his eyes appeared to weigh down the rest of his ruddy face.

Deet didn't remember much about Aunt Betty since she divorced his uncle when he was just a tike. Yet seeing Louie put the brakes on his line of conversation convinced the boy that his uncle still missed her to some degree.

Louie renewed his rant. "You know how pissed I get having to get off my creeper in the middle of an oil change because the phone is ringing? I mean it could be a customer or could be a doctor's office calling old man Maddox about his constipation problem."

Deet grinned as his old man snorted beer through his nose, and the three of them shared some heaving laughs at Arch's expense.

"Next game?" After a prolonged recovery from Arch's hysterics, the words creeped out of Louie's mouth as his eyes seemed to swell behind his dark rimmed spectacles.

"Wednesday night at 6."

"I know you could whiff at least eight guys with just half your stuff, Deet . . ." Arch interrupted himself as he clutched the neck of his bottle as it rested on a sheet of paper atop a crude, wooden side table. "This being your second week at Consolidated, you might want to ask Simmons to just put you in the field and pitch you only in relief. Don't just focus on the sixty cents an hour you'll be making at Consolidated."

Deet zeroed in on his father's bandaged, cracked fingers. The heel of his palm was as callused as a turtle shell.

That hand could never throw a fastball, let alone a curve.

"I think I'll be alright, Dad. Besides, it didn't seem to bother me last Wednesday."

"Ok but remember—." Arch started to take a final swallow from his bottle when he noticed the paper. "What's this?" He picked it up and tilted his head from one side to the other, holding the paper at a distance with his extended arm. "This looks pretty nice. Take a look, Louie."

"Thanks," Deet said.

Louie looked at the drawing of the neighborhood, which—despite the watermark of the bottom of the beer bottle—depicted bold, sharp lines and angles of the roof lines, utility poles and wires, windows, sidewalk, and brick-paved street while the lightly shaded trees, bushes, and grass seemed to be ghostly images. "You should be an artist, Deet."

"Just a hobby, Uncle Louie, just a hobby."

Arch picked up where he'd left off. "As I was saying, even though it's the grave digger shift, that mill room is no place to catch shuteye".

Deet rolled his eyes. "Don't have to worry about that, Dad. I got that lesson loud and clear on my first night."

Chapter 2

Cleveland, Ohio

June 1937

The lake breeze blew through seventeen-year-old Hugo Geller's dark, wavy hair, but he barely noticed it. The last day of his junior year at West High ended in unexpected ecstasy. Months of feeding nuggets of information to his classmates at last produced some interest, at least someone willing to engage him about his beloved beliefs. In blond-haired, blue-eyed Mary Ellen Schneider, he'd not only gained a potential political confidant but a beautiful one at that.

Walking down Franklin Boulevard towards their home neighborhoods in this industrial district on the west side of Cleveland, Mary Ellen clasped her hand around his. "I really appreciate a guy who's passionate about his beliefs, Hugo. I know you've taken some hard ribbing from some of the screwballs at West, but you've never backed down."

For some time, Hugo had accepted his role as a square peg in the circular cliques at West. He'd zig when everyone else zagged, ignoring football, basketball, and baseball in favor of playing soccer at German American rec fields on the weekends. Although handsome, he rarely dated while preferring symphonies to swing jazz, or *Jew music,* as his father put it.

The touch of her hand jump-started a tingling from his groin to his brain and momentarily jumbled his view of America's future. He'd experienced these primal urges before but never over discussing his world view. "Geez, Mary Ellen, thank you. I'm glad that I found at least one person who sees the value in America following Germany's lead in stopping the communist menace." He stopped there on the sidewalk and took her other hand as a steady stream of traffic spewed its exhaust alongside them. "This country is meant for people *like us.*"

"Like us?" Mary Ellen tipped her head to one side and sucked him in with her sky-blue eyes.

I could drown in those pools and never want to be rescued.

Engrossed in his dream world, he stood in awkward silence for several seconds as his face turned to gelatin. "I mean . . . like us— good, white, *American* Christians." His face hardened with sincerity.

"Oh, Hugo." The blond curls dangled from her temples, hiding her ears, as she pulled him close to her and kissed him.

A few cars honked their approval as she held him by the shoulders buckling his knees. He hadn't kissed a girl in over six months, not since after a dance late last fall when he felt obligated to kiss homely Betty Warren goodnight. That had been a charitable chore at the end of an arranged date by his parents, but this . . . this was a full-blown honey cooler. Hugo's lips stayed for the duration until Mary Ellen called a truce. "Wow, I mean . . . mean, I'm surprised at your interest, Mary Ellen."

"Hey, I have an idea!" An ear-to-ear smile lit up her flushed face. "Let's go over to St. John's for a dip in its therapy pool."

Woo-woo! Woo-woo! A locomotive's blast from the tracks behind the nearby refinery interrupted Mary Ellen's impulsiveness as diesel fumes wafted in the air about them.

"The hospital?" Hugo coughed, further handicapping a mind which never worked well with spontaneity.

"Come on, Hugo." Mary Ellen pulled him by the hand toward the West 80th intersection. "My mom's a part-time nurse there, and I know of an outside entrance door to the pool that's never locked. I also have a good idea that it's empty on Friday afternoons."

"What will we use for bathing suits?"

"Who needs a suit?" Her nose scrunched together as they both giggled.

Everything about the availability of the pool turned out just as Mary Ellen predicted. Hugo eased himself into the water, the scent of chlorine stirring his nostrils, as full immersion acclimated his body to the tepid water. Wiping the chlorinated prickle out of his eyes, he was glad his boxers remained tight around his waist. Before Mary Ellen entered the women's locker room at the far end of the pool, they'd agreed to at least keep their undergarments on, just in case.

Now, he eagerly kept watch at the far end of the pool, awaiting her arrival. A good swimmer, he extended his arms, cupping his hands, as he cut through the water. With each stroke allowing him to ride on top of the water, the more he appreciated today's good fortune and wondered what future bliss between the two might bring. It only took a few seconds to cover the fifty-foot length of the pool, but it took much longer to overcome the shock of seeing a fully clad Mary Ellen standing at the entrance to the locker room bending over in gut-rolling laughter.

From the opposite end of the natatorium, a familiar voice of a classmate tormentor yelled out, "Crummie Hitler-heiler!" as an exit door shut with an echoing *thud*. By the time he turned around again, Mary Ellen had vanished.

Heartache and shame raged emotional warfare within as he discovered all his clothes, including his shoes, had been swiped.

****

Frederich—*Fred*—Geller, stood by a darkly varnished secretary with a poster advertising tonight's German American Bund Rally perched above it. A Bund member in uniform clung to an American flag while a three-dimensional Nazi swastika rose just below it as if reaching for the star-spangled banner. A plumber by trade, he had fought for the Fatherland in the Great War before emigrating to the states in the early twenties. Now, Germany's impressive rise under Hitler filled him with pride, and he became an ardent member of the German American Bund upon its inception a year ago.

"Let's not have any foolishness like you got yourself into a few days ago." Hugo's father pronounced each word in precise German, the only language spoken under the Geller's roof. His long fingers straightened the knot on the boy's black tie before securing it with the gold-colored tie clip to his khaki shirt just above the diagonal, leather belt—a Sam Browne belt—which ran over his shoulder to the black belt around his waist. "You won't be running with the jackals who tricked you into that pool. These are solid, good people—merchants, tradesmen, attorneys, . . . even doctors.

"It is fortunate that the officer found you before you wandered beyond the hospital grounds and brought you directly home in his police car. Word of this could have damaged our standing in the Bund. You might have been stripped of tonight's honor."

Fred inhaled and shot a stern glare towards his only child. "You're not like your cousins down in Akron and that uncouth American father of theirs." He pointed toward the poster. "You almost let the Bund down . . . and Herr Hitler . . . and me. It was only because of the pity that the officer took on you that we were spared great embarrassment. Hugo, you are of German ancestry. *No one* should ever have to pity you."

"It will never happen again, Father." Hugo admired his father and looked him straight in the eyes. A man who worked with his hands and dirtied himself almost every hour on his job for his family, Fred Geller cleaned up nicely, believed in discipline, and doing things the right way, not necessarily the easy way.

"Aren't you ready yet?" The voice of Hugo's mother climbed the stairs. "Frederich, you know the two of you need to drive across town. You're going to be late."

Fred gently clapped his son's cheek with the palm of his hand. "I believe you, my son, I truly do." He turned toward a mirror and made sure the pleats in his pants were sharp, and he adjusted the special belt with the leather cup, which would cradle the base of the pole of the Nazi flag he would carry leading the Bund procession into the auditorium.

Their arrival, along with that of other Bund members, didn't go unnoticed.

"Nazi swine!"

"Bastards!"

Dozens upon dozens of protesters milled about the sidewalks, overflowing onto the paved street as they shouted at the Bund procession entering through the wrought iron gates of the mansion on Euclid Avenue. To Hugo, their simultaneously hurled insults reminded him of the yipping hyenas often shown in the various Tarzan movies.

With his father holding the swastika flag next to the red, white, and blue American flag held by another member, pride and angst churned as one in Hugo's stomach. In brown shirts with black pants, boots, and their own Sam Browne belts strapped over their shoulders, fifty stormtroopers followed behind the flags from the sidewalk down the concrete drive to an auditorium behind the house. He stood with five other teens in their Hitler Youth attire upon the front porch of the three-story manor on *Millionaires' Row*. The luxurious house, built in the 1890's, had recently been renovated with the addition of a large, brick hall behind it.

Hugo faced significant schoolyard teasing and pranks in the past year-and-a-half over his staunch support for Adolf Hitler's Germany, but nothing like what presented itself in the street beyond the iron fence and a jagged line of dark police uniforms. Crazed fury warped each face as screams in English and German replaced the mechanical clatter of usual late afternoon traffic.

"Murderers!"

"Sie sind verrückt!"

Several protestors broke through the police line and clung to the black iron fence atop a low brick wall.

How could true Germans be against us? How could they think father and I and the other Bund members were crazy?

Volksbund jugend, marsch! The order was given for the boys to march single file off the porch, down the terrace, which ran parallel to the fence and street, and turn left on the driveway toward the auditorium.

"Baby killers!" Not more than five feet away from Hugo, a woman in a pinkish-white dress bellowed as loud as a taxi driver in a traffic jam before a policeman pulled her off the vertical iron.

"Go back to your concentration camps, you blood suckers!" A man in a shirt and tie tried to breach the low wall and attached fence only to be wrestled to the ground by officers.

Outwardly, Hugo maintained a disciplined pace down the concrete path, pivoting sharply at the driveway away from the street. While the taunts and slurs faded with each step closer to the auditorium, inside his chest beat as if he'd just finished a soccer game.

****

"Heil Hitler! Heil America!" Rising from their wooden chairs, Hugo and several hundred Bund members gave the stiff-armed Nazi salute as the meeting came to an end.

He mingled about, making small talk with his peers when his father tapped him on the shoulder. "Hugo, there are several people who would like to meet you." He extended his left arm in order to guide his son towards the dais where the national and Cleveland Bund leaders smiled as they spoke among themselves.

"Herr Kuhn," Fred spoke with pride, "this is my son Hugo."

Kuhn, a large man with dark hair and eyebrows and a prominent triangular nose, beamed from ear to ear and offered his hand. "A pleasure to meet you, young man."

Even as Hugo offered a firm shake, Kuhn's bear paw swallowed the boy's hand. "The pleasure is much greater for me, sir. I've heard so much about you." To the boy, the national head of the German American Bund looked larger than life while being framed on either side of him with the Nazi flag and a photo of Adolf Hitler hanging down from the ceiling.

"And Hugo, this is Herr Schmidt, leader of Cleveland's chapter of the Bund." With his black side cap firmly in place, Kuhn bowed his head in homage to his local host.

"Your father tells us you are very eager to work for the cause." Schmidt, a stocky man with a receding hair line, shot Hugo a wide grin as he, too, shook his hand. "Enthusiasm will take you far, Hugo."

"I wish I could do a better job in getting my message across to my classmates." Upon seeing his father's lips tighten, Hugo wished he hadn't opened that door.

"Not to worry, Hugo." Kuhn chuckled and swept his extended arm back towards the banners, where a portrait of George Washington and the American flag hung to the right of Hitler's image. "As I mentioned in my speech, the swastika and the Stars and Stripes will blend together in proper time. It can't be forcibly rushed. However, when democracy's clay feet give way in the face of communism, Americans will flock to us . . . to you, my dear Hugo." The imposing Kuhn pressed the tip of his forefinger on the boy's chest.

"Besides, young master Geller," Schmidt joined in, "there are already roles for young people such as yourself. For instance, Bund Camp next month at the Central Farm in Parma. We can use older boys such as you as squadron leaders."

Fred beamed. "My wife and I have already registered Hugo for the camp, and he was recently notified that he would be a squad leader."

"Excellent!" Kuhn's eyes danced as he placed his meaty hand on the boy's shoulder. "Remember, your time . . . *our time* . . . will come soon."

Glowing from their interaction with the Bund's hierarchy, father and son mixed with the small talk in the crowd for the next hour. For Hugo, the evening couldn't have gone better—he kept his focus in the midst of screaming protestors, and he was introduced to important members of what would become the future leadership of the nation. The sour coating of last week's embarrassment had been cleansed—or so he thought.

Because of limited parking at the auditorium, Fred had parked his car a block down on Euclid Avenue. By the time he and Hugo left the auditorium, only a few vehicles remained in the hall's parking lot. At eleven o'clock and free of police and deranged demonstrators, the street tempted Hugo to be his personal, paved boardwalk under the artificial golden haze of periodic streetlights. After a short stroll down the sidewalk, the two oversized headlamps of his father's Chevrolet were within less than a dozen strides.

"This whole evening makes me look forward even more to next month's camp leadership experience."

"*Ja*, perhaps that will lead to more opportunities—"

"You Nazi bastards!" A man wearing a fedora lurched out from behind a line of hedges, his hand held high.

Hugo saw an object in the man's hand and pushed his father out of the way as the stranger's arm came down. The weight of the object, or perhaps the alcohol the boy could smell, caused the attacker to lose his balance, and he stumbled. Meanwhile, something hard gave a glancing blow to the boy's shoulder before he righted himself.

Crack!

From the sound of it hitting the sidewalk, the object must have had the mass of a brick or rock. As the pool prank and other peer-related indignities reared their ugliness in his consciousness, Hugo took vengeance against the attacker in the shadows of the hedges. Even though no one ever considered him a brawler, the teen let his right fist release his pent-up venom as he pummeled the stranger about the head and mouth. Straddling him and holding the man by the scruff of his shirt, Hugo pounded blow after blow into his face until his knuckles were raw and warmed with the blood of his assailant.

"Hugo! No more, that's enough!" Someone grabbed his right hand, so it couldn't land another punch.

Dazed and heaving in tears, the boy looked to his left where his father, having been knocked aside by his son, was just regaining his feet. Hugo turned. "*Herr* Schmidt?"

"You can't kill him, Hugo, even though from the looks of that brick," Schmidt pointed a few feet up the sidewalk, "he'd have it coming." The Bund leader turned towards Hugo's father. "Fred, are you alright?"

"I believe so." He rubbed the back of his head as he repositioned his side cap. "I must have hit my head on the sidewalk when the boy pushed me out of the way."

"The two of you need to get in your car and go home." Schmidt knelt next to the bloodied man and held his wrist. "He's still alive . . . barely."

Hugo wiped the tears from his face while his insides twisted at the reality of his rage, and his face began to tremble.

"We will wait with you, *Herr* Schmidt until the authorities arrive." Fred stood erect as if at military attention.

"Unless you want the three of us to undress to our underwear, which will pose a different problem, you need to go. The Bund doesn't need such publicity." Schmidt motioned with the fingers of both hands to his uniform. "I will make sure to get an ambulance here. The two of you go . . . now."

"Come, son." Fred was already opening the door to the brown 1930 Chevrolet sedan.

Hugo took a step toward the vehicle when Schmidt latched onto his arm and handed him a clean handkerchief. Getting close enough that the boy could smell the tobacco on his breath, the Nazi leader added, "The Bund needs *men* like you. I won't forget."

Chapter 3

Akron

June 1937

❝ Well, as far as I'm concerned," Lacey Frazier, Deet's off and on girlfriend, said, "Simmon's decision to fake a bunt to draw in the third baseman and have the runner on second steal third . . . that was the key to you guys winning today." She sipped on a chocolate malt as the foursome, including Deet's brother and his date, sat in a corner booth of Bob's Diner on East Market, a half dozen blocks down from the Consolidated plants. A bunch of the younger Consolidated workers knew about Bob's because he never served slugburgers, so they knew their dime was paying for all beef and no stale bread.

Deet doodled, or so it seemed, on a napkin, using a short pencil. Every now and then, he nodded.

"Well, that led to the game-winning run with a sacrifice fly, but . . ." Ricky, Deet's sixteen-year-old brother, gave a wry smile, which stretched just a few of his freckles. "But, let's face it, Deet's complete game shutout might have had something to do with it."

Deet looked at Lacey seated next to him, tightened his lips, and gave an *I told you so* smile.

Wearing a blue ball cap, an old Legion jersey, which masked her torso, and shorts, Lacey put an index finger and thumb to the side of her head. "Well . . . that might have helped . . . a bit." Her laughter started a chain reaction around the booth.

"Knucklehead." With a gentle underhand swipe, Deet knocked the cap off her head exposing her wavy bob hairstyle, popularized by the movie actress, Greta Garbo. Her ample light brown hair swept over both sides of her head, hiding one eye. Then he showed her and the others a precise diagram of a ball diamond and the play she just described.

She laughed and planted a kiss on his cheek. Known as a tomboy with a plain Jane face and oversized clothes throughout her high school days, she never stood out as a female to be pursued. A year ahead of Deet at Central, she lured him to her small apartment last fall on the pretext of showing him some valuable baseball trading cards. Apparently, she ended up schooling him in another game, one in which the teen came away seeing a lot better curves than the spinners Bob Feller threw for the Indians.

"I just wish the city would let us girls have a crack at playing ball. Hell, if Jackie Mitchell can strike out Ruth and Gehrig back-to-back, why not let us have a shot playing in a league of our own right here in Akron?"

"Lacey, a girl striking out Ruth and Gehrig? Think how whacky that sounds. You just don't have the skinny on that." Inside, Deet disliked Lacey constantly swimming against the current on topics ranging from girls playing ball to the shorts she wore in public, although he'd give her a pass on that more times than not.

Lacey's busy eyes took the temperature of the booth before they settled on her blond-haired beau. "Damn it, Deet! It was reported in the *New York Times*, and the *Times* don't lie."

In a nutshell, this was the conundrum that drove Deet wild—the same love of the game, which drew him to her like a magnet, came back to knock him on his ass like an Australian boomerang in her relentless ackamarackus about girls playing ball. Whenever he tried to put the kibosh to her silliness, she'd give him the cold shoulder for weeks on end.

"Do you think there'd be enough girls in Akron who'd want to play ball?" Mousy Sally Clark, Ricky's date, spoke up and innocently stirred the pot.

"Enough girls?" Lacey's eyes flashed, although hardly a facial muscle twitched. "Sally, let me tell you. I can get fifteen young ladies from the flipper beading department at Consolidated on any given evening in the summer to join me in playing a pickup game of softball at Seiberling Park."

Deet inhaled and sucked in his cheeks as Maria, the waitress, came over to check on them.

"You folks need an-n-ything else?" She put the tab down, dipping her words in an Italian accent as two perfect rows of brilliant white teeth sparkled.

"Maria," Lacey interrupted. "If you had the chance to play softball with other girls, would you?"

The tip of the waitress's tongue traveled across her compressed lips as a weak smile broke over her olive face. "*Si*, if I had the time."

"What did I tell ya?" Lacey dug her elbow into Deet's ribs.

Ricky and Sally chuckled.

"Lacey, why you ask me again?" Maria cocked her head to one side as the softness of her forehead rumpled into ridges like an accordion. "I told you last week I love to try to play ball."

Everyone stared at Lacey before the table erupted in laughter.

"So much for an unbiased opinion." Deet finished his Coke and dug out a dollar of his first paycheck from Consolidated.

"Did I say something wrong?" Maria's grin shrunk a bit.

"Absolutely not, Maria." Ricky ran a finger over one of the pinstripes of his uniform. "The joke was on Lacey."

"You're fine, Maria." Lacey forced a tight-lipped smirk and bobbed her head up and down.

"Keep the change, Maria." Deet handed her the dollar bill for the eighty-cent tab.

"*Grazie*! *Grazie*!" The waitress covered her mouth before apologizing as she headed toward the cash register at the other end of the diner. "I sorry, thank you very much."

"Well, so what if I knew she was interested in playing ball," Lacey argued, "it's not like I twisted her arm. I just knew before you guys did. Besides, the point is Akron should allow girls' leagues to play ball. You guys have Legion ball, why not us?"

Just then, Deet saw the answer to his prayers. Jack Acker, an attorney and the councilman for the ward where he and his family lived, walked into the diner. Acker recently responded to Arch

Jenkins' request to get a sewer line fixed after a heavy rainstorm, and his father introduced the politician to Deet.

"Excuse me, I think we can settle this issue right now." Deet made a bee line to the front of the diner, where Acker's broad, closed-mouth smile acknowledged the younger Jenkins. After a brief discussion, the two made their way to the teens' booth.

Deet sat down, introduced everyone, and laid out his cards. "Mister Acker, as a city councilman, we'd like your opinion on something we've been jawin' about."

"Oh-h, what might that be?" Acker ran his hand across his combed-back blond curls. "I hope I can be of some service to Akron's youth."

"What are the chances the city can *and will* start a girls' softball league?" With her brown eyes focused on Acker, Lacey wasted no time in getting to the point.

"Well miss, I certainly appreciate your frankness. I can tell you that youth recreation is very important to me." Acker's baritone voice greased each syllable of every word with the sophistication of a church bishop, so it sounded as if he were talking from a pulpit. "I know from talking to the Parks and Recreation director that new programs will be introduced in a forthcoming council meeting."

"When might that be?" Lacey's words came out like fastballs popping into a catcher's mitt as she glared at the overdressed councilman.

Deet quietly hoped he hadn't overplayed his hand. *Please, Lacey, be polite about it.*

Acker flattened his dark blue tie before buttoning his herringbone suit coat at the waist. "Let me see." He rested his chin on his index finger. "Department directors report quarterly, and I believe . . . Parks and Recreation . . ." He counted with his fingers. "Yes, July. Its last report was in April, so the council meets routinely on the third Monday of the month. Next month on July 19."

"So, nothing will happen this summer?" Ricky asked.

"I believe that to be an accurate statement, young man."

"Can the public attend these council meetings?" The tone of Lacey's voice softened a bit.

"Surely. But be advised, certain business takes place in closed sessions. However, you may come to hear the department reports, and there is a period for addressing the council with questions or comments, provided of course if you put these questions and/or comments on an official form by the Thursday before the council meeting."

"Where does one get these forms?" Lacey asked.

"At City Hall. Just ask the receptionist for one."

Mission accomplished, Deet wanted to make sure nothing awkward resulted from his pulling the councilman into his problem. "Thank you, Mister Acker, for sharing your time with us."

"You're most welcome. Thank you for your input. I'll keep it in mind during the July meeting. A pleasure meeting you all." The councilman bowed his head. "I trust I'll see you next month." Acker brushed off some lint from his trousers, smiled and left the diner.

"Well," Deet looked at Lacey next to him, "there you have it. The time, place, and procedure by which you can talk to council about a girls' softball program. Satisfied?"

"Depends on the answers I get. Besides . . . " Lacey's vision stayed glued to Acker's exit.

"Besides what?" Deet's voice held a noticeable edge. In the past several months, this would be the point where he'd just walk away from her.

"He knows we can't vote until we're twenty-one." Lacey's eyes stayed glued to the councilman's walk down the sidewalk.

"So? What's that—"

"Hey, anyone got a nickel?" A smiling Sally stood up. "How about some Benny Goodman?"

"Sounds good." With a toothy grin, fair complexion, and a nest of curly red hair, Ricky playfully pushed his brother's shoulder. "Really good."

****

Deet gagged, then coughed hard several times, as the fog of carbon black leaked out of the compounding mill.

"Maybe you should wear a mask." Dixon looked him in the eyes. "This shit'll eat your lungs for sure."

"I'll get one from the supply room during lunch."

"You got that much time, Jenkins?" Dixon almost bent over with a belly laugh. "You eatin' at the Ritz?"

The 3 AM bell rang for the meal break, and Dixon was certainly right. Lunch, snack, meal, whatever one wanted to call it, was a fleeting experience in Consolidated's world. Fifteen minutes to whoof down a sandwich and some milk only aided indigestion, adding another possible ailment to the list of potential injuries in this arena of black-smudged faces. Deet already knew if he and Dixon were behind on expected production, food would be consumed next to the running mill. Fortunately, today they were on schedule.

Dixon split from Deet upon entering the breakroom. Along with a half dozen other coloreds, he went into the back storage room, which the white workers called the Mill Room Cafeteria. On his first night on the job, Deet mistakenly followed Dixon into the cramped quarters where Black men sat on old crates to eat their food under the beacon of a single, low wattage light bulb. Dixon wasted little time in setting the teen straight.

Deet sat across from a hulk of a man at one of the circular tables in the main breakroom. All he knew about his table mate was his words fought their way through a thick, dark beard with a heavy Slavic accent, and that he was known as "Big Mike". While the other tables had at least three or more employees engaged in quiet conversation, Big Mike didn't speak.

Five minutes into lunch, Chaw Nelson—a hillbilly gummer with a constant wad of chewing tobacco between his cheek and gum— breezed into the breakroom. "Jones got scalded in the Pit. Steam hose ruptured as he took out a tire and burned his arm and half his face." He settled in at the last table and made no bones about his frustration.

"Damn it! I'm tired of this shit! We need a real union!" After his outburst, he hunkered down, spat out his wad, and wasted little time stuffing his face with whatever sandwich greeted him out of his paper bag. The pocket of food under his cheek bent his moustache at an upward angle.

Deet surveyed the room. Besides Nelson's brief display of anger, the other couple dozen or so men did little more than quiet grumbling. Big Mike's blue eyes stayed focused on his cheese sandwich and a canning jar of red beets while his mouth, hidden behind the well-kempt whiskers, never broke its rhythmic chewing.

A few minutes before the bell would end the meal break, Deet got up and threw away his wrapper and bag as he finished his pint bottle of milk. A thin, middle-aged man strode into the room, acting like a supervisor, talking to no one in particular but addressing everyone. "You've heard about Jones, I presume. When will you accept that capitalists don't care about you. Cleave to the party of the workers and be set free." He held up a leaflet before putting a small pile of them down on Deet's table and leaving.

"Who was that?" Deet's brain short-circuited, and the words left his mouth just as he looked at the notice from the Summit County Communist Party, easily identified by its hammer and sickle emblem. Every high school kid had been warned about those jokers.

As Big Mike rose to his full six-foot-five or six frame, Deet took a dry swallow. Mike's massive hand crumpled all the flyers with ease. His accent coated his gruff voice. "Just an ash-hole, keed . . . just an ash-hole."

"Did you see that guy, that communist, come in and make a little speech?" Deet didn't wait for Dixon to walk away from his Black co-workers outside the breakroom.

"That was Jimmy Bryant." Dixon grinned. "He's in his own little world. Like the snakes I grew up with down in Carolina, harmless . . ." Dixon's grin evaporated. ". . . unless you get too close."

"I thought we had a union to deal with these safety issues." Deet's thoughts spun like a hamster on its wheel.

"You got a union card, go see how the Consolidated Congress works. Since Simpkins' injury last week, we got a temporary union rep. You can bring it to his attention."

"I'm just the new kid here, why wouldn't you?"

"Me? I'm just a tap-dancing Negro." Dixon's mocking smile stretched from ear to ear without exposing a single tooth.

"He the best juke joint tapper around, boy," one of the other Black workers laughed, as Dixon showed off some spiffy juke moves with his feet, finishing his short act just as the bell rang to end the break.

Dixon stopped his schtick, and the smile dissolved from his face. "No, Jenkins, if you have safety issues, you need to talk to that man. He's your temporary rep." He pointed toward their machine where Harley Kershaw waited with arms crossed over his chest. "You want a real union, work over at Apex. Apex just recognized the United Rubber Workers."

Chapter 4

Akron

July 1937

❝ You know your mother won't stop riding me until we get that bald tire replaced before you guys go up to Parma, or wherever that place is your mother's family meets, next month." Despite the lowered visor, Arch Jenkins squinted into the western sun above the tops of the buildings framing Market Street on either side as Deet sat next to him in the family's '32 Pontiac Six sedan. A cigarette dangling between his lips, launching smoke toward the velour ceiling, the older Jenkins grumbled under his breath, "It gets old."

"So, Uncle Louie has a tire to fit the spare's rim in back?" Deet expressed little interest in his parents occasional squabbles, although it made him wonder at times about the value of marriage. If he got hitched to Lacey, how would he react to her constant harangue of a women's softball league . . . or other nonsense?

I'm only eighteen . . . not to worry.

Arch took the cigarette out of his mouth as its exhaust streamed through his nose. "Yeah, and he's got the tire changer to boot, so it shouldn't take too long."

"Hey Dad, I thought we were part of a union at Consolidated?" Deet took the pause at a traffic light to have his father shed some light on factory life.

"Well, yes and no . . . mostly no." A bead of sweat meandered down Arch's temple and through some wrinkles near his eye. "What brings this up?" He pushed in the clutch pedal with his left foot and engaged the floor-mounted gear shifter.

"Another guy got hurt, hurt bad, last night. This time in the pit. Dixon basically told me we didn't have a real union like what Apex has." Deet's eyes wandered about the passing cityscape, but his ears were peeled to his father's words.

"Yeah, he's right." Arch took another puff. "Apex workers held a six-week strike to get the company to recognize the URW. The Consolidated Congress is horse shit. It's a company union. The company picks the representatives to be on it, and then Consolidated chooses to accept or reject any suggestions it makes. We, the workers that is, don't have any real say in what goes on." Arch plunged the remnant of his spent cigarette into the pulled-out ashtray on the dash.

"Now, it makes sense."

"What?" Arch flicked the turn signal lever as he approached Union Street.

"Dixon told me that Harley Kershaw was appointed temporary union rep since Simpkins got hurt."

"Kershaw? Really? A supervisor? That's even a new one for Consolidated." Arch turned right on Union where traffic lessened. "Well, that should tell you all you need to know . . . for now."

A couple more turns, and they were on Bluff Street, named for the ridge which it straddled overlooking a shallow valley occupied by several rail lines. They pulled into Uncle Louie's drive between his shop and house greeted by the usual clutter of a man who loved working with his hands—a stripped car chassis, old water pumps, radiators, an engine block or two, rusty 55-gallon drums filled with scrap metal, an old ice box, and even old models of early gas-powered lawn mowers, among other junk. As a rat scurried a slalom course between the barrels, Deet couldn't help but notice how the junk yard had grown since he'd been here last Christmas.

There's no grass on this lot to cut.

He looked up and down Bluff Street. One house across the street teetered over the valley while others featured abandoned washing machines or furniture holding down hayfields posing as yards. At least one was boarded up.

Don't think the neighbors will be complaining.

"Louie!" Arch knocked on the back door of his house. "Louie!" Grimacing, he walked toward the garage. "Where is he? He said . . ." Arch's voice trailed off as he turned his hands into blinders as he looked through a dirty glass pane on one of the two eight-foot garage doors. "Let's check his shop." He fished out a key ring from his pocket and unlocked one of the large doors before heading to the service door.

Deet lifted the unlocked door of the stall only to be faced with more junk—body panels, fenders, wheel rims, worn tires—all piled as if delivered by a dump truck.

"Shit," Arch whispered under his breath just loud enough for his son to hear as he flicked the light switch. The oil change pit stood out as the star attraction of an empty bay. "The only place left to work in and it's empty. He's probably off on a bender."

"What?" Deet asked.

"Your uncle has had more than his fair share of trouble with alcohol since he got back from France in '19. Some times are worse than others, but I've never seen him sacrifice a bay in his garage for pack rat storage. Normally, he'd have two vehicles in here with a couple more outside either ready to be picked up or worked on. Then again, I haven't been here in over a month."

"You fellas looking for Louie?" A female voice, which sounded like it crawled out of a chimney, called out from the driveway behind them.

"Hello, Missus Ryan," Arch answered. "Yeah, we were supposed to meet my brother here to get a tire put on a rim. Have you seen him lately?"

Thin as a rail, with a fabric wrap around her hair, the elderly woman exhaled cigarette smoke. "He left about an hour ago. Can't be sure, but I suspect he's over at that clip joint on Furnace Street." She took another drag on the smoke. "Booze downstairs, lottery gambling upstairs. He crowed last week how he bet a penny and won five dollars."

Arch closed the service door and locked it. "This place . . . I mean the saloon . . . does it have a name?"

"*O'Doule's.*" She spit on the weeds infesting the gravel drive. "Shitty-looking brick building where Broadway meets Furnace. You can't miss it."

"Thank you, Missus Ryan." Arch made sure the garage got locked tight before they headed several blocks on foot towards O'Doule's.

"Aren't lottery games illegal gambling?" Deet asked as a locomotive pulled a couple empty coal cars below Bluff Street.

"Yep. And if the police raid the place, Louie's in the hoozgow."

The two walked deeper into one of the seedier sections of Akron as Deet almost fell after stubbing his toe on a hooved section of broken sidewalk. "Cripe!" His mind spun on a dime. "Is that what pissed off Mom last week when Uncle Louie dropped by?"

Arch glanced back at his boy, making sure he remained upright as they started to cross the bridge over the tracks. "Yeah, your mother's opinion of Louie has nosedived since your Aunt Betty divorced him years ago. Then again, Louie came back from the war with a bad case of shell shock. I guess Betty could never get used to his nightmares, and his drinking grew over time."

"Why did he drink?" Deet took a gander over the bridge's steel railing at the puffing engine some forty feet below.

"To escape the ghosts . . . ghosts he's never been able to describe to me, but they're real to him."

Arch's thumb pointed over his shoulder toward's Louie's shop. "The bays in his garage were always spotless before the war. Even up to recently, he'd never turn either bay into a rat's nest like what we just found."

Within a minute after leaving the bridge behind, they came upon a dilapidated two-story brick building where Broadway t-ed into Furnace. Parked cars lined the curbs of both streets. Outdated posters for local attractions covered the inside of one of the two windows on the first floor. *O'Doule's . . . Beer . . . Spirits* in white script took up the center of the other window surrounded by even more old posters. *The Parlor Club, Second Floor* stenciled on the entry door's window gave the two reason to look up at a row of four double sash windows on the second floor, each with the shade drawn.

"Whorehouse?" Deet wondered aloud.

"Might have been once, but Old Lady Ryan talked about some lottery scam. Let's go in and see if he's just drinking."

The wooden door swelled in the humidity, and Deet had to yank on it before it popped open. A mix of burnt rubber and clogged crappers assaulted Deet's nose, forcing him to bum a cigarette from his dad. He coughed as he inhaled, since he hadn't yet become used to the tobacco sticks. He took another puff as a means of producing a smoky barrier to the joint's stink. Dead flies and other bugs in each of the half dozen globe fixtures suspended from the embossed tin ceiling further dimmed the feeble light they offered. As Deet's eyes adjusted to the saloon's dim interior, the worn paneling of the bar caught his eye. Years of shoe scuffs left it dull with the bead board's outer layer completely eroded in several areas.

Only two of the eight stationary bar stools were occupied as the bearded bartender gave the two a wary stare. Something was off about his eyes, but Deet couldn't make it out from the doorway. The half-dozen wooden tables stood abandoned atop the dirty, plank flooring. The decorative ceiling groaned under the weight of a sizeable gathering upstairs as the dead insects in the lamp globes bounced a bit from time to time. Muffled shouts sprouted here and there in the mysterious upper room. Louie wasn't here, at least not on the first floor. Arch and Deet's gaze went up the dark staircase on the wall opposite the bar.

Arch walked over to the end of the bar, his eyes still on the stairs. "Have you seen a guy a bit shorter than me with wavy, salt and pepper hair and glasses come in here in the last hour or so?"

"You don't see him in here do ya?" The slim bartender's odd gaze focused on Arch while he wiped the top of the bar with a white towel.

"If I would, I wouldn't ask you." Arch reached across the bar and grabbed him by the collar. "How 'bout upstairs?"

Deet closed in next to his father, crushing his half-sized smoke in a metal ashtray on the bar before instinctively retreating a few steps.

A glass eye . . . the man's got a glass eye. It's lifeless.

"That's for Parlor Club members only. If he's a member, he could be there, I-I-I . . . don't check everyone coming through those doors."

"Look asshole, we're not the cops. I'm just looking for my brother. Business isn't that crowded that you couldn't have noticed him if—"

The stairs creaked their displeasure as someone began his way down. Louie's chin hung almost to his knees as each step was so deliberate making Deet think he could easily miss the next one even though his uncle clung to the rickety railing with his right hand.

The lean, muscular teen marched towards the stair's landing, thinking ahead of catching his uncle's possible free fall. "Hey, Uncle Louie, we missed you at your place."

"Oh!" Louie faked a hand slap to his forehead. "The tire . . . the tire . . . the tire . . ."

With his uncle two steps from the landing, Deet got a whiff of booze that cut through the joint's aroma of rubber and sewer.

"Check his pockets, Deet." Arch called out from the bar.

Louie stood trance-like, his eyes dancing in different directions as his nephew found his wallet. "Empty. Whatever he had is gone."

"Tell your Mister Big, or whoever runs this show, someone's coming to shut you down." With both hands, Arch grabbed the barkeep by his vest.

"My name isn't Big, it's Mahoney." Clearly overdressed, a man in a white shirt with a blue-striped tie, and pin-striped, gray pants stood half-way down the stairs. "What's the problem, gentlemen?"

Arch released the bartender and took a couple steps across the room to hold onto his brother's shoulders and stare into his vacant eyes. "You guys specialize in robbing soused citizens?"

"No one kidnapped your brother and forced him to play our lottery." Mahoney pointed to the street first, and with his other hand, back to the top of the stairway. "You'ins think these folks were hijacked? Besides, your brother was sober enough to climb these stairs on his own."

"You took ad—" Arch didn't have a chance to finish his sentence.

"You'ins . . . just wait here." Mahoney went back upstairs and came back within a minute holding a small bag in one hand and a carriage of sorts with what looked like three small, hourglass-shaped baskets, each with a single die. He attached two of the baskets to the carriage's center rod, which was attached to a crank handle. "Now, if we were using just one die, the player's chances of winning would be one in six, so we use two as the minimum, upping the odds to one in thirty-six." He cranked the handle several times and allowed the baskets to spin themselves to a stop.

Arch's jaw set. "But of course, *The Parlor* usually uses three baskets for one in two-hundred and sixteen odds . . . better yet, four baskets for one in twelve-hundred and ninety-six odds." He folded his arms across his chest. "Listen, you overdressed hill jack—"

Deet noticed a shadowy figure from the waist down of a man high on the stairway wearing workman's trousers with a pistol clutched in his hand at his side. He grabbed his father's arm and pointed toward the mystery man.

"Right. Louie, here, won three times last week on the two-basket game, playing with nickels." Mahoney's facial expression never changed as he spoke as if he was the only one in the room. "He lost it all in just under ninety minutes playing the three-basket game. Just to show you'ins there's no hard feelin's, here take it all back, Louie." Mahoney dropped the canvas bag with a clang. "A hundred nickels . . . a metal Lincoln. Why don't you'ins go to Spankies on Howard Street? Just don't ever come back here . . . ever."

****

Deet gawked at the skeletal works of horizontal, vertical, and parallel, steel rails taking carts of filthy, raw rubber up, over, and into mixing and milling machines. For someone who had been an average student at best, the teen always held an affinity for geometry. He noticed the parallel and perpendicular as well as the obtuse and acute throughout nature and in man's contraptions. In one isolated way, this enormous, benzene-dipped, vibrating room made him feel in his element.

A glimmer of light on the outside of Plant One's windows announced dawn's arrival, and with it, the start of the last hour of Deet's shift. In just under a month, he'd learned clock-watching prolonged the grind of work much worse than any classroom lecture he'd endured at Central. It was only Tuesday, but he already had

Saturday night on his mind, dancing with Lacey at one of the local juke joints.

Just an hour to go. Work your way through it, Deet.

A whiff of solvents from a bucket that Dixon opened brought him back to the present, and he pulled a cart of raw rubber along the steel rollers onto the scale. There, he cut one chunk of raw rubber off the loaded cart before deciding that another subtraction had to be made. From the far side of the factory's first floor, he thought he heard someone's voice drowning among the noise of the mills.

" . . . down!"

Dixon, who'd meandered down the aisle between mills for no apparent reason, stepped alongside him. "Don't dump that cart into the mixer just yet. Wait till I tell ya."

Deet had just finished scratching his head over the Negro's order when someone flipped the power switch off to all the mills. The eerie silence in the vast facility amplified the echoing of a simple command from Chaw Nelson, in his West Virginia twang. "Shut 'er down! Sit down!"

"Shut 'er down! Sit down!" The hilljack operator repeated his command. He had become a leader of sorts in trying to form a union, at least in this department. To Consolidated, he was an *outside agitator.*

Deet looked at Dixon with a hanging jaw as he surveyed the factory stand down into near silence. Only the voices of the workers disrupted the otherwise stillness as some laughed, others whooped, but most who spoke ratcheted down to their *off-the-job* voice.

"What just happened?"

"It's your first sit-down strike, Jenkins." Dixon wiped the sweat off his brow and the back of his neck with a relatively clean rag before rubbing it between his hands.

"What caused it?" The boy used the dirtied shoulder of his once pristine tee shirt to clear the sweat off his face.

"Don't rightly know, yet. Don't worry, scuttlebutt will catch up with its cause. All you have to remember is to stay in sight of your mill. Don't let it, the rubber, the run of ply, or the compound be damaged. We might be strikers, but we're no vandals." The Negro flashed a toothy grin.

Deet then presented his most important question. "How long will it last?"

Dixon shrugged. "Who knows? A couple hours? A couple days?

Hours? Days!

The Black man looked the teen over and read his mind. "Don't be pissy-faced about it, kid. Yeah, no one leaves until this is settled. Nelson and his cronies will secure the entrances in due time and, if necessary, get us food. Without a real union, we have to pull this petty shit from time to time. I understand you play baseball."

Deet nodded.

"Even if you're the star, sometimes a sacrifice bunt is in order. This is one of those times."

"Hey Taps!" One of Dixon's Black friends stood next to his machine across the aisle. "Let's play some cards." He turned over an empty crate for a makeshift table, and another man added a couple buckets for seats.

"Sounds like a good—"

A metal service door slammed at the end of the building closest to where Deet was stationed. Harley Kershaw, his face beet red, stormed down the aisle with his two fists pounding on each other as he glared at most every operator. "If you value your jobs, you better get your asses back to work right now!"

Absent the roar of machinery, Kershaw's voice boomed about the massive room. He stopped halfway through the building and pointed back to the entry door. "Security's been called, and they've been ordered to take over this shop in *whatever manner they choose!*" He picked up a small pry bar and splintered an empty rubber crate with it. "You've got less than a half an hour to make the right decision." He walked out the door opposite the end from which he entered.

Deet's stomach fluttered, and his breathing quickened. Even though he'd read about the sit-downs over the past year or so and his dad downplayed their existence as nothing more than a game of chess, the teen hadn't expected to be in the middle of a labor war within his first six weeks on the job. He looked at the large wall clock next to his mill. It was 5:25 in the morning, and his shift would be extended indefinitely.

So, this is the labor version of a sacrifice bunt. Would it help men from getting hurt on the job?

Deet looked over at Dixon, throwing down a card on the overturned crate and laughing with his pals as if nothing had happened. He turned to find an empty bucket for himself and almost walked into *Big Mike*. "Sorry," Deet said within inches of the Slav's well-trimmed beard overlapping a broad chest, covered by a moth-eaten, denim shirt.

"I not like that guy."

Gassed by the man's garlic breath, Deet turned back toward where Kershaw had stood. "I can imagine not many folks in here do." He stepped back a bit before looking back on the dark-haired man with pot-marked cheeks surrounded by beard. As rough as he looked, Deet thought his deep set, blue eyes soft enough to be approachable. "By the way, I'm Deet Jenkins." The boy extended his hand.

"Mykhailo Kobenko." The fortyish man held out a massive hand, but his grip was less than enthusiastic. "Just call me Mike."

Knowing little about the foreigner, Deet decided on simple questions. "You been in Akron how long?"

"Ten years."

"How long have you worked at Consolidated?"

"A year." Not a line in Kobenko's face shifted.

Deet stumbled forward. "Where's home?"

"You the police?" Big Mike's recessed eyes steeled, and the lengthy carpet around his jaw rippled as he ran a hand through his greased hair. "You ask so many questions. Why you care? Maybe you spy for Law-and-Order League. Eh?"

The young Jenkins stepped back, realizing he'd overstepped his bounds. "Sorry, I was just trying to be friendly."

"Then don't inter- . . . inter-gate me!" The Slav's forceful tone and hardened face conveyed his anger as his twisted tongue tightened, and he turned away.

"Interrogate?"

"That's what I said." Mike snapped around with the cold eyes of a Karloff monster and arms flailing. "First the czar, then the Bolsheviks. Now vigilantes and hookman. Are you Consolidated spy? Maybe communist spy?"

"No." Although his frame remained square, Deet let his eyes drop to the floor as he walked away. "Just someone who wanted to strike up a conversation."

Thud!

A solid metallic thump to the nearest service door caught the attention of Deet and most everyone on that side of the cavernous room. Dixon sauntered up to the young Jenkins' side as raucous voices clamored just beyond the fragile metal barrier.

"Break some heads!"

"Break this damn union!"

"Send these Reds back to Stalin!"

Deet jerked his head and lifted his heels as Dixon put his hand on the boy's shoulder. "It appears Consolidated put some finks in as tire inspectors on the second floor and trumped up some phony inspection reports to get some guys fired."

Deet felt the hand leave his blackened shirt, and he turned to see the Negro grab an iron pry bar. "Kershaw's bark is usually worse than his bite during these sit-downs, but I have to be honest with ya, kid. Get a bar or break off some lumber from a skid. You're probably goin' to need something to fight with against those company gorillas."

The teen's stomach roiled as he recalled the few occasions he'd fought. Because of his long arms and wide fists, he'd won every time . . . against boys. Now, he searched about his mill for the most convenient weapon, and he found it—a five-foot piece of pipe used to give added leverage on some machinery handles.

The agitation outside the door grew louder, and Deet's hands fused to the makeshift, metallic bat in them. "Sounds like there could hundreds out there."

Dixon shook his head. "Probably not hundreds . . . but fifty or so I'd say. Don't go after anyone until they try to hit you or mess with the goods."

Deet gave the senior co-worker a rumpled look.

"You thought I was blowing smoke up your ass when I said earlier we weren't vandals?" Dixon chuckled. "We're not . . . we're protect-"

Silence at the door cut off Dixon's lecture as he turned toward a single voice apparently addressing the *security* mob. Everyone else in the massive facility was riveted as well to what was unfolding out of their vision.

"Are you guys sure you want to make your reputation by attacking your fellow workers?" A lone voice spouting reason spoke loud enough for even the ears on the inside to hear. "Five, ten years from now, you want everyone in Akron who runs into you on the street to say, *Hey, weren't you one of the thugs that tried to break up that sit-down strike at Consolidated in '37?*"

By now, Deet could have swore he recognized that voice, and he inched a bit closer to the door.

"I trained some of you Squad members . . . Pete, Dennis . . . Rick and a few others who got *promoted* to security. Shorty, remember when I helped get you time off because of your sick wife? You do realize you've been lumped together with the finks, gorillas, and missionaries Consolidated recruited from some clip joints along Howard Street, don't you? Don't you remember what Momma always said, *You'll always be judged by the company you kept.*"

"Enough talking, what are we waiting for?" One rough voice got shooshed down by a volley of others.

"That's my dad," Deet whispered before he trailed back to Dixon and others in direct earshot. "That's my dad." Tears welled in the corner of his eyes.

"One last thing . . . once you go in there, who knows what might happen to the machinery and product. That'll be on you guys as well, no matter who does it, and you can't think Consolidated will be happy with the results, can you? I do know the newspapers will have a hay day with what you're about to do. Well, I've had my say. Time for you guys to piss or get off the pot."

An indiscernible murmur overtook the outside gathering, gradually dousing into silence like the last drops of a sudden summer shower. Inside, the gummers filtered back to their sit-down stations around their mills. Dixon and his friends continued their card game, and Deet plopped himself down on a crate next to his mill. A heavy hand landed on his shoulder, and he turned to see a smiling Mike holding a bucket of his own. "I can join you, yes?"

Chapter 5

The German Zentrele (recreational park) near Parma, Ohio
August 1937

Having a driver's license surely had its perks, but this wasn't one of them. With his father begging off of the semi-annual visit with the family of his mother's sister, Deet became her chauffeur. His only consolation lay in Ricky's forced enlistment to see the Hitler-heilers. Last Christmas, the Gellers visited the Jenkins' house on Laird Street and spent the better part of the meal peddling the virtues of *Der Fuehrer*—full employment in Germany, industry booming, Christian nationalism growing a new self-respect among the German people, and as for the Jews . . . only the corrupt ones had anything to be concerned about.

What would George Washington want if he were alive today? With his fist planted on the dining room table, Fred Geller had asked. *He'd want a white, Christian nation.*

His dad offered some resistance, but his mother cut him off at the knees before the argument ruined the holiday spirit. Since there wasn't any August holiday, Deet thought that he could at least have some fun by getting Uncle Fred to blow his wig.

"So, what do you think of our camp, Dietrich? Richard?" Deet's uncle Fred ladled another spoonful of potato salad onto his plate as his Sam Brown belt sagged to just inches above the dish's bowl.

Caught with a mouthful of food, Deet held up one hand for a time-out.

A breeze wafted through the large pavilion, causing Trudi to brush loose strands of her dark hair out of her eyes. "I'm sure the boys are much impressed by the sheer size of this park."

Deet saw his uncle's jaw twitch and his flushed face tighten, although his stern eyes never wavered, staring across the table at him. He doubted Fred cared about his nephews' opinion of the camp in general. He sensed his father's absence disappointed his uncle, and therefore he'd indoctrinate Ricky and him by seeking their approval of the German American Bund's youth march from the entrance of the camp into the pavilion. With brass horns blaring and snare drums tattering, one hundred children from ages six to seventeen paraded in their brown shirts and black shorts while singing some German song. Of course, Hugo, holding the pole of the Nazi flag, marched near the front wearing a smug smile while his arms and legs moved with machine-like precision. When they came to the end of their procession by encircling the flagpole near the pavilion, the entire troop stopped and gave a crisp stiff-armed salute to the American flag waving in the wind just above the Nazi flag.

"Looks like something right out of the movie newsreels . . . straight from Berlin." Ricky broke Deet's thoughts as he cut off a chunk of bratwurst and shoved it into his mouth only to stop in mid-chew. "The parade I mean."

"Don't speak with your mouth full." Deet figured his mother's tone wasn't aimed at Ricky's table manners. "You're not a small child anymore."

Deet looked down at his plate of red cabbage salad, brats, and potato salad before scanning the attentive eyes of his aunt, uncle and cousin seated across the wooden picnic table. He knew his Aunt Petra, Uncle Fred, and Hugo wanted something more than a candy-coated response, but he wouldn't give them the satisfaction that they wanted. "Yeah, like Mom said, it's huge. If Hugo has the time, I'd like a tour to see what it has to offer."

Fred's eyes dropped as he shoveled more food into his mouth. "Naturally, he will gladly give you a tour of the *Zentrele*."

Still, Deet felt the need to chisel an angle at needling his German relatives. "Why is the Nazi flag on the pole with the American flag?"

In the middle of a beehive of conversation around them, all of their eyes turned toward Fred, who took a swig from a bottle of beer before answering. "We are Americans first, but we cannot turn our back on our German ancestry." His robust voice rose over the pavilion chatter. "Both flags represent our faith in God and country."

Deet couldn't resist playing the devil's advocate. "What if we end up in a war with Germany?"

"I highly doubt it, Dietrich." Petra responded in a voice reserved for putting a frightened child to bed. "Besides, we are for religious freedom and the code of moral behavior under which we and *your parents* were educated." She brushed a loose strand of her fading blond hair from her eyes. "We will not allow your generation to be lost to the atheists."

By now, Deet felt like a kitten with a ball of yarn even though he saw Ricky and his mother share a concerned look. "So, everyone is to follow one particular religion—the one our family grew up with?"

Aunt Petra's ears reddened. "Whatever the *Fueh*—"

Her teeth barely missed biting her tongue as Fred put up his hand like a policeman directing traffic. "No!" His shoulders arched. "That will be left up to Congress to decide when the time comes."

Deet had been an average student, but he knew the basics, so he decided the ball of yarn needed one more swat. "What about the Constitution and the First Amendment?"

"Both of those documents were written by men with the distinct ability to be changed by other men. The Constitution can be changed and more quickly than that turtle-paced amendment process . . . I assure you."

Deet listened politely as he finished off his plate. He nodded with his last bite rolling around the inside of his mouth before swallowing.

"Hey, Hugo, how about that tour?" Ricky spoke up, rescuing his mother from further embarrassment.

Deet would make it up to his mother somewhere down the road. Right now, he knew he wasn't necessarily a good German since he had too much of his father within him.

****

"Physical fitness is important to us." Hugo pointed to the tennis courts located behind the pavilion where several Bund youth and their guests began volleying white balls with their rackets. "I know it's important to you guys because you play baseball and—"

Deet and his brother ogled a well-endowed blond bounding across one of the courts to return a serve. Perhaps a bit older than Deet, the pig-tailed woman offered a striking figure. The upper portion of her white blouse rolled like swells on Lake Erie during a gale.

"Who's the dish?" Ricky's mouth moved, but his eyes never abandoned the buxom blond.

"That's Gertie . . ." Hugo smiled before his voice lowered with a sense of exasperation. ". . . and Vogel." His voice shifted into a higher gear once again. "She's a fine example of Aryan breeding. She and Vogel are camp instructors from New York City."

"Not big on Vogel, Hugo?" Ricky asked. "Want to get Gertie in a phone booth all to yourself?" The younger Jenkins broke into a convulsive laugh while Deet smiled.

"Why is it American boys are always obsessed with sex? Gertie is quite accomplished in throwing the javelin and playing the piano, not like so many American tramps I've met." Hugo started along a path that dissected a wooded area. "This way."

"So, tell us more about Gertie's *fine breeding*." In the rear of the file of the three, Ricky snickered as he blocked the backlash of a slender branch from a maple sapling.

Hugo stopped and faced the younger Jenkins. "Ricky, you seem to be as vulgar as your father."

Ricky came chest to chest with his cousin only to have his brother slip between them.

"Ricky, no. Let's not screw this up for Mom." Up to this point, Deet kept silent, enjoying the coolness under the shade of mature oaks and maples and the invigoration of breathing uncontaminated air. However, his patience with his host ran out, and he turned toward his cousin. "Hugo why does it seem you always have a stick up your ass?"

Hugo took a step back from the more imposing presence of his older cousin as he wiped strands of his dark hair backwards over his ear. "I have my own question for you, Dietrich. Why were you such an ass when you spoke with such disrespect to my father?"

"Just asking legitimate questions, although I have to wonder if the Germans in the Fatherland are allowed to ask questions any more."

"What would give you that idea?" Hugo marched forward along the trail.

"I bet Hitler does all the thinking for whole damn country. I mean from what I've heard from my dad and occasionally in the newsreels at the movies, no one dares to speak out against him. Everyone just goes around *heiling* him."

Ricky began a goosestep pantomime with his right arm in a stiff-armed salute.

Ignoring the mockery, Hugo stepped backwards toward an opening out of the woods about a couple hundred feet away. "You can't appreciate what Herr Hitler has meant to the German people."

"Ok, so explain it to me," Deet demanded.

"For one thing, he has taken charge." The young Geller resumed walking while speaking. "Time isn't wasted with numerous parties arguing about this or that. Democracy is such a waste of time, money, and energy. It's like an overboiled stew that has lost its flavor and texture." Hugo's hands danced in front of him as he spoke with his back to his cousins before turning around with clenched fists. "Herr Hitler has given the people a well-cooked beef roast in the form of a renewed efficiency in Germany that the people have clamored for, and they love him for it."

Deet listened to Hugo's words as they passed a grassy gulley half-way through the forested area. However, its peaceful, secluded scenery diverted his thoughts to how it would be the perfect place to picnic with Lacey.

"Americans would be wise to imitate *Der Fuehrer's* achievements." Hugo turned back toward Deet and Ricky, almost stumbling before righting himself.

"So, give me some specifics about his *achievements*." By now, Deet saw a wide-open area begin to emerge at the end of the path.

"He's built-up industry and virtually eliminated unemployment and with it, the people have regained their self-respect." Hugo sprinted the last fifty feet toward acres of a well-kept expanse. "This is our athletic field." He beamed with pride, holding out his right arm as a formal introduction. Netted goals at opposite ends of the groomed field indicated its use for soccer matches. "We march and drill here as well, and down there is our shooting range." He pointed to the right where the field seemed to drop off into a valley.

"March and drill?" Ricky sneered. "You really want to be a stormtrooper?"

Deet didn't want to lose his cousin's focus, so he jumped over his brother's wisecrack. "What else has Hitler done for Germany?"

"He has reigned in the undesirables in the nation and has either imprisoned or deported most of them." Hugo led the group toward what appeared to be the limit of the open field on the right-hand side. "He's created laws that will enhance the lives of Germans—no spitting or littering in public and no walking on the grass of public buildings."

Deet looked at his brother, who shook his head.

The manicured field sloped down into a shallow basin with a string of benches, each protected from the weather by an overhang at one end and a row of paper targets on a long, wooden wall in front of an earthen mound at the other end several hundred feet away.

Again, Hugo smiled. "Herr Hitler's built up the military, so Germany will become great again, no longer the bootlicker in Europe." His eyes widened into a two-mile stare onto the pale blue horizon. "Someday, I might have the honor of fighting for the leader who the communists fear the most."

Hugo outstretched an arm to the area below. "Here we have our own shooting range. We practice our shooting numerous times a week. I am almost certified to instruct the younger campers."

"You're really dig this, Hugo, don't you?" Deet said.

"If you mean that I am proud of what my fellow Germans have accomplished in a few short years, yes, then I *dig it,* as you say." The Cleveland cousin folded his arms in front of him. "You know there are many Americans who've taken notice of Herr Hitler's accomplishments and want to bring them here."

Deet saved a curve ball for his last challenge. "What about the Jews?"

"What about them?" A slow smirk crossed Hugo's face. "You've watched too much propaganda on those newsreels, Cousin. He has only dealt severely with the corrupt Jews, but the rest of them will have a place in the New Germany."

There was no conversation on the walk back to the pavilion. Deet stewed over how his mother's family could be so taken with this nitwittery to the point of suggesting of importing Hitler's ideas to the states. He reflected on things Uncle Fred boasted about last Christmas.

How could people connect Hitler with George Washington unless they were whacky twits?

Halfway back on the footpath, Deet accepted the fact there was no reasoning that would penetrate his cousin's family's shell of steadfast Nazi beliefs, so he consciously opted to enjoy what was often lacking in and around the rubber mills—the rustling of trees in the wind, songbird melodies, and the passionate human groaning off to the left-hand side of the footpath. "Listen!" He held his finger to his lips.

"What?" Ricky and Hugo whispered in unison.

"Over here." Deet walked off the path toward the grassy ravine.

Soft moaning rose from the sunken area as Deet led the threesome to peek through the brush along the path. Some fifty feet away, a half-clad Gertie writhed atop her tennis partner, Vogel.

After sucking in the peep show for a while, Deet sensed Hugo backing away from the sight.

Deet grabbed his cousin by the bicep and brought him back to the group. "Fine Aryan breeding . . . my ass," he whispered. "Take a good look, Hugo. That's plain old making whoopee."

Chapter 6

Akron

August 1937

❝ Hey, Jenkins." The partially balding man waltzed into the lunchroom and sat, uninvited, next to Deet, munching on a sandwich. "Aren't you Arch's—" The man pinched his nose. "Phew! Boy, what the hell are you eating?"

The teen swallowed and without flinching any facial muscle, answered, "Limburger cheese."

The man retreated to a seat directly across the table from Deet and scooted his chair back a foot or two. "As I was saying, aren't you Arch Jenkins' boy?"

Deet looked at the bespectacled man with the physique of a pencil and certainly didn't recognize him from the milling area. "Yeah, I am." He chased the morsel he'd just devoured with some milk before taking another bite of the stinky cheese held together by two pieces of sturdy rye bread.

"Allow me a few minutes of your time. I'm Jimmy Bryant. I work up in the labs most days. Sometimes . . . ," Bryant's hands danced in front of him as his head moved back and forth. ". . . sometimes, I like to come down here and get the pulse of the men who mill the rubber. For instance, what improvements could be made to make your working conditions better?" His blue-gray eyes darted back and forth, giving him the appearance of a squirrel deciding whether or not to cross Market Street.

With no available place of retreat, Deet stopped in mid-chew. The young man felt as if he'd been transplanted onto a car lot, only his dad wasn't there to handle the dickering. "Well, it seems like a lot of men —"

Jimmy Bryant . . . He's in his own little world. Harmless . . . unless you get too close.

Suddenly, Dixon's warning of the slender man from a few months back haunted him.

"Yes . . . " Bryant forced his chair to the edge of the table. "A lot of men . . . what?"

"Well . . . ah . . . it seems like a lot of men get hurt on the job." Deet wiped his mouth with his fist and stared back at Bryant, who peered at him over his metal-rimmed glasses, scrutinizing each word out of the boy's mouth.

"How is improved safety on the job ever going to happen? The union . . . Consolidated's union? Not hardly. Even with men like your father working to bring this plant into the URW, don't bank on it." The defense offered by the odor of the cheese seemed to be crumbling as Bryant moved one seat closer to Deet at the round table. "The greed of the bosses won't allow it to happen. There has to be a bigger change."

Deet wished the break buzzer would ring as Bryant's conversation pinned him against the ropes in an arena, with his fellow gummers as the spectators. "I don't know much about that."

"Last year's strike at Consolidated made some modest gains, but it didn't push the bosses to recognize an outside union, probably never will. All you have to do to see the writing on the wall in this place is to see what happened up in Cleveland back in May at Republic Steel."

What's this pitch all about?

"What happened?" At that moment, Deet really didn't care, but those words kept the focus off of him.

"Steelworkers struck, Republic brought in scabs, kept the plant running, National Guard came in for a while, left, and fights broke out. Bottom line—the strike failed, no union, and men lost their jobs. The government stood by and did nothing. We need some real power when dealing with big bosses. We need the government on the side of workers . . . a government run by the workers." Bryant smiled and pushed a folded pamphlet over to Deet. "Think about it, kid. A guy like you will be here for a long time. It'll pay to make the best of it."

Bryant stood up and smiled, exposing at least one gold tooth, and left, leaving Deet to lift the edge of the leaflet and take a peek at its other side. At the sight of the hammer and sickle emblem, his hand crumpled it with thoughts of stuffing it into a pocket of his blackened pants. Contaminated by the encounter, he turned around and noted that while a number of men were engaged in their usual break conversations, Chaw Nelson and his buddies interrupted their meal to chuck emotionless stares his way. He wasn't going to risk losing the goodwill shown him since his father's stand during the last sit-down strike, so he made a deliberate show of tearing up the propaganda piece and throwing it away with the rest of his lunch time trash. Deet turned around and found himself in the shadow of Big Mike Kobenko.

"You did good." Mike mumbled somewhat as he ditched his trash before the power of his sullen face paralyzed Deet. "Don't talk with that ash hole again. Nothing good can happen."

****

Arch and Trudi sat in their living room during the dying moments of a late August evening. A streetlamp near their house offered an island of ghostly light as darkness settled in over their neighborhood. Trudi knitted under the glare of a goose-neck lamp as tobacco smoke wafted about the light painting the air a bluish gray tone. Arch puffed on a Lucky Strike stuck between his lips as he read the local paper. Faint sounds of music drifted down from Ricky's bedroom and mixed with occasional traffic noise on Laird Street.

"How's your head?" Trudi asked without looking up from her knitting.

"I told you when I came home this afternoon, it didn't seem to be any big deal, *and it still isn't.*" He snapped the unfolded news of the day in between his hands.

"Must you contaminate the living room?" In a voice lacking the compassion of her previous question, Trudi interrupted her row of cream-colored yarn links by batting smoke back and forth with one hand.

"Got to . . ." Arch turned the page of the paper. ". . . got to get the stink out from tonight's meal." He stuck his head out from behind the paper. "Trudi, you're a fine cook, but why do you insist on poisoning me with that stew every couple of months?" With an over-stuffed upholstered chair cushioning his behind, Arch continued his imitation of a chimney as he fixed his interest in an article about the National Labor Relations Act. "Says here that the Wagner Act, the NLRA, guarantees workers the right to unionize. Did you know that Trudi? I bet most folks either don't know or don't want others to know about it."

So how does Consolidated get away with its sham union?

"It reminds me of hard times in Germany when I was a child, just like these past years." The yarn came together on the needles between her fingers with machine precision.

Still surrounded by his paper, Arch piped up, "At least, I've had steady work the past—"

"Hey, Arch!" A voice cried out from somewhere in the shadows of night outside of the house. "How does a Red like you sleep at night?"

Arch crushed his cigarette in a pedestal ashtray and put down his paper while Trudi dropped her needlework as her face fell with fear.

"Come out and convince us you're no commie!" A second, deeper, voice yelled out.

"Turn off your lamp!" Arch commanded Trudi in a low whisper as he reached for the ceiling light switch. "Get down—"

A high-pitched burst of shattered glass erupted from the adjacent dining room as something heavy crashed through it.

An arm around his whimpering wife, Arch helped her crawl into the foyer.

"What the hell is going on!" Ricky stomped out of his room as he accidentally kicked several wadded pieces of paper all the way down the stairs.

On the thread-bare carpeted floor and holding on to Trudi, Arch called up to his youngest son, "Ricky, stay upstairs . . . but first, get me my pistol out of my nightstand."

"What? Dad—"

"No time to explain now, just do it. Put it on the third step from the top of the stairs."

While he heard Ricky's footsteps sprint across the second floor, he looked through the faint light offered by the streetlamp at the candlestick phone resting on top of an old, oak plant stand. "Trudi, honey," he sat up and coaxed his wife to do likewise. "I want you to call the police. Can you do that for me?"

Trudi inhaled the congestion her tears had caused. "Yes, yes." She brushed her hair off her face and got on her knees. "Wh-wh-what are you going to do? You can't go out there . . . with a gun. A gun? Oh, Archie." She clutched her husband around his shoulders and convulsed into more tears.

"I've got to shed some light on those cockroaches, or they'll make a habit of this shit." Arch kissed her on the forehead, scrambled up the stairs, and picked up the Smith and Wesson off the step where Ricky left it. He came down just as quickly. "I'm—"

Another bang of broken glass exploded on the front porch.

"Come on, Jenkins! Quit hiding behind your wife's skirt!" A raspy voice, a chain smoker's voice in Arch's mind, joined the other two. "You commie unionist!"

Still hunkered down on the floor, Trudi flashed panic in her eyes as she looked at her spouse. "Please, don't Archie."

"Call the police . . . now!" Arch left the words hanging in the air of the kitchen as he dashed out the back door.

He grabbed the flashlight out of the Pontiac and worked his way down the alley which hugged his house. With the .38 Special in his right hand and the unlit flashlight in the other, he crept around a hedge lining the corner of the front porch. He saw three men—two around a large maple on the tree lawn across the street and a third about twenty feet down the curb from the other two. From the edge of the hedge, with one hand he cast the beam of the flashlight on the two by the tree —one tall and blond, the other lean with dark hair. He cocked and aimed the pistol with the opposite hand. "Hold it right there, assholes!"

At that moment, a car followed by a delivery truck crawled towards Market Street as if they were in a parade. Just like that, the men were gone. Arch saw at least one man already more than a block down Laird as a police car pulled into the alley's entrance with its side spotlight focused on Arch. An officer sprung out of the passenger door and yelled from behind it. "Drop it, mister!"

Blinded by the spotlight and no longer aiming the weapon, Arch slowly lowered it to the crumbled brick of the alley. Hands held high, he called out, "You guys got this all wrong!"

****

Deet walked down Market Street before turning on Laird after having played pool with some pals at a neighborhood billiards hall. Thoughts of a cozy meeting with Lacey later in the week entertained him as if she were the tonic with which to stomach the upcoming six-hour shift. Within a block of his home, he noticed a flashing turn signal of a vehicle with its headlight beams illuminating the side of his house as if it were a giant Consolidated billboard on Market Street. With a few more hurried steps, he recognized a newer model police car, a '37 Plymouth with black and white body panels. Just as he came within speaking distance, he heard two officers talking to his father as one of them holstered his pistol while the other one picked up a pistol off the alley.

"What's going on, Dad?"

"I was just telling these gentlemen that while your mother and I were quietly minding our own business in the living room, three company goons threw a couple rocks through our windows and threatened me."

"Mind if we go inside and check out the damage Mister Jenkins?" the taller of the two patrolmen asked as his partner called in on the car's radio.

"Of course not, look for yourself." Arch wiped strands of his blond hair out of his face and back behind his ear.

To Deet, the warm evening air became tropical as he noticed moisture around his father's shirt collar and in his armpits. "Is Mom alright?"

"Yeah, go inside and check on her, will yeah? I'll give these guys the tour."

Deet walked in through the kitchen door, and the patrol car's headlights helped guide his fingers to depress the *on* button for the ceiling light fixture. Unfortunately for him, the stench of the rutabaga stew his mom served for dinner hung in the air as a lasting reminder of the root vegetable's potency.

Dog farts.

Sobbing from the foyer overrode self-pity. "Mom!"

Angular rays of light fell into the front entrance room from multiple directions—the kitchen, the stairway, and through the side window at the base of the stairway. Where they intersected, Deet found his mother in a heap, weeping on the floor near the phone. "Mom!" He knelt down beside her and held her as footsteps thundered halfway down the stairs.

"Is that you, Deet?" Ricky eased his way down the remaining stairs.

"Yeah." He lifted his mother up as the police followed his father into the kitchen. "Mom, come into the kitchen and sit. Would you like some warm milk?" It was a question he'd never asked anyone, but he remembered how his mother smoothed rough spots in his childhood with a cup of warmed milk at night.

She groaned *ja* in German just loud enough to be heard over the crunching of glass in the dining room as the police investigated the damage.

Digging out a saucepan from a cabinet and a quart of milk from the icebox, his curiosity got the best of him. "Here," he ordered Ricky, "see that mom gets a cup of warm milk."

"This was the first one . . . about nine." Arch pointed to a worn brick with a jagged coat of old cement on one side and stamped with the name *Robinson*, a local brickmaker, on the other.

Deet beat them into the living room and turned on the ceiling light and was somewhat surprised to find nothing disturbed other than his mother's knitting on the floor.

"It's on the porch, son." Arch called out as if he anticipated Deet's reaction. "Let the police check it out first."

On the enclosed porch, the police found a similar brick touching the front skirting of the old sleeper sofa. "You said the men taunted you with words like *Red, unionist, and commie*?" The taller officer scribbled notes on a paper pad.

"Yeah," Arch lit another cigarette. "They had to be some company thugs." He rubbed the back of his neck before running his hand over his forehead. "I'm starting to feel kind of shitty . . . almost like I'm getting the flu."

"Just a few more questions, Mister Jenkins. Did you get any kind of look at any of them?" With the officer's nose mere inches from the pad, Deet wondered about his eyesight.

"Yeah, I got a glimpse of two of them from across the street." Staring through the broken window, Arch took a long drag on his cig, exhaling an extended trail of smoke before continuing. "One was tall and young, at least six feet . . . yeah." Arch turned his head toward the officer and hesitated for a bit. "Couldn't have been more than twenty or so, with blond hair. The other guy was shorter with dark hair." He put the cigarette out of its misery in a glass ashtray next to the sofa. "Oh, one other thing . . . the voice of one of them was gravely, like he was a two-pack-a-day guy."

Deet found irony in his father's description as his voice became increasingly raw as he spoke to the policeman.

Still writing, the officer asked, "Why do you think the company would harass you?"

"Because I've expressed my opinion about joining the URW. Who else could have been pissed off about that?"

"Well," the officer seemingly in charge put away his pad and pencil, "we've heard reports of some vigilante activity—people getting rousted and threatened. But most of those cases have involved immigrants." He stepped off the porch steps and looked up at Arch and Deet. "We'll get these details processed and see if there's some common threads with other cases."

The second patrolman came around from the alley, having made a cursory search of the postage stamp lot. "Nothing important around the house."

"We'll be in touch, Mister Jenkins." The pad and pencil cop made his way to the driver's side of the patrol car.

The officer who'd searched around the house walked up the concrete steps to the porch door with Arch's pistol in one hand and the bullets he had ejected from the cylinder in the other. After giving the weapon back to Arch, he pushed up the bill of his cap, and his face shifted to one side. "You know, if you wouldn't push this union thing, these types of events wouldn't happen."

"I'll share that thought with the other gummers the next time the city needs more tax money for police."

After he thought everyone else had gone to bed, Deet readied himself in his room for another shift at Consolidated. As he got dressed, thinking about slogging through another night his mind could be greased by fantasies of Lacey but not an attack on his family. Clenching his fists, Saturday night paled in importance to beating the guilty party's ass. He would share this incident with Dixon and Chaw, and scuttlebutt would take it throughout the plant.

Shortly after eleven, with the air thick and oppressive, he noticed a pale light creeping in the hallway outside his open door. He followed the sneaky glow as he crept downstairs in order not to wake anyone, only to find the lights on in the kitchen. His father sat statue-still at the kitchen table, hands on the table and chin against his chest. "Dad, why are you still up?" Deet put his hand on his father's shoulder.

Arch slumped over with his forehead resting against the table exposing a bluish-black bruise on his neck where it joined the skull.

"Mom!" The teen raced upstairs. "Mom!"

Chapter 7

Akron

September 1937

❝ Why aren't you on your way to school?" Deet's pulse pounded. Whether it was from the three-story climb to this hospital floor's waiting room or the anxiety of his father's undetermined condition, he snapped at his brother.

"Just wait a minute." Ricky stood up from his wooden chair and stuck his arm out toward the wall clock above the doorway through which Deet just entered. "Somebody had to walk with Mom the half-hour up Market Street in the middle of the night. She was blubbering most of the time, and who can blame her. Was I supposed to let her go alone?"

Looking over his shoulder to realize it was only ten till seven, Deet threw up both of his hands. "Alright, alright. I'm sorry." He peered through the windows of the double doors of the hospital ward where his father lay motionless. The lone patient in some sort of small isolation room, he was covered in bedding from his neck down. His mother sat near his father's feet speaking with a white-robed doctor who stood with both hands on the bed's tubular foot rail. "Any news about Dad?"

"Nope." Ricky plopped back down in the chair and folded his arms. "She's been in there since he got wheeled in on a gurney over an hour ago." Restless, he walked over to his older brother by the entrance to the ward. "They must have had him somewhere doing tests . . . maybe, I don't know. The doc just came in about fifteen minutes ago." The tops of a few flecks of blond beard stubble tightened on Ricky's chin as he grabbed his older brother's attention by the shoulder. "Hey, do you think this has anything to do with those brick-throwing bastards?"

"I'm not sure . . . but I doubt it." Deet's attention remained at his father's bedside where his mother stood up and started walking toward him as the doctor exited by another door. "Both bricks came nowhere near hitting him or Mom. The only thing I know for sure is that I want to pound the shit out of those guys." Now, tension across his forehead started a headache.

"You and me both." Ricky retreated a few steps as his mother opened the door, handkerchief still clutched in her hand.

"What's going on, Mom?" Deet asked as the trio sat in a tight cluster of chairs which Ricky arranged.

"I'm too warm." Trudi rose and, with Deet's assistance, took off her woolen overcoat before sitting again. "Your father is in a como . . ." She shook her head in frustration. ". . . a coma. The doctor believes your father is suffering from brain fever, a swelling of the brain."

"Does it have anything to do with what happened at the house last night with those men?" Ricky asked.

Trudi shook her head. "No, as bad as that was, it has nothing to do with it. Doctor Salter says it's some sort of virus. Apparently, a lot of people were getting it about ten years ago but not many lately. We think your father passed out at work yesterday. He didn't know what happened, just that several men were looking down on him when he awoke. He said they were concerned for him, but he refused to be examined and kept working."

"Why didn't you guys tell us?" Deet spoke to his mother as if he were the parent.

"Your father didn't want to alarm either of you. He didn't want to make a big deal about it. He felt fine when he came home yesterday." Her knuckles turned white as she kept kneading the handkerchief.

"So that's how he got the bruise on the back of his neck?" Deet took hold of his mother's hand.

"Bruise on his neck?" A canyon formed in Ricky's freckled cheek.

"Yes," Trudi said. "Doctor Salter . . ." she pointed toward the ward where Arch lay, "Doctor Salter believes, more than likely, the brain fever caused your father to pass out at work, and the bruise came about when he hit the concrete floor."

"So, the brain fever caused him to pass out twice, and now he's in a coma, right?" Ricky stood up and looked out toward Market Street through one of the gridded windows. "For how long?"

"Even the doctor doesn't know for . . . how . . . long," Trudi's voice fell off to a whisper.

"Did anyone see him fall?" Deet asked.

For the first time in almost eight hours, Trudi appeared composed as she straightened her posture and hid her handkerchief in her purse. "There were four or five workers around him when he came to, but your father said none of them saw a thing."

"What if someone hit Dad from behind?"

****

Deet's body went through the motions at the mill that night, but his mind was caught between his father's hospital bed and the assault on his family home the night before. He pushed the rail cart off the scale towards the mixer.

"Hold it, boy!" Dixon's large hand shot out and grabbed the rail car before Deet could dump its load. The Black man stared into his face with the whites of his eyes swelling. "I knows where your mind's at, Jenkins, but that's the second mistake you've made on that scale in the last hour. This load's too light. Geez, if Kershaw'd been around, you'd be out on your ass . . . no matter what shape your father's in."

Deet cocked his head and pursed his lips. He told everyone the night before about the attack on his parents' house, but he hadn't said anything yet about his father's condition.

"Word gets around fast, Jenkins. Coma is it?" The same large hand that stopped the cart now cupped Deet's shoulder.

"Yeah, doctor doesn't know when or if he'll snap out of it. Damn brain fever may very well have caused him to pass out at work yesterday."

"I can imagine it'll be tough on your family . . . not having sick pay for your pop . . . having to scrape by on yours."

The boy twisted out of Dixon's grasp. "Hey, can you think of anyone in this plant besides the bosses who'd hate having a real union?"

"Like I told you from Day One, don't trust anyone around here. But the honest answer is no." A smirk crossed his stubbled face. "Leastways, no one of my color. And another thing, just because fortune has frowned on your family, the worst thing you can do is become some nit-witted tough guy. You're the man of the house now, act like it."

Deet spotted Harley Kershaw walking out of his office at the end of the aisle between milling machines. "Quick, Kershaw!"

Dixon corrected the weight on the rubber cart before dumping it into the mixer while Deet began loading another cart with chunks of raw rubber. The teen's insides churned as the shift supervisor approached his mill.

"Jenkins." Kershaw's voice missed its usual bite.

Deet turned to face him, hoping his boss hadn't noticed his errors on the scale.

"I'm sorry to hear about your dad." Arms at his side, Kershaw's rough exterior had softened a bit. However, his shaved head and pot belly still gave him the look of a hard-boiled egg. "I hope he recovers as soon as possible."

"Thank you, sir."

"At the end of the shift, I want to see you in my office."

"Alright."

Deet finished loading his cart and pushed it toward the scale before scanning his surroundings for Kershaw's presence. With the coast clear, he looked at Dixon, who seemed to know the boy's mind.

"No," the Negro yelled over the clatter of the machinery. "You're not getting fired. He would have done that on the spot if that were the case. He *loves* doing it out here to make a show of it. Just might be your time for movin' on up, *Traveler.*"

****

Somewhat calmed by Dixon's assurances, Deet used the thighs of his pants to wipe the sweat off his palms before he knocked on the door to Kershaw's office.

"Come in!" Harley Kershaw's voice boomed in an unusually jovial manner.

Deet walked into a space not much bigger than a broom closet where Kershaw sat on a swivel chair behind a small, oak desk. Another man in a shirt and tie with dress trousers sat on a wooden chair between the desk and the square window through which Kershaw could view the milling operations. A pair of shiny, black galoshes rested on top of the desk. Deet stood against the closed door.

It's just the end of September. What the hell are these galoshes all about?

"Deet, this here is Alvin Bailey from Consolidated's marketing department." The floor supervisor bowed his bald dome toward the executive.

"How do you do, young man." Bailey stood up and reached out his hand.

As the younger Jenkins shook hands, he realized Bailey's smooth as silk appearance extended to his soft hands.

Don't trust anyone around here.

Dixon's warning played out in the boy's head as he gave a weak grin to each of the two men in turn.

Kershaw rested his elbows on his desk and interlocked the fingers of both hands. "Alvin is in charge of introducing Consolidated's new household products—like these rubber galoshes—into the community." He allowed one hand to touch the metal buckle at the top of the mid-calf boot before letting it trickle down the remaining three buckles.

"It's an overshoe, Deet." Bailey said with some enthusiasm, grabbing one of the rubber boots and slipping it over one of his black patent leather shoes. Without any hesitation, he buckled the boot with ease, encasing his shoe and the lower part of his trouser leg. "This will protect any man's feet and lower legs from the worst an Akron winter can throw at him. And they're just two dollars and forty-nine cents a pair."

"They look very impressive, Mister Bailey, but . . ." Deet looked through the square window as his stomach growled. ". . . but I don't think I can buy those right now."

Kershaw and Bailey looked at each other and laughed before Kershaw coughed out, "Buy?"

"No, son, we don't expect you to buy these." Bailey shook his head. "How'd you like to sell them?"

Deet cocked his head and scratched the blond curls on the edge of his forehead.

"Look, Jenkins." The spring on Harley's chair creaked as he leaned back with his hands behind his head. "We know your family is facing hard times with your dad being laid up. Alvin thinks he can use you to sell these door to door."

"That's right." Bailey patted the sharp crease on his trouser leg and placed the galoshes back on the desk. "If you can spare three hours an afternoon three days a week over the next few months, I think it'd be worth your while . . . how's five dollars an afternoon sound?"

"Five dollars for three hours' work?"

Bailey nodded.

Even with modest mathematical skills, Deet realized that was more than twice his pay rate in the plant. "Fifteen dollars a week?"

Kershaw leaned back far enough for his belly button to show as his shirt pulled out of his pants, smiled broadly and bobbed his head. "We here at Consolidated like to view ourselves as good people. Thought this might help you out . . . but don't go broadcasting it about. We can't do this for everyone."

Sixty dollars extra a month! Don't trust anyone in this place. What's the catch?

"You do a good job out on the street," Kershaw stood up and squirmed his bulk around the desk, "and you just might qualify to be trained for the Squad."

"The Squad?"

"It's a specialized unit of younger workers." Kershaw pulled up on the belt of his trousers. "They learn to do numerous jobs throughout the plant and can be put in place in a minute's notice, just like the time the Simpkins fellow lost part of his hand at the mill next to yours. They make a lot more than what you're making now."

"When do I start?"

Chapter 8

Akron

October 1937

The intermittent rays of sun and occasional chorus of songbirds along Pilgrim Street didn't fool Deet. In a modest, relatively new neighborhood dotted with immature trees lost in the forest of giant utility poles, his basic senses grounded his existence. The stench of rubber ruled as Consolidated's black smoke billowed skyward less than a mile to the west.

"Take it in, Deet." Alvin Bailey smiled, closed his eyes, and inhaled. "That's the smell of money."

During an uneventful second afternoon of accompanying the snazzy dresser as his pack mule, Deet carried a sample case of various boot types as well as some inventory in a second one. He learned to make a polite first impression on the various housewives they met and always played up the positive features of the product.

"Make them feel like their family can't live as well without it ," Bailey preached as they walked the outer edge of the Eastern Hills allotment built by Consolidated itself some decade or two earlier for purchase by their employees.

By three o'clock, Deet's church shoes pressed on his feet like heated tire molds.

"You take this one, Deet." Bailey surprised him as they walked up a half dozen concrete steps to an open front porch.

Stomach churning, the apprentice salesman knocked once on the wooden door of the brick house before it swung open. He stood face to face with a tall, slender blond with curlers encasing her head and a cigarette stuck to her pale lips. "Good afternoon, ma'am. My name is Deet Jenkins, and this here is Mister Alvin Bailey, and we sincerely hope you're having a fine day."

"Well," she blew smoke past Deet's ear, "it hasn't been great so far, but it may be looking up. Whatcha sellin'?"

Deet maintained an awkward smile, concentrating on the general script of his pitch. "Well, with winter fast approaching, Consolidated has come out with new winter footwear for men and women designed to protect one's feet from the harsh weather that will soon be upon us." Dry-mouthed, he felt like he was back on stage of his lone high school play in which he had to sing his only lines. Embarrassed by his performance, he had left the theater forever.

"By the way, is it Missus Perkins whom we have the pleasure of addressing?" Bailey's question highlighted Deet's first mistake—not confirming the customer's name.

"Yeah, that's me. Come on in." Have a seat on the couch. I'll be right back." The woman vanished up the stairway hidden behind the entry door

Deet and Bailey sat down on a floral print sofa with rounded, upholstered arm rests. The boy looked around as his mentor opened the samples case. Furniture was clean but sparse. A single overstuffed chair rested across the room from the couch. Light streamed in from double hung windows on two of the four walls. A third window had its blind pulled down.

"Sorry to keep you gentlemen waiting." Missus Perkins, curlers removed, and lips painted ruby red, walked down from the second floor as if she were an actress making a grand entrance. "We've just bought this place last month, and we're still moving our stuff in." With her plain house dress unbuttoned near the neck, she sat in the large chair and stroked the skin under her chin with the tops of the fingers of one hand. "Now, what do you have to show me?"

Actress Jean Harlow came to mind as Deet admired the woman's medium length, curled, blond hair. "Well, Missus Perkins, as you and your husband need to deal with the upcoming winter, we have a sample of Consolidated's newest galoshes for men and women." He held up one of the men's rubber boots and described its features before doing the same for the more stylish women's outer shoe. As he gave her each sample to inspect, a hint of lilac drifted about the room.

"Yeah, I can see those rubbers would really protect . . . your feet."
She slid her tongue across her upper lip as she ran her fingers along
the shiny black outer surfaces of each boot. "How much did you say
they cost."

"Ah, two forty-nine for the men's pair and a dollar ninety-nine for
the women's." Deet had been around the block enough to know when
a girl was making a play. He strained to keep his mind in his head and
not letting it fall below his waist.

"As you can see, my husband works third shift at Consolidated
and often stays at the URW hall afterwards. He doesn't come home
till late on Wednesdays. Those rubbers would be mighty useful . . .
walking from downtown that is."

"A-hem," Bailey coughed. "Is it true, Missus Perkins, I've heard
the URW is infested with Red agitators. That can't be a good thing . . .
if it's true, that is."

As if he'd been dunked into ice water, Deet glared at Bailey. His
heart pounded as he remembered Bailey making a similar comment to
a woman on Newton Street on his first afternoon two days ago. Bailey
mentioned *rumors* of union thugs roughing up workers outside their
homes.

"Never heard about such things, Mister Bailey. I have other
agitations. I will take one pair of each of those rubbers, if you'd be so
kind . . . a medium in men's and also in women's. How much will that
be?"

Deet took out a paper pad and pencil and began figuring. "With
the state sales tax, that'll be four dollars and sixty-one cents."

"Excuse me while I get my purse." Missus Perkins' hips swung in
a mesmerizing rhythm as she walked out of the living room to the
back of the house before she stopped and looked back. "I won't be
long."

"Yes, ma'am," Mouth open, Deet hoped his face hadn't flushed
too much. When she vanished from sight, he turned toward Bailey
next to him. "What's this talk about commies in the union?" Deet
whispered.

"Not now." Bailey wagged his forefinger back and forth before wiping his hand across his greased, dark hair.

"Here you are, gentlemen." Missus Perkins came back around the corner near one end of the sofa, a fiver in hand. "Who . . . wants it?"

"Allow me, ma'am." Alvin Bailey stood up, dug out some change from his trouser pocket, and exchanged the coins for the five-dollar bill.

Deet wrote out a receipt and set out one medium-sized pair of each style of boot and placed them on the black and burgundy area rug in front of the sofa. "Thank you, again, ma'am." With both cases in hand, Deet gave a cursory bow as he backed out of the house.

Bailey followed and stood on the porch by the door. "Thank you, Missus Perkins, for your time and purchase. You won't regret it. You can trust Consolidated products."

The Perkins woman stood in the doorway with one arm extended against the door casing. "Do come back anytime, gentlemen. I'll be here."

Deet waited until they were down the sidewalk to voice his objection. "What did you mean the union is loaded with commies?"

Bailey put down the sample containers and held up his hands. "Hold on, Deet. First, do you realize what was happening back there? I mean were you getting uncomfortable in any way before I made that comment?"

"Sure!" Deet wave both outstretched arms. "You'd have to be a complete twit not to see she wanted whoopee."

"Precisely," Bailey said as he inhaled with utter resignation on his face, "when she mentioned the union hall, I was hoping to change her frame of mind . . . getting her off her one-track mind."

"Do you run into this often?"

"Often, no, but there's always a dame or two in any neighborhood that's looking for *adventure*." The salesman folded the back of the front seat and returned the sample inventory to the rear seat, "I was working to get us out of an embarrassing situation."

"So, what were you getting us out of on Wednesday with that old crow on Newton Street when you brought up *union thugs?*"

Bailey kept silent as he lowered his head to get into the driver's seat.

"Is this part of the script, or at least to be added once a day?" Deet opened the passenger door to the navy blue '37 Ford coupe.

As he got behind the wheel, Bailey lit a cigarette and started the V-8 engine before turning toward the teen. "Alright, I'll level with ya, kid. You want the extra dough? Then you're going to have to play along and be a missionary."

****

You do realize you've been lumped together with the finks, gorillas, and missionaries Consolidated's recruited . . .

Within minutes of exiting Bailey's Ford, Deet connected *missionary* to how his father had stood up to the company thugs the day of the boy's first sit-down strike. With his father still lying unconscious with a tube stuck down his throat, the teen knew he'd have to spill the beans to someone on his Saturday shift before he got sucked so deep into Consolidated's plan, he'd drown under the failed expectations of his dad and his co-workers. He shared his suspicions with the only man who he could trust, Dixon. Prohibited by the color of his skin to be in the union himself, he thought it best for the boy to confide in Chaw Nelson. The hillbilly floor leader grimaced when Deet explained Bailey's sales pitch, but it didn't surprise him that the company put its hooks into Deet, considering his father's condition. According to Nelson, this was typical Consolidated advertising. Company missionaries canvassed the streets of Akron, especially the neighborhoods where many rubber workers lived, like Eastern Hills, posing as salesmen peddling the company goods. All the while, the real objective was to raise doubt about unions among the wives and other family members of those workers.

His dilemma lay like a tractor tire on his chest during his twenty-minute walk to Lacey's place. By the time his shoes pounded metallic *thuds* on the permanent fire escape to Lacey's apartment above a hardware store on Exchange Street, his head ached, and his stomach gargled. Inside her door, his welcoming embrace didn't meld them together as one inseparable body as usual, and he didn't spend several minutes reconnecting with the full lips he'd missed for a week. Rather, after a few, fleeting seconds of bonding under their noses, he gave her a peck on the cheek and released her. He took off his jacket and draped it on the back of her second-hand couch.

"Glad to see you, too, fella." Lacey's deadpan face alerted Deet as she wore her emotions on her sleeves.

"I'm sorry, Dollface." He threw up his hands and plopped down on the worn, green fabric of the sofa. "I don't want to be a pill, but I got myself into some trouble, and I need some advice." He patted the seat next to him.

"Alright, tell me about whatever it is." Hand on her cheek with her elbow dug into the sofa's back, Lacey sat sideways in order to eye Deet square in the face.

Deet spent the next five minutes explaining the bind between making extra money for the family as a missionary fink or remaining true to his fellow workers. Having leveled with her, he felt the urge to really kiss her, but as she tugged on the side seam of her new jeans while offering a poker face, he thought better of it.

"Did Kershaw and Bailey tell you up front these anti-union comments were part of the job?" Her suspenders stretched over the contour of her chest as she repositioned her arm against the couch.

"No. It was all about selling galoshes." Deet prayed to himself that Lacey would offer some wisdom which wouldn't upset anyone at the factory.

"How long have you worked at Consolidated?"

"Four months."

"How about your dad, before he got hurt?" Seemingly tired of the sideways position, Lacey swung her hips around for her torso to face forward while keeping her face turned toward Deet.

"Twenty years."

"Who's that Black gummer you work with . . . D—?"

"Dixon."

"How long has he been there?

"Nine years . . . yeah, he told me once, nine years."

"Look." She gently cupped her hand over his. "Tryin' to deal with your father being in a coma is tough, and like I've told you before, if there's anything I can do to help, you know I will."

He wiggled his hand out from under hers, so he could squeeze it. "I know you will, Lace."

"Before I give my thoughts, let's start from the top." She leaned into him and presented her lips.

This time Deet didn't hesitate and buried his hand in her bobbed, light brown strands at the back of her head while their lips exploded with wanton sensations. The aroma of rose water perfume engulfed him as his torso pressed against her white blouse. For nearly a minute, all his problems evaporated as she became his anesthetic. Then, she broke away, tilting her head into a *this is going to hurt you more than it hurts me* moment.

"You . . . fresh out of high school, want to put the kibosh on the goals these workers have fought over and gone on strike over for years? You know how damn dangerous that plant is, or have you forgotten about your first night on the job?"

His emotions whiplashed, Deet's eyes stared at Lacey while he relived those horrid moments where he helped Dixon rescue Simpkins and his mangled hand.

"Consolidated saw you in a bad way and wanted to take advantage of you at the expense of the other guys." Her caring eyes remained locked on Deet as she exhaled a bit. "I get it. You won't make that type of money for three hours work elsewhere, but you can pick up some extra dough legitimately at some mom-and-pop store or delivering papers . . . or you can play Judas."

Deet recoiled. This time he didn't feel the soft curves of romance over his face, rather the sharp contours of a scowl. Although he grew up in the church of his mother's choice, as he'd grown older, he'd drifted. Yet, enough teachings of his early years in Sunday school remained to make the reference to Jesus' unfaithful disciple sting.

"That's easy to say if you're not standing in my shoes."

"In your shoes," she straightened her posture and looked him in the eyes, "that's true. However, in the Consolidated world, that's what you'd be— in the shoes of a Judas paid by the company pharisees to betray his fellow workers."

Then she crossed her arms in front of her and stared ahead at a bare, wall-papered wall. "You weren't in my shoes on that picket line at Consolidated over a year ago when police and vigilante thugs tried to roust us back to work. You didn't have to breathe in the tear gas. You didn't have to see a fellow flipper worker getting a finger shot off." Lacey paused and a tear coursed down her cheek as she mumbled, "And you haven't had booze blow up your family to the point your mother begged you to leave for your own safety."

Deet inhaled as his ego smarted. "No, I haven't." Louie came to mind, but he never had to live under the same roof with his uncle. He pulled her close to him with both arms. "I'm sorry." His head on her shoulder, he caressed her hair. She had opened a part of her world just as he had his. He always associated strikes with men. As far as her home life was concerned, it hadn't come up, and it wasn't any of his business. He always knew her as a strong-willed individual, but now he got a glimpse of what made her gears tick.

Content in a mutual embrace, minutes passed before Deet kissed her on her forehead before noticing the clock behind her. "Hey, it's almost movie time. Maria and Casper, . . . they'll be waiting. Bogart, right? *The Black Legion?*"

"You got it."

****

A glum Maria held a solemn-faced Casper Miller's hand as Deet and Lacey approached them in front of the movie house.

"Maria, Casper what's the matter?" Lacey asked.

74

"Mister Bob . . . Mister Bob," through huge brown eyes, moistened by tears already shed, she struggled getting the words out through an anguished face. "Mister Bob, he fire me."

"Fired you?" Deet's face crumpled in disbelief. "For what reason?"

"He say my English is not good enough . . . customers complained." Maria's hurt painted the darkened crescents under her eyes of a woman years older than she was.

Deet looked at Lacey, Casper, and Maria. "That's bullshit. You've served me . . . us . . . a lot in the past several months. We've never seen anyone hassle you. Right?" Deet looked at each of his three companions. "That doesn't sound like the Bob I know."

"No," they said in unison, each shaking their heads.

"Has anyone ever complained to you, Maria?" Lacey asked. "Especially recently?"

With eyes glued to the sidewalk, she shook her head.

"You'd have to live with the high and mighty not to have brushed shoulders with folks who've emigrated." Lacey looked down Market Street in both directions. "There's quite a few different languages at Consolidated. There's certainly a good number in the flipper beading department."

"What work is done there?" Maria dabbed her eyes with a dainty handkerchief.

"We girls put a thin circular rubber bead inside a small rubber tube that eventually anchors a tread to the body of a tire." Lacey's eyes lit up. "Hey, Maria, why don't you come down to Consolidated Monday morning and ask to apply for work in the flipper department? We're always in need of new girls."

Maria's eyes finally rose a bit, and her dazzling white teeth became visible as her lips relaxed. "*Si*, I do."

The group got their tickets and popcorn with about ten minutes left before showtime. Lacey and Deet held the bags while Maria and Casper went to their respective restrooms.

"Who'd be behind such shit?" Lacey glanced over her shoulder as if the enemy could be lurking anywhere.

"Vigilantes . . . maybe." Deet scanned the late arrivals. "Least ways, Dad's mentioned them."

"Vigilantes?" The complexion of Lacey's lightly tanned face darkened as creases sprouted from her forehead to her chin.

"There's a fair number of people in this town that can't stand foreigners . . ." Deet whispered as Maria came out of the restroom. ". . . and union members."

Chapter 9

Akron

October 1937

❝ It's been over three weeks. Is he ever coming back to us?" Ricky stood almost toe-to-toe with the slender, middle-aged doctor in the waiting room. While a good wind could have blown the doc on his ass, his nerve in the face of the boy's outburst proved unflappable.

"Take it easy, Ricky." Deet stood up and created a physical barrier between the overwrought sixteen-year-old and the composed physician, who came out of their father's ward to brief the entire family.

Ricky backed away toward the windows while Deet pleaded with the doctor. "Is there any hope for him to snap out of it?"

"I'd say there's a fifty-fifty chance he'll come out of his coma. To be even more honest, that chance diminishes with each week he remains in it. This brain fever apparently is caused by a virus of which we know very little. There was an epidemic when I began my practice right after the war. Trouble was the Spanish flu pandemic hit, and not much attention was paid to something we didn't understand . . . and we still don't.

"I can tell you this. If he comes out of it, he won't be the same man he was before the illness."

"What do you mean, Doctor?" Trudi looked up at the white-clad physician with her hands interlocked as if in prayer.

"Most cases of survivors of this illness are weakened and in a palsy-like state for the rest of their lives. I'm sorry, but he'd be an invalid."

Trudi inhaled quickly to stifle a sob as Ricky pounded a fist into the palm of the other hand.

Deet lowered his head and shook it back and forth. "Thank you, Doctor Salter."

"Great!" A deep voice roared into the room. "Just the people we need to talk to."

Deet and the others gawked at two men who looked to be complete opposites. Cloaked in a dark brown overcoat, the shorter man who announced their presence possessed a bowling pin shape. Slits for eyes atop a flabby face hid any clue of eye color. The other man stood well over six feet with a dark blue knee-length coat covering a trim figure. Wavy, jet-black hair was combed back with a part in the middle of the taller man's scalp.

"I'm Detective Gerald Ragmon, APD," the chubby one said as he flashed an ID card. "This here is my partner Detective Kelly." The other man showed his identification as well. "I presume you're Missus Jenkins," Ragmon said after putting his wallet away and removing a brown fedora from his mostly bald head.

Trudi nodded. "Yes."

"And these are your two sons?" Ragmon wondered out loud.

"Yeah, I'm Deet, and this is Ricky." The older brother spoke with a touch of sass, annoyed at the intrusion of the two strangers.

"Excellent." Ragmon grinned, ignoring the slight. "That brings us to Doctor Salter, I presume."

The doctor chewed on his lower lip for a moment before nodding as well. "What is this all about Detective Ragmon? I'm a busy man and have many other patients under my care that need my presence."

"We hope to make this quick, Doctor." Kelly spoke for the first time and his voice sounded confident but not overbearing.

"Downtown got an anonymous phone call last evening about a mysterious incident at Consolidated a couple weeks back." The multiple chins of Ragmon bobbed up and down as he spoke, but the slits between his eyelids never parted. "The caller indicated there might have been some criminal intent behind your husband's accident, Missus Jenkins. In fact, although the call was somewhat garbled, the word *union* was mentioned."

"After three weeks, it's going to be a slog to try to connect the dots." Kelly walked over to take a casual glance out the window. "We might not have even come to talk to you, Missus Jenkins, except that in reviewing the department's records, we noticed there was an incident at your residence the very night of your husband's misfortune at work."

"Excuse me, Detective." Salter exhaled and looked at Ragmon. "Whatever you need to know from me, can you get on with it? I'm needed elsewhere."

"Certainly, Doctor. What's your diagnosis concerning Mister Jenkins?"

"In layman's terms, brain fever. Technically, viral encephalitis . . . a swelling of the brain caused by a virus."

"Did you see any outward signs of foul play, any bruises, cuts or other such obvious wounds?"

Salter inhaled. "There was a dark contusion at the base of the neck."

Deet observed Ragmon's surprise as the detective's blue eyes appeared from behind the eyelids.

Dr. Salter must have caught on as well. "Don't jump to any conclusions on that Detective. Passing out in a factory setting could have caused that bruise . . . anything from the edge of a work bench to the concrete floor. His symptoms are classic for encephalitis *lethargica*—feverish upon admittance, muscle rigidity, sleepiness which probably led to his collapse, and his present coma."

"Would there have been any obvious symptoms while he was conscious, Doctor Salter?" Kelly asked.

"Well, sleepiness and flu-like symptoms—fatigue, headache, dizziness. I believe Missus Jenkins said she didn't notice any other symptoms but maybe the boys did."

"Thanks, Doctor." Ragmon's face turned into a smiling cartoon character. If we need to talk again, we'll get in touch at a more convenient time for you."

The bottom of the doctor's white medical coat fanned out behind him as if caught in a sudden gust of wind as Ragmon turned back to the family. "Well, Missus Jenkins, boys, what about it? Did you witness any of those symptoms from your husband or father leading up to his accident?"

"No, Detective, my husband was fine until that night when he became unconscious at the kitchen table." Calm, Trudi still clutched a handkerchief in one hand.

"I did." The two words came out of Deet with little energy, and he swished his tongue around the inside of his mouth to gain some moisture. He felt four sets of eyes on him.

"What?" The blue of Ragmon's eyes made an unexpected encore.

Deet leaned over a bit and extended his arms to brace himself on the back of his wooden chair. "On the porch that night of the brick-throwing incident, I was with him as he was answering questions from the patrolman. He said he wasn't feeling well, and that he had a headache. His voice almost sounded like it was getting a sore throat. Until the doctor mentioned those types of symptoms, I never thought much about it."

"Say," Ricky chirped as his freckled face flushed, "we haven't heard boo from the police since my parents were attacked with bricks on that night. And the only reason you're here now is because of some crackpot phone call about something at Dad's work." He started pointing a forefinger at the detectives as if the finger were the barrel of a pistol. "Why don't you bother those guys with these stupid questions?"

"Take it easy, Ricky." Deet dropped his hand on his brother's wrist and lowered the offending arm before speaking to Ragmon. "My brother might be a bit out of line in style, but he makes a fair point. Why aren't you guys working on finding who assaulted our house and folks?"

"There's a lot of dirt that needs to be cleaned up in this city, Deet. It takes time and more men than we have." Kelly wasted no time in answering the boy as he took a single step towards him.

"But as Ricky put it, chasing down a bullshit phone call is more important than an obvious assault?" Deet felt his spine tighten.

"Well, look at this way," Kelly said as he walked toward his partner, "it did bring renewed attention to the case you're interested in . . . didn't it?" With that the two detectives walked out and met someone in the hall with whom they engaged in laughter and conversation.

"Don't worry, Mom." Deet pulled his chair next to his mother and sat down as he placed his hand on hers. "I'll keep turning over my pay to you in order to cover the hospital bill."

"Bill Mowery said he could use me to help make furniture deliveries for this antique dealer." For a change, Ricky's demeanor swung towards the positive. "That'll help with the cost of other things, Mom."

Deet inwardly cringed at the mention of Bill Mowery, a chronic troublemaker at Central who was a year older than him. However, this wasn't the time for more drama. "I'm gonna look for a part-time job during the afternoon, if I can find one. He'd never mentioned a word about the door-to-door sales position, and now that he had a change of heart about it, he was glad.

"You're such good boys." Handkerchief in hand, Trudi sniveled as Deet grabbed her around the shoulders, and Ricky sat next to her on the other side.

When the three of them looked up, there stood Jack Acker. "Excuse me, Missus Jenkins, Deet, Ricky. I'm sorry to have walked in on you like this." Dressed in a camel-colored overcoat, not a strand of blond hair out of place, he bowed and spoke with that distinctive voice as if he was narrating an opera. "You folks have my utmost sympathy for your family's trying situation."

Trudi offered a weak smile while she nodded, and her two boys sat emotionless.

The councilman's appearance produced the first smile of the day in a wide-eyed Trudi. "Thank you, Mister Acker, but I'm sure you have more important things on your schedule than to make an extra trip to the hospital."

"To be honest, Missus Jenkins," Acker patted her hand, "My brother-in-law just had his appendix removed, and I came to check on him. I heard about the dreadful incident at your house several weeks back, and I've been meaning to get in touch with you about that." For a change, the slick talking lawyer groped for words as he looked around to each of the boys before focusing on Trudi again. "Well . . . then . . . then I just bumped into Detectives Ragmon and Kelly near the nurse's station, who informed me of Arch's unfortunate situation. My law practice allows me breaks in my schedule, but the hours are unpredictable. So, having this opportunity, I made it a point to check in on Arch."

"That's very kind of you. You're good people, Mister Acker."

Acker gave a forced smile and a dip of his head before he edged to the windowed double doors and peered into Arch's room. "He's still in a coma, is he?"

"Yes, he's got viral encephalitis." Deet spoke up.

"Oh-h," the councilman's mouth dropped. "So, it wasn't any criminal attack similar to what happened at your home some weeks back?"

"No," Trudi shook her head.

"Rumors swirl like leaves off the trees this time of year." Acker took the few steps necessary to return to the family.

"No, it wasn't criminal." Ricky snarled like an injured animal. "Our father's sick! A pip like you has enough pull in this town. Get the word out!"

"Ricky!" Trudi was on the verge of tears.

"Relax, will ya?" Deet went to usher his brother out of the room, but Ricky stomped out on his own. "I'm sorry you had to listen to that, Mister Acker."

"Think nothing of it, Deet. Your father's condition is extremely stressful for all of you. If you need any type of assistance, please don't hesitate to call me either at home or my office. If I'm not home, just leave a message. I'll get back to you." Acker left.

"He's such a good man." Trudi rested her head on the tips of a thumb and two fingers.

Deet reflected back on Lacey's unsuccessful attempt to lobby for a softball league. "Yeah, Mom, he appears to be a good man."

****

November 1937

Before Monday's first shift began, Deet dropped by Chaw Nelson's locker to explain his decision to quit the *salesman* position.

"You told Kershaw, did ya?" Chaw plucked a wad of loose-leaf tobacco out of a paper pouch and stuck it in the back corner of his mouth.

"Yeah. He wasn't necessarily happy about it, but he didn't flip his wig."

"Well, that's good, kid." Nelson dug out an old soup can from his locker, and the two started out to the mills. "Just the same, keep a watch out. I wouldn't trust that bastard for as far as I can throw him." He accentuated his point by spitting some tar-colored juice into the can.

Deet met Dixon at their mixing machine, and the Black man issued his own warning. "Jenkins, you've just made some strong buddies, but just like a stung cow'll kick, a few powerful enemies will try to get even. Be sure to stick with the scale on every cart you fill."

As he'd done for the past five months, Deet filled each cart with the shoe-box-sized chunks of raw rubber as the black mist from the milling machines swirled about and settled upon him. The penetrating odor of benzene, so prevalent his first few weeks on the job, had become a mere occasional nuisance. Cart after cart, he made sure each load was within the half-pound tolerance at the scale. Shortly before the meal break, he had another load at the scale, which read two ounces over, well within the weight specifications.

Br-r-ring! Br-r-ring! Br-r-ring!

Someone switched the nearest milling machine—the one on which Simpkins mangled his hand—on emergency shutdown.

"Shit!" The recognizable voice of Carver, one of its operators, was easily heard.

Instinct, honed by experience, took over and Deet rushed over, fearing the worst. Instead, he found a sheepish Carver scratching his head as he stared at a crushed broomstick in between the mill's rollers.

"Tried to fish out a specs sheet before I lost it forever in the compound." Carver stood with the brush end of the broom in his hand.

"Get a couple pry bars and dig out the handle." Dixon shouted before his eyes widened at the sight of Deet at the mill.

Deet realized his error and rushed back to the mixing machine only to find a smug-faced Kershaw. "Your load is five pounds over, Jenkins."

"Bullshit!" Deet snapped. "That load was within two ounces of specs when I rushed over to help Carver . . . that is, until I realized he didn't need my help."

"Well, it's your ticket." Kershaw held up the paper identifying the loader. "And the scale is accurate and five pounds over."

"Someone messed with my load! Someone—" Deet felt a strong hand hold him back from going after Kershaw.

Dixon nodded his head in the direction of the entry doors—the same ones behind which Arch had talked down a company mob from entering—where now two burly company guards stood, cross-armed, each with a billy club in hand.

"Clean out your locker and get the hell out of here," Kershaw sneered. "You're done."

Chapter 10

Cleveland

November 1937

Not even the stink bombs lobbed by protestors outside the assembly hall on the east side of Cleveland and a strong police presence could dampen Hugo's enthusiasm for tonight's festivities of the German American Bund. Having turned eighteen and in good standing with the Bund, he graduated into the uniform worn by his father—light khaki shirt and black trousers held together with a matching Sam Brown belt. A black tie and side cap atop his greased back hair highlighted his outfit as much as his glossy black boots, on which he labored over an hour to obtain just the right sheen.

Another national leader of the German American Bund was scheduled to speak to several hundred Cleveland-area members. Even though Hugo saw a few men in civilian suits, including several with dark blue side caps, there was a buzz of excitement in the large room as Nazi-style uniforms milled about. Hugo smiled and allowed his fantasy to take over.

Some day . . . some day, I will be in Berlin . . . among those who've rubbed shoulders with Der Fuehrer.

"Good evening, Herr Schmidt." Fred Geller called out as father and son walked to their assigned row of wooden seats. Hugo felt his father's hand on the small of his back push him along.

"Hello, Fred, good to see you again . . . and Hugo as well." Wearing a khaki suit coat with black upper lapels, the local Bund leader shook each Geller's hand in turn. "Hugo, I haven't forgotten about your daring exploit earlier this year in rescuing your father. In fact, word filtered down to me that you were one of the top marksmen at the youth camp in July."

"Thank you, Herr Schmidt. It would be my greatest honor if in the not-too-distant future, I would be able to use my skills by fighting the communists for the Fatherland."

"Let's not get ahead of ourselves, first things first. Remember, on that night in June I told you the Bund could have use for *men* like you?"

Hugo beamed and nodded.

"The Bund is growing, especially here in Cleveland. In fact, that is why we felt confident enough to invite some of our American brethren from the American Legion to hear our speaker this evening. Anyway, with growth comes the need for more men. I understand you will graduate from high school next spring. Freed from the responsibilities of schoolwork along with a driver's license, opportunities for you will open up."

Fred's face froze in self-satisfaction. "He already has his driver's license. He will be a good soldier for the cause."

Pride swelled inside Hugo. "Perhaps I could start my duties early?"

"We shall see." Schmidt offered a faint smile and a slight nod. "For now, remain patient and dwell on the words of Herr Jurgens. We hope to plant seeds this evening." Schmidt excused himself and walked up the few steps to the elevated stage where several Bund dignitaries awaited him.

In short order, Schmidt introduced Oscar Jurgens to a warm ovation from the crowd. A man of medium height and build, Jurgens wore the same dress uniform as Schmidt but with fancier epaulets on the shoulders of his jacket. Close enough to the stage to see the shine of Jurgens' balding forehead reflect off the speaker's combed-back hair, Hugo listened intently.

"Bund members are you not patriotic Americans cut from the same cloth as George Washington?" Jurgens cried out as he turned to one side and extended an arm towards the first president's portrait.

The crowd of a few hundred roared its approval.

"Yet by our ethnic makeup, we also have strong ties to Germany." He pointed to the American and Nazi flags side by side in the middle of the stage behind him and the large photo of Adolph Hitler hanging next to that of Washington behind the national banners. "Let me make this perfectly clear." He began to pound his fist on the podium. "As long as the Stars and Stripes sits next to the swastika, America will remain free. Only the hammer and sickle can doom America."

Hugo felt shivers as he joined others in clapping that stung his hands.

"The phrase *America first* is becoming more popular by each successive year, each successive month, and with good reason. We Americans need to tend to our own affairs on this continent and not be dragged into the connivance of distant foreign lands. We must be sure to keep Jewish wishes from derailing the goals of this great nation." His voice became more strident and harsher. "On a more personal note, the Bund and Nazism stand for the religion under which you grew up. We believe in the freedom of religion which made this nation great and intend to keep it great." Once again, a fist to the lectern punctuated his point.

Like some globular millipede, hundreds of arms were raised and shaken as the crowd cheered its approval. Hugo joined in the raucous cheers of the audience, dreaming of holding power in such a future government, spurning the pleas from all those who'd mocked him at school.

The pitch of Jurgens' voice fell somber again. "However, there is a condition which we must confront similar to how Herr Hitler has successfully steered Germany out of its economic and societal decay. Democracy can become like a sickness, much like overeating leads to flabby stomachs, weakened muscles, and the deterioration of overall health. Too much freedom weakens the national resolve and allows a mix of mongrel cultures to rust the iron will of the people.

"Under Herr Hitler, the Germans have undertaken this challenge, and it has resulted in the renewed vigor of the German nation. America, as well, can throw off the shackles of its present economic and moral decline. There is an antidote to this malaise which has hung over America this decade. The Constitution, and with it the Bill of Rights, must be significantly altered so as to give an elected leader supreme power and elevate the religion of our fathers as that of the state!"

Again, the crowd thundered in agreement. However, when the clamoring died down, a lone voice pushed back. "Hold on there! You post George Washington next to *Herr Hitler*, the American flag next to the banner of the Nazis, and claim the German Bund is loyal to America."

Hugo and those around him turned to see a man standing in a civilian suit, wearing his own style side cap—the dark blue one of the American Legion. A few others with similar caps sat near him.

"We fought one German government in the Great War to preserve our democracy and our constitution. And now you're all for destroying the most important part of our nation's past and present for some goose-stepping future?"

The fervent crowd erupted in an attempt to shout the man down, but another man in a dress suit rose to the legionnaire's defense. "I am a German American," the man spoke with a strong accent and even deeper conviction. "I agree with this man."

Loud mumblings and agitated movements surged across the crowd as the immigrant continued to make his point. "America is devoted to democracy and millions of German Americans such as me resent your traitorous remarks."

Jurgens' screamed a response as dozens of Nazis got out of their seats and swarmed toward the two dissenters from multiple directions. "The moral decay of America is here in this hall for all to witness." He pointed at the immigrant speaker. "You have chosen to lift a dangerous, decrepit ideology as a faith rather than submit to the religion of your fathers."

All hell broke loose as uniformed Bund members tried to physically remove the two men. With the help of five other legionnaires, the first protestor turned the hall into a bar room brawl, swinging haymakers and landing most of them. The immigrant squirmed and fought his way toward the American Legion contingent, but police funneling in through the lobby interrupted the events with swinging bull clubs, intent on making numerous arrests.

Hugo began toward the fray, only to be held back.

"No, Hugo." Local Bund leader Schmidt put a vice-like grip on the boy's shoulder. "You want to help our cause, right?"

With a scrunched and confused face, Hugo nodded.

"Then I need you clean!" Schmidt needed to raise his voice to be heard. "I need you to have a clean record. I don't want you arrested. Fred, take him out the back way, and both of you go directly to your vehicle and home."

Disappointed, Hugo followed his father. He was good at taking orders.

Chapter 11

Akron

November 1937

At two in the morning, while the night hid rubber's soot but not its smell, Deet hoped to sneak in the back door to his family's kitchen. Just as he bumbled his way through the door, he ran into a shadowy figure, who he wrestled to the ground. With one hand pinning the intruder to the wall, he punched the button switch to the ceiling light with a finger from the other.

"What the hell are you doing this time of night?" Deet tried his best not to scream his surprise.

"I could ask you the same thing." Dressed in a dark cap and second-hand leather jacket, Ricky's freckled complexion and fringes of red hair seeped out of his garb as he pushed himself away from his brother. "Bill's got a load of antiques that need moving."

"In the middle of the night!" Now, Deet's voice couldn't be restrained. "I told you Mowery's nothing but a cheap ass hoodlum." He grabbed his brother by the shoulders. "What do you expect you're going to be doing at this time of night?" In just a few weeks, his father's illness turned Deet's outlook on his brother. He'd never bothered with Ricky's comings and goings before the disaster. Then again, he never knew his brother to stalk the streets of Akron in the middle of the night. Gradually releasing his pressure on Ricky, Deet succumbed to the only resistance his younger brother offered—a cocksure stare.

"I'll answer that if you answer my question first." A mischievous grin spread across Ricky's face.

Still clutching to the scuffed leather, Deet took a deep breath and exhaled. "Alright, shoot."

"Why aren't you at work?"

Deet released his hold on Ricky's jacket. "I was canned."

"Sh-h-hit." The profanity hissed out between Ricky's lips. "What for?"

"They said I overloaded my cart of raw rubber." The older brother sat down at the kitchen table. "That was bullshit. I'm sure Kershaw sabotaged my cart while I checked on an emergency at the mill next to me."

"That's all the more reason for me to be working for Bill. Look, you know piddly part-time jobs are few and far between. You can talk about finding extra work, but it's still tough to find something regular that pays more than peanuts. Now, you're out of work, there'll be no money coming in, and Mom's got those hospital bills, let alone food, electricity, the house payment."

"So, what's Mowery told you about tonight's *job*?" With no logical argument to counter what Ricky just said, Deet turned away, unable to face him.

"He told me that this dealer needed furniture from an estate sale cleared out of his warehouse before eight this morning, because another load was arriving then."

"To where are the two of you hauling this old furniture?"

"Bill said we're to take it to the guy's shop somewhere on Exchange Street. He'd be there to open up."

Already weary of being his brother's keeper, Deet raised the white flag. "It's going to be a tough day at school tomorrow."

"Yeah, I'll figure it out."

As the light on the staircase spread across the entry to the foyer, Ricky made his way out the back door, leaving Deet to explain everything while consoling his despondent mother.

****

A semi-conscious Ricky left for school on a blustery morning the next day. Over oatmeal and an egg, Deet still offered his mother hope. "I'll stop by a couple of the smaller plants on either side of Consolidated today. I might have a chance of getting in one of those."

Trudi laid her hand on her son's wrist. "Tell me something, Dietrich."

Deet stopped mid-chew and knew something was bothering his mother, something beyond wondering about his father's chances of survival. "Sure, Mom, anything."

"Your girlfriend Lacey works with many women at Consolidated, yes?"

Deet nodded.

"You think you could ask her if I could get a job at Consolidated?"

His mouthful of oatmeal turned to cement by the time it hit his stomach. The soft warmth of his voice tried to coat his cold, hard logic. "You wouldn't make even as much as I did, Mom, because you'd be doing piece work. The place wreaks of burnt rubber and benzene, and in the summer it's hot as hell inside those brick walls. Besides, the name Jenkins isn't very popular there right now." Deet pushed parts of his fried egg across his plate as if it were a hockey puck. "And . . ."

"And what?" his mother challenged.

"And when Dad comes home, wouldn't you want to be here to take care of him?"

"Of course, of course." Trudi clutched her apron as her face melted into wrinkles of agony. "But I don't seem to have much choice, Dietrich. Even with your pay, all the bills were too much before yesterday, and now—"

A knocking on the back door interrupted her, and Deet went into the mudroom to see who it was. Upon opening the door, there was a stubble-faced Uncle Louie under a gray flat cap holding a bag of groceries in one arm. "May I come in?"

"Sure." Deet hadn't seen his uncle recently except for a brief *Hello* at the hospital shortly after his father's admittance. "Mom, it's Uncle Louie."

Trudi stayed seated, milking her coffee. "What brings you around, Louie?" She glanced at him for a moment before finishing the last bites of her toast.

"I went in to see Arch last week and, to say the least, I was upset by what I learned." Louie put down the bag on the counter. "I've had some decent repair work recently—"

"Have a seat, Louie." Deet acted as the graceful host. "Would you like a cup of coffee?"

"I wouldn't mind some." He took off an old, full-length coat with a noticeable hole in one elbow and sat across from Trudi. "As I was saying, I've had some decent repair jobs of late, and I just figured you folks might be able to use some extra bread, cheese, and eggs."

"We don't need charity, Louie," Trudi said with an emotionless face.

Deet exhaled deeply as he poured his uncle some coffee. "Yeah, Mom, right now, we do."

During the next ten minutes, the boy explained their plight ending with yesterday's termination.

Louie took a sip of warm coffee and shook his head. "Damn, that's tough. At least Ricky's got some work."

"I'm going to check out some of the smaller factories today and tomorrow—Phillips, Acme, Jones . . . hope to find something there."

"Ah, there was one other reason for my visit." Louie's face sounded like sandpaper as he ran his hand over his chin. Blackened deposits under his nails testified to recent work.

"What's that?" Trudi commanded as she began to clear dishes off the table.

Behind his metallic spectacle frames, Louie's green eyes swelled as he looked directly at Deet. "I could use your help to remove an engine from a '30 Model A. I already have most everything detached, but I need another person to help take off the motor mounts and guide the engine off the chassis cross members when I have my shop crane attached to it."

Deet shrugged his shoulders. "Sure, why not."

"I'd really appreciate it, Deet. There'll be a couple bucks in it for you."

After Louie left, Deet confronted his mother. "You really don't care for Uncle Louie, do you?"

Trudi shrugged, seemingly more interested in the dirty dishes. "Not really."

"Why not?"

Trudi placed some dishes in the sink and snapped her head towards her oldest son. "He's a drunk, been a drunk, and will always be a drunk. That's why Aunt Betty left him. That's why his business is in ruins."

"You don't like Dad hanging around him either?" For the first time, Deet noticed the crows' feet at the edges of his mother's eyes had sprouted more branches and a few streaks of gray dappled her brunette bun.

"I won't lie to you, Dietrich. Yes, they're brothers, but your father always seems to drink more when Louie is around. I never wanted your father to . . . to . . . " The tears began to flow. " . . .to become like him." Trudi's emotions boiled over into a waterfall as she rushed upstairs.

****

Deet drove the Pontiac over to Louie's around eleven that morning. Somewhat shocked, the teen found an organized, fully functioning repair garage. The scrap metal trash behind the house, next to the garage still remained—a cemetery to steel, a memorial to rust, and a dumping ground for several fifty-five-gallon drums of empty beer and whiskey bottles. However, the hoarded clutter, which had consumed one bay inside the garage had been removed, replaced by a Model-A with a shop crane in front of it. Meanwhile, Louie worked bent over the front fender of a dark blue '32 Chevy in the other bay.

"Hello, Deet." Louie popped up with a wrench in his hand. "Let me just put the finishing touches on this Chevy's fan belt." He got in the car and started it up, producing a high-pitched squeal that made Deet cover his ears.

Louie turned off the vehicle and hopped back over the fender, a ratchet in hand this time. "You know, Deet," his voice somewhat muffled by the confines of the engine, "if you don't get the tension just right on a fan belt, you can open yourself to a number of problems." After a bit of a grunt and downward jerk of his arm, he stood erect again.

"Such as." Deet stood nearby with his arms folded.

"If it's too loose, you get that nasty squeal, which is telling you just that. Left unchecked, your water pump won't function right, and your radiator will overheat." Louie got back in the Chevy and started it. The engine purred as the fan whirred.

Deet's uncle got out and checked over his work. "If its tension is too tight, the same thing can happen, and in either case, the belt can break."

Deet walked toward the mechanic as he turned off the Chevrolet. "That's good to know, Uncle Louie. I'll be sure to pay attention to the sounds of the Pontiac's belt."

"It's more than that, Deet." Louie stepped over to a workbench next to the Chevy and returned the ratchet to its rightful place in a toolbox. "It mirrors life . . . certainly mine."

He grabbed a pack of Lucky Strikes and offered one to Deet, who shook it off, before lighting one for himself. "Betty couldn't handle my drinking. It caused too much tension. It wasn't a shock when she left and eventually got a job as a mail carrier."

Deet cocked his head. He wasn't used to Louie being philosophical.

"Yeah, take that Consolidated plant you used to work in." Louie took a puff and exhaled smoke, which was quickly kidnapped by a breeze. "The guy who owns this Chevy dropped it off yesterday and said that the plant had another sit-down strike yesterday. For all I know, it's still going on. Who knows the reason? I don't, but the point is there has to be just the right amount of tension between labor and management for that factory, any factory, to function properly. If either side presses too hard or gets too lax, things break down. Over the past eighteen months, the tension at Consolidated has been totally out of whack. Something's got to give and soon."

"Well, it's not going to be including me, whatever happens." Deet felt the need to shift gears. "Hey, the garage looks a whole lot better than the last time I was here with Dad."

"I have some good stretches at times when I can think clearer." Half a cigarette still in his mouth, Louie wiped his hand with a rag as he walked to the far side of the Model A. "I'm clear now because I can't remember."

He picked up a different ratchet out of a second toolbox, slightly larger than the first. "I got to make a living while I can." He took a final drag on his smoke before crushing it with his boot in the gravel. He nodded his head to the bottle-filled barrels and handed the ratchet to Deet. "I've got almost everything detached that needs to be taken off." Louie picked up his own ratchet from the top of the stripped-down engine. "I've got four motor mount bolts—two on my side down below and two on your side . . . attached to the crossmember that we need to take out. Then we can finagle it out with the crane."

Looking between the crane's parallel vertical chains, Deet realized a new portrait of his uncle, at least new for him. Curiosity egged him deeper into Louie's past. "Louie, why do you drink?"

"To forget that which I can't bear to remember." Louie's head and arm were bent down toward the ground. "Come on, Deet, get with it on your end. It's best if we can loosen each side in tandem."

Deet found it took considerable strength to break the bolts loose. The lower of his two required a pipe for added leverage on the ratchet handle and for him to lay on the pitted, oil-stained concrete floor. Within an hour, they removed the bolts and worked the engine out of the vehicle's front cavity.

"Thanks, Deet." Louie dug out two crinkled dollar bills and handed them to him. "The guys delivering the new engine tomorrow will take this one off my hands and help me slip the new one in."

Deet put up his hand. "No, Uncle Louie, think of it as a favor."

"Nonsense." Louie stuffed the bills into the boy's jacket pocket. "Just remember what I said about tension. It applies to families as well, and yours is really being torqued at the moment. Loosen it wherever you can." He took another smoke off the workbench, came outside and lit it. "God knows I busted the tension all to hell in mine."

The ringing from a phone in the garage interrupted any further prodding Deet might have had.

"Wonder who that might be. Never can tell with these damn party lines." Louie marched into the garage and called out, "It's for you. It's your mother."

"Why would she be calling?"

Dad! Oh my God, no!

Deet picked up the receiver of the candlestick phone. "Hello. Mom, what's wrong?"

"A Mister Nelson called. He said you're to come back to Consolidated tonight on your usual shift."

Chapter 12

Akron

November 1937

Cliff and the High Notes belted out Louie Prima's *Sing, Sing, Sing*. With the clarinet's melodious dazzle leading the drum beat and blaring brass, Deet picked up Lacey at her waist and swung her legs to the ceiling, allowing her to tumble over his back landing feet first on the hardwood floor. One of a dozen frenetic couples gyrating on the union hall's auditorium floor, they amazingly kept their limbs to themselves as other duos threw their elbows and feet in various directions as each pair choreographed their own dance to the rhythmic swing.

Invigorated by the release of energy and a feeling of sexual tension, Deet clasped Lacey's hand after the music ended and headed to the refreshment table. He relished the fact that she was one of only a few women wearing pants. Just as with her interest in baseball, she had her own sense of style.

As if at Consolidated, a shift change occurred at the URW hall as older couples reclaimed the floor with tepid ballroom music. "Now that's the way to celebrate a birthday!" Sweat beads dotted Deet's face and neck as his chest heaved under a broad smile.

"You're only nineteen once. I want you to enjoy it." Disregarding the perspiration, Lacey kissed him under his ear.

"You cats were tearing it up out there," Casper Miller, Deet's old high school buddy, said as he squeezed Maria Rossi around the waist. "I know I kept one eye out for the two of you . . . and the other for the cement mixers out there who didn't know their left foot from their right. Didn't want to be caught in your buzz saw." His chuckle led to some light laughter.

"You ladies want something to drink?" Deet asked.

"I think lemonade," Maria said, looking at Lacey as if for guidance.

"Me too." Lacey bobbed her head as she smiled at Maria. "But first, we ladies need to go powder our noses."

"You want a beer, Deet?" Cass asked.

"No, I got to watch my pennies. I'll stick with lemonade as well."

"I understand. Let me buy you one; that's the least I can do." Cass held up two fingers to the bartender. "Two Burgers."

"Sure, but what are you talking about?" Deet felt the lines of his face curve upward as he was relieved that he wasn't reduced to grade-school party drinks.

"It was you and Lacey that hooked me up with Maria, well . . . Mama Mia Maria." The sandy-haired Casper let his hands form an invisible, curvaceous hourglass figure in front of him. "She's a fun dish in more ways than one, if you know what I mean."

"Well, okay, ah, you're welcome." Deet tipped the top of his bottle to lightly clank in a toast with Cass' bottle.

"And that double date flick with Bogart, *The Black Legion*? Had her crying on my shoulder after we left you guys. Worked out perfectly." With a toothy grin, Casper twitched his head to one side.

Deet stopped tipping his bottle for another swig. "About that . . . both Lacey and I didn't know the whole plot . . . I mean we thought *Bogey, must be cops and robbers*." He finally took another sip. "Anyway, had we known, we'd have never picked that movie for her. I can see how that hoodlum group of vigilantes picking on foreigners would have upset her."

"Hey, Deet!" A giggling Jake Carver grabbed Jenkins from behind by the shoulders. "Good seeing you here. How's it feel to get back to work?"

"Jake, this is my good buddy, Cass Miller. He works at Apex. Cass, this is Jake Carver, fellow gummer at Consolidated's milling department."

The two young men shook hands after which Carver ordered a beer. "We shut down the plant on account of Deet this week, at least for a day." He took a swig from his bottle.

"That was you?" Cass almost choked on a mouthful of beer as small streams trickled out of the edges of his mouth.

"Floor supervisor fired him on the spot for supposedly overloading the raw rubber cart." Carver shot the extended thumb of a closed fist over his shoulder. "We were suspicious from the start because Deet wouldn't become a missionary, even to make more dough for his family, them being in hard times now. Anyway, one of Dixon's Black buddies saw the supervisor put a big chunk of rubber in the cart while Deet was checking on an emergency on my machine. When Chaw Nelson got wind of it, he's about as close to a real union rep as we got, he shut off the power, and by the end of the shift, all of Plant One was down. We sat there till almost noon the next day before Consolidated saw the light."

"Good to have guys backing you up." Miller patted Deet's shoulder. "You guys need to get recognized by Consolidated. We walked out and shut everything down last winter, and Apex finally recognized the URW. We don't have that kind of shit your floor supervisor pulled. It would have been handled by a grievance committee. No, we don't do sit-downs anymore, but someone from the outside ends up settling the grievances. No *company union* bullshit."

"Sounds like what we want," Carver said. "Hey, I heard you talking about vigilantes as I walked up to you guys."

"Vigilantes?" Deet furrowed his brow for a moment. "Oh, yeah, that was in a Bogart movie we saw."

"Well, be warned. Some vigilante group called *the Brigade* has come in from Toledo. They want to cause trouble for unions, because they say we're commies. They're also not so fond of foreigners either. Just be on your toes and keep your eyes open wherever you're at . . . including right outside those doors." Jake pointed to the double doors of the auditorium which led to the front entrance of the union hall on Market Street. "Besides, I saw you guys with some real lookers tonight, if I might say. You don't want anything to happen to them."

Flashes of *The Black Legion* raced through Deet's mind—floggings and shooting down foreigners, burning them out of their homes. Maria's and Lacey's return snapped him back to the present, and he introduced Carver to them. Deet handed the lemonade to the ladies as he and Jake excused themselves for a trip to the men's room.

As he and Carver were exiting the restroom, Deet made unexpected eye contact with a raven-haired woman with a Shirley Temple curly top in one corner of the dance hall. Dressed in a white blouse with black pants, she looked to be in her late twenties by his estimation. Arms crossed, she stood with one hand supporting a lit cigarette between full, rose-colored lips. She blinked twice as if to send him Morse code, *I want you.*

How could she be all by herself? Why would you leave her unguarded?

"Jake," Deet said, turning away from the woman, "don't stare, but who's that dame in the back corner to our left, the brunette in pants, smoking a cigarette?"

"Oh, quite the hot mama, isn't she. Supposedly, she's from New York, some union organizer who got them started for garment workers. Sophie's her first name, I think. Didn't catch the last name."

Guilt coated the lust, which had taken hold of his body since he laid eyes on *Sophie.* For the sake of his relationship with Lacey, he hoped the shame wouldn't become a meaningless cover hiding his yearning for the exotic brunette.

The band played the opening notes of Benny Goodman's *Bugle Call Rag*, prompting legs and arms at right and acute angles to create a dense forest of swing dancers obscuring his view of Sophie. He raced back and grabbed Lacey by the hand, "Let's dance, Babe."

****

"'Twenty-five damn minutes! Twenty-five damn minutes!' That's what he shouted over and over again while he took a folding chair and starting smacking his table with it at Doogan's Bar." The mustachioed, pot-bellied police sergeant stopped half-way down a narrow corridor at the police station and turned back towards Deet. "Then . . . then he hunkered down behind a booth and shouted '*I'm not going over again! I'm not going over again!*'" The officer flailed his arms toward the ceiling. "It took two of our stoutest officers to pull him out. I'll tell you that was a helluva way to remember Armistice Day." The red-headed sergeant opened the door to a small room with only a wooden table and a folding chair on either side of it.

A stench packing the power of a heavyweight's punch smacked Deet across his face as he sat down across from his uncle. Unshaven, with disheveled hair, a torn shirt and downcast eyes, Louie looked and smelled like shit. "What happened, Uncle Louie?" The nephew spoke softly as if comforting a sick child at his bedside.

"I remembered," Louie mumbled through vomit-crusted lips as he buried his head into the palms of his hands.

To forget that which I can't bear to remember.

It didn't take long for Deet to reflect on his conversation with his uncle from a few days earlier on why he drank. He looked up at the sergeant. "Could I have a few minutes alone with my uncle? I think he'd open up more if it were just me talking to him."

"Well, it's not standard procedure. Then again, we're not dealing with Dellinger here. I'll be right outside that door." The sergeant pointed to the door through which they'd entered, which had a square window in its upper half with wire mesh embedded in the glass.

Ignoring the odor as best he could by wiping a hand over his nose, Deet whispered, "Tell me what you remembered."

"The eleventh hour . . . of the eleventh day," Louie's words breached his lips like rusty hinges trying to swing back and forth. " . . . of the eleventh month. By nine that morning, most everyone in my regiment knew the war was to end at eleven . . . just two damn hours."

He finally raised his head and stared his blood shot eyes at his nephew. "We were back-slapping each other in the trenches. The attack planned for that day must have been called off. What possible purpose would it have had? The war was all but over. Some men were singing while others slouched their weary bones against the walls of dirt they called home for the past several weeks and had a smoke. My dear friend Henry Wallings of Duluth, Minnesota, took out some paper and a pencil and wrote a letter to his girl, Sally." Louie took a moment and cleared his throat. "When he had finished it . . . he read it to me. He told her of the joy we were experiencing and how he couldn't wait to see her again so they could get . . . get mar-ried." A tear zig-zagged down through Louie's stubble.

"Around ten o'clock, word came down that the attack was still on." A sliver of Louie's teeth peeked out between his lips, just enough to let Deet know his uncle was grinding them. "Some regimental bastard had to be ass-kissin' in the name of glory." The edges of his ear lobes turned red. "At 10:35 we attached bayonets, the whistles blew, ordering us over the top into no-man's land. Why?" Tears flowed easily by this point. "The Germans were just waiting it out. Why the hell couldn't we have done the same?"

A small puddle had formed on the table below Louie's head. "Hun artillery opened up, and a Doughboy got thrown into the air twenty yards ahead of me while one of his arms and one of his legs flew in opposite directions. Maxims opened up on us as we got closer and sprayed a chest-high line of lead.

"We made two unsuccessful charges before they ordered one last attempt to take a meaningless prize—some skeleton of a village. This time Henry Wallings happened to be just to the right of me, and the Germans seemingly had retreated because the artillery had stopped, and machine gun fire was only sporadic. As we came within thirty yards of the Hun trench, a single Maxim opened up again, and Henry crumpled to his knees.

"Through a terrain messed up by so many bomb craters, I raced toward the trench, which had basically become a mass grave, but one last Hun was trying to climb out on a rotten ladder. My rifle jammed, but I wasn't going to let him get away, not after what they'd done to Henry.

"The German's ladder broke under his weight, and he fell back onto the corpses of his buddies. Helmetless and on his back, he looked up at me with his arms over head. *Ich gebe auf! Ich gebe auf!* He kept screaming. He just wanted to surrender.

"He wasn't more than eighteen. He had a peach fuzz moustache." Louie began to ball like a baby. "He was just a kid." Heaving sobs interrupted his story. "But a rage . . . within me grew after I saw Henry shot all to hell, so . . . so . . . I ran him through with my bayonet." Louie's head collapsed to the table as he blubbered, "I murdered the poor son of a bitch."

By now, several tears trickled down Deet's cheeks as he started to understand the invisible prison in which his uncle lived.

After a minute or so, Louie pulled his head up and wiped the tears off his face with his hands. "We took the line, and I raced back to Henry who lived just long enough to look at me as I turned him over and gurgled 'Sally' as he died in my arms."

Deet knew five minutes had long passed, so he glanced towards the door as his uncle pounded his fists on the table. The police sergeant, vigilant at his post, didn't intervene. Deet guessed he could hear everything anyway and decided to let Louie vent the venom trapped for decades within his memory.

Louie stopped abusing the table, took off his specks, and wiped his face with each arm in turn. "In less than half-an-hour . . ." He stopped to inhale snot up his nostrils. "In less than half-an-hour, my best pal and over a dozen other guys in our outfit died, and I murdered a German boy. " He locked eyes with Deet. "For almost twenty years Henry and that German boy have haunted my dreams." He closed his eyes, rumpling his eyelids before screaming the question which had tormented him for so long. "Why did we have to go over the top with less than a half hour before the armistice?"

"Alright," the sergeant said as he entered the room with another officer, "time to be shown to your quarters, Mister Jenkins."

Louie grabbed Deet's arm before being led away. "I don't want no sympathy, Deet, understand?"

Deet wiped away his own tears and nodded as the second officer led his uncle down the hall towards the cells.

"Shell shock," said the sergeant. "I experienced it for a while after I came back from France. It's a bitter destiny that some can't ever escape."

"What will my uncle be charged with?"

"Most likely drunk and disorderly . . . perhaps resisting arrest." The sergeant rubbed his jaw line above his chin. "Of course, he'll have to pay for the damages at the bar as well."

"How long will a judge give him?"

"Hmm. Could be anywhere from ten to ninety days . . . depends on his record . . . depends on the judge."

"Will a judge consider his shell shock?"

"I'd be lying if I said they would. Too much time's passed. Many a judge don't even believe it exists. What I can tell you, young man, is when your uncle does get out, it's best he finds someone to whom he can talk. Sounds like a lot of demons have built mansions in his mind."

Chapter 13

Akron

November 1937

A sliver of light welcomed Arch Jenkins' consciousness, if you could call it that.

What is that?

As if he'd been on an overnight bender, he felt like assuming the fetal position and hiding under whatever sort of fabric draped his body. However, this was different. Although he couldn't feel any pain, he could barely move and was clueless to his surroundings. He was a prisoner to the horizontal beacon. His back was cushioned, but he didn't know whether he was horizontal or vertical. He tried to move his arms to feel the world within inches of him, but they were lifeless.

Have I died? Is this the entrance to hell? Heaven?

As the light grew from a sliver to an orb, blurred images materialized but still left him bewildered. One thing crystallized in front of him.

Where am I? What's this tube doing in my nose?

Again, he tried to lift his hands, this time towards his face, but his arms were as stiff as a two-by-four. The clatter of metal and muffled voices signaled the presence of others.

Hey! I'm here. I'm someone. Don't you care?

The ultimate fear tingled in his core—his mind eternally trapped within his body. The fog lifting from his vision offered him hope.

A hospital bed? Do Trudi and the boys know I'm here?

Although Arch's head felt as dense as a bowling ball, a soft pillow cradled it. While he strained to turn his head toward the left, his motionless legs felt as anchored as his arms. His eyes followed the course of the flexible tube as it exited his nose only to dive off the bed before ascending to the bottom of a bag suspended on some metal rig. Behind the stick-figure stand stood the first ray of hope.

Woman in a white apron dress, blue blouse, and white cap tucked in her blond hair from ear to ear. A nurse! Please turn around.

"A-a-a-a-a."

This damn tube is strangling my words. How long have I been here? Please, please turn around.

With mounted effort, Arch lifted the fingers of his left hand and allowed them to drop on his blanket. With his eyes pinned on the nurse, he repeated the tapping gesture several times until she turned around with a tray holding medical instruments.

"A-a-a-a-a." Arch blinked several times in succession.

The young nurse's blue eyes swelled, and she dropped the tray, causing a tremendous crash, before bolting out of the room "Doctor Salter, Doctor Salter!"

Well, that worked alright . . . I think.

A slender doctor in a white coat, with a head mirror banded around his buzz cut, marched into the room and put his fingers on Arch's pulse. "Welcome back. I am Doctor Salter. Can you hear me?"

"Ye-a-a-h."

Shaking his head with a rumpled brow, the doctor must have second-guessed himself. "For now, just blink . . . once for yes, twice for no." Salter put the cold metal of the stethoscope to Arch's bare chest.

Arch blinked once.

"H-m-m. Good." Doctor Salter nodded but remained hovered over him and looked into his eyes. "Please stare at my mirror."

Arch looked at the round glass perched above the field of dark stubble on the doctor's head as he smelled the coffee on his breath.

Salter nodded and stood up again before taking Arch's right hand in his. "Squeeze my hand as hard as you can."

Arch felt the tips of his fingers press the doctor's flesh, but he was unable to take hold of the doctor's hand.

"Nurse, get a cup of ice ready." With meticulous care, Salter pulled the rubber tube out of Arch's throat and positioned it over the bag hanging from the rig. "That should make things a bit easier for you."

The removal of the tube left Arch's throat like sandpaper. Like some cowboy stranded in the desert in one of those cheap Saturday afternoon matinees, he couldn't wait for one of life's basic necessities.

The nurse held the paper cup to Arch's lips and allowed slivers of shaved ice to coat his tongue.

That feels like a bubbling stream going down my dry throat. More, please.

Arch tried to lift an arm to control the cup but couldn't.

"That's enough for a start. Before the day is over, you'll actually get real water." Doctor Salter held a clipboard chart at the foot of the bed. "Can you say your first name?"

"A-r-rch." Even with the coating of melted water, his throat still felt like it was lined with broken glass.

"Alright, I won't strain your voice. I'm going to ask you some basic questions." The doctor put down the clipboard and grabbed on to the circular tube of the bed's footboard. "Again, just blink once for yes and twice for no. Alright?"

Arch blinked once.

Salter began questioning. "Is your last name Jordan?"

Arch blinked twice.

"Is your last name Smith?"

Arch blinked twice and felt a scowl cross his face.

"Is your last name Jenkins?"

A single blink and a smile reassured the doctor. "That's a good sign. Mister Jenkins. Are you married?"

Again, Arch blinked once.

"If you can, hold up the number of fingers equal to how many children you have."

Arch struggled but managed to lift the index and middle finger of his right hand an inch off the bed covers.

Doctor Salter beamed. "Excellent. Remembering your family is a very positive sign. Now, do you remember what happened that caused you to be here?"

Arch blinked twice.

"Six weeks ago, you fainted at work and hit your head. You regained consciousness shortly thereafter, but you lost consciousness at home that evening and ended up here at City Hospital. It's my professional opinion that your condition was caused by viral encephalitis, what many folks call brain fever."

Six weeks! Trudi and the boys must think I'm halfway into the grave!

Arch closed his eyes in despair.

"Mister Jenkins, please look at me. Since you've been in a coma for over six weeks, your body is extremely weak. It's going to take some time to get your strength up so you can return home."

Arch's eyes drifted upward, and his head slowly rocked back and forth.

My family needs me.

Salter sat down along the side of Arch's bed, braced an arm on the mattress, and looked his patient straight in the eyes. "Whatever you're thinking right now, there are two things you need to understand. First, your recovery will take time, weeks, probably months. Second, your family will be thrilled to know of your renewed consciousness. I will inform them of the good news as soon as I order you some broth. Your body's been shut down for a month-and-a-half, so we have to start slow—broth and soups. No solid food for a couple days."

"B-b-b-e-er?"

"Absolutely not. No alcohol for some time. Your brain needs to recover even more than your body. I can't stress this enough, Mister Jenkins—This will be a struggle."

What kind of mess am I in?

****

Bill Mowery used his gloved hand and removed a tire iron from under the driver's seat of his 1929 Dodge pickup. The cold, crisp air of the middle of the night morphed whistles from the central railyard several miles away into looming locomotives a mere block around the corner.

Ricky Jenkins blew into his hands as he stood on two inches of fresh snow in the back of a South Main Street pawn shop. "What's that for?"

A nearly full moon's light reflecting off the frozen, white blanket made the architecture of a six-panel door stand out in an alley where flat doors and padlocks were the norm.

"Got to get in, one way or other." Bill smiled with his knitted cap pulled over his hairline while leaving his pronounced ears uncovered.

Ricky knew better than to mention anything about Mowery's ears. Bill had been known to pummel those who teased him about how his ears stuck out like miniature wings.

In an instant, a frown replaced Bill's smile. "Where's your gloves?"

"I forgot them, but it's no big deal." A cloud of carbon dioxide hovered over Ricky as he continued to warm his hands. "The more I work loading, the less I'll notice the cold. Say, what's going on?"

"What do you think?" With the tire iron in one hand, Bill shone the beam of a steel flashlight against the brass lock plate of the door.

"We're supposed to be hauling stuff for some guy, 'who needs inventory at certain places on certain days'. At least, that's what you told me a couple weeks back when we got a load of tires from that warehouse."

Bill spoke to the door as he focused on prying it open at the lock with the flat end of the iron bar. "Well, the boss gave me a key for the warehouse, but she doesn't have one for this place. And she needs certain things from here."

"She?"

"Yeah, *she*." Mowery put his weight into the bar and broke the lock. "So just shut up, and don't touch anything with your bare hands unless I tell you to."

"Bill, this is breaking and entering!" Ricky stuck his head passed the splintered door casing

"Quite right, genius." Mowery's voice faded as he worked a path into the bowels of the shop with the help of his light. "Once we take what she wants, it will be considered grand theft as well."

"I didn't sign up for this." Ricky remained in the doorway.

"Tough. Once you helped move those tires you were up to your eyeballs in it." Unseen, Bill's voice seemed to animate the shop in chastising the redheaded sixteen-year-old. "And your eyes were wide open when I handed you those three sawbucks. Not bad for a couple hours of night work, right? Don't tell me your crippled old man can't use it either. Now, unless you want the cops to know you were here, don't touch anything except what we're loading."

I told you Mowery's nothing but a cheap ass hoodlum. What do you expect you're going to be doing at this time of night?

Deet's warning ran though Ricky's mind, stunning any momentary action. The beam from Bill's flashlight zipped back the way it entered and further mesmerized the youngest Jenkins.

"Jenkins, get your ass in here." Mowery stormed out from the darkness of the shop with his coat unbuttoned. "We got guns, jewelry and watches on our list. Remember, I'll tell you what to touch."

Something hard jabbed Ricky's thigh as Mowery got into his face. The peripheral rays of the flashlight allowed Ricky a glimpse of a pistol stuck into Bill's trousers at the belt.

Oh, shit.

Chapter 14

Akron

November 1937

Deet lived for Saturday night. He knew the end of high school would at least begin with the responsibilities of a job. Not only had he begun a life's work in Consolidated's gigantic rubber mill, but he'd also lost and regained it within thirty-six hours. Unfortunately, the strain attributable to a man twenty years his senior weighed on him as his father's illness, his uncle's drunkenness, and his brother's questionable choice in companions landed in his lap. Saturday nights with Lacey became a liberation ritual from the slabs of tension pressing him in recent weeks.

Buoyed by his father's escape from a coma, this Saturday night celebrated the removal of an extra weight. After stopping to check on the security of his uncle's house and shop while Louie served a thirty-day sentence for drunk and disorderly, he picked up Lacey in the family Pontiac and took her to a new entertainment establishment.

A harmonious mixture of stunted conversations and the intermittent cracking of Bakelite balls greeted Lacey and Deet as they entered Duke's Billiard Hall. Since Duke's recent opening near downtown, Deet got wind that one could play a table for a quarter an hour, a half-an-hour longer than other pool halls. That was a deal when money had become all too tight.

Deet waited at the bar to pay the bartender, who fiddled with the radio dial as various stations came and went through the staticky airwaves. "Table Three?" Deet put a quarter on the bar after the bartender's eyes acknowledged him and waved him on.

Cue stick in hand, Lacey waited for her boyfriend's return at one of the two empty tables in the business's group of six. "So, when do you think your pop's coming home?"

"Doctor Salter said that unless there was some unforeseen complication, Dad could be home a week or two before Christmas." Deet chalked up his cue stick. "Eight-ball?"

Lacey nodded as he racked the fifteen balls together.

Deet paused as Lacey took her first shot after he had broken the stack. She dropped the seven ball in one of the side pockets while he silently marveled at his luck.

How many guys have a gal that not only loves baseball, but shoots a good game of pool?

Once it was his turn, he focused on the striped balls on the table and nothing else. His first shot sunk the fifteen ball with the cue ball's carom effortlessly passing between two solid balls without hitting either of them. That set up his second shot in which he stunned the cue ball, stopping it exactly where he hit the ten ball, depositing it in a corner pocket. Deet continued, making six shots in a row before finally missing.

"Thanks for giving me a chance." Lacey narrowed her eyes and smirked. She dropped the number six ball into a nearby corner pocket before missing a long shot. She left Deet with a challenging, but not impossible, shot on his final striped ball.

Deet sized up his shot on the last ball, which lay roughly six inches from one side pocket. The challenge lay in the fact the number eight ball stood between the cue ball and the last striped ball, number thirteen. Rules dictated he couldn't strike the black eight before hitting the thirteen.

"Behind the eight ball," Lacey chuckled. "Guess I'll still get another shot."

Deet shook his head before splitting the middle and index fingers of his right hand and putting them down next to the thirteen ball. "One has to play the bad lies as well as the good ones."

"Something new?" Lacey asked.

"Sort of." Deet chalked his cue stick and laid it almost on top of the table to mimic the angle he'd created with his fingers. "The split fingers gives you a thirty-degree angle which can help you direct the shot while redirecting the cue ball in a favorable direction." With the sincerity of a surgeon, he double-checked the angle again with his stick. Finally, he banked the cue ball off the opposite side's cushion causing it to drop the thirteen ball in the side pocket. The cue ball ricocheted off the thirteen ball and banked off the cushion a couple of times before positioning itself directly in front of the eight-ball.

"Eight-ball in the corner pocket." Deet pointed to the exact pocket, struck the cue ball, which stopped dead in its tracks, and won the game. "How about a beer?"

Lacey smiled and nodded. "You should be making money off this game."

"Then it probably wouldn't be fun anymore." Deet headed toward the barkeep, whose elbows kept his shoulders propped up to support a head which looked like a medium-sized pumpkin despite the parallel horizontal ridges on his brow. From the creases of his ears to a number of chin-to-cheek etchings on his weathered face, vertical lines on his round face were his dominant features.

Within a few feet of the bar and the palm of the barkeep's hand up as a barrier to business, Deet realized the bartender's focus rested on what the radio spat out—the baritone rantings of America's most popular radio preacher—Father Coughlin.

I dedicated my life to fight against the heinous rottenness of capitalism because it robs the laborer of this world's goods. But blow for blow, I shall strike against communism, because it robs us of the next world's happiness.

"America has been led to a crossroads. One leads to communism, the other to fascism. I take the road to fascism. The Rome-Berlin Axis is serving Christendom in a peculiarly important manner."

Despite the barman's turned head, Deet decided to interrupt the Catholic priest. "Two beers, please."

Without acknowledging Deet's presence, the bartender reached down and opened an icebox underneath the bar. Then, as he placed the unopened bottles on the polished maple bar, he addressed Deet as if they were old chums. "You know that priest's got it right."

"Excuse me?"

"The Reds and the Jews are what's behind all the trouble in this country." The barkeep popped off the bottle caps with a wooden-handled opener. "The Jews control the money, and the commies try to mess up society by claiming they can make a eu-eu-tipia."

"Eutopia?"

"Right, that's what I said, eutipia, where everyone gets treated fairly. Bullshit. Never been treated fair in my life. That's not the way it works. Anyway, Hitler's got it right over there in Germany. Put down an iron fist and take no shit from anyone. That's what we need here."

A younger man, with dark, slicked-back hair, in a blue work shirt and rolled up sleeves came through a back door behind the bar and whispered something to the bartender.

"What? Speak up, Pike." The younger man pulled the bartender through the door.

During this odd exchange, Deet noticed something strange about the guy's deep-set eyes. Despite his dark hair and olive complexion, his eyes were blue! Before the younger man left, Deet couldn't help notice one other thing, something much more ominous than eye color —a tattoo on his arm—*Brigade*—with what looked like two crossed lightning bolts beneath the word.

"How much for the beers?" Deet asked the bartender after he reappeared from his short meeting with Pike.

"Two beers . . . that'll be a buck."

"Fifty cents for a beer?"

"What'd I tell ya, life ain't fair."

Deet and Lacey played another game, finished their beers and left. Deet knew they'd never go back.

****

December 1937

The heat of the milling room comforted Deet for a change as the midnight air outside the plant hovered in the single digits. However, other things remained oppressive. The black grime of powdered carbon black still covered his clothes and smeared his skin as he wiped his brow with his arm. Harley Kershaw still spent an extraordinary amount of time near his machine as if conspiring to rid his world of Deet's presence. It reminded him of what the bartender at Duke's had said.

Life's not fair.

Was it fair that his father contracted brain fever, seemingly out of nowhere? Was it fair that while one in three gummers had lost their jobs in the past two years, he got one because of his father? Was it fair that Consolidated still didn't address various safety concerns? Was it fair that anonymous hoodlums attacked his parents, and no one had been brought to justice?

Powerless in the face of these numerous unjust circumstances, Deet drifted into gratitude for the things he did have—a job, no matter how menial, fellow workers who had looked after him in a time of need, his father out of his coma, his mother and brother, and Lacey.

Standing twenty feet behind the scale, Kershaw's glare put the brakes on his introspection. His load was a pound light, so he went over to a raw rubber stock cart and cut off a piece to add to it. He'd do everything in his power not to give Kershaw further excuses to can him.

"You know, Jenkins," Dixon yelled as he came around the milling machine after inspecting the flat belt of tread it spat out, "I can't call you *Traveler* anymore."

Deet took a 360-degree turn, making sure Kershaw wasn't lurking. "Oh, why's that?" He walked over to the raw rubber supply cart.

"Don't worry, Jenkins, ole Harley's headed back to his office. Besides, I don't think Kershaw's goin' to want you to leave." Dixon offered a half-hearted grin. "Think of him as a jailer who's got the keys to your freedom. He can keep you locked up down here for as long as he likes."

"Sort of like you, Dixon?" Deet looked at his Black mentor before he cut a chunk of rubber.

The Negro lost his smile. "Yeah, just like me."

"Well, and I mean no disrespect, especially because you and your friends helped me get this job back by letting Chaw know what happened. But because of that and what's happened to my father, I'm just grateful to have a job right now." He patted Dixon on the back of his shoulder and reweighed his load.

Dixon said something as he turned away from the tall teen, but the noise of the floor's milling process devoured his words.

"What?" Deet asked, thinking he heard the word *father*.

"I said how's your father doing?" Dixon made sure his voice carried over the machinery's roar.

"Doc said he'd probably come home next week. He's regained his strength." Deet pushed his cart of measured rubber down the short track and dumped it into the compound mixer.

"Oh-oh." Dixon looked down the aisle while the mixing machine blocked Deet's view.

"What?" Deet remained focused on dumping all the cart's rubber into the mixer. This was no time for spillage.

"Kershaw's headed this way with Detective TB."

"Who?" The teen tugged the cart along the rails back to the scale and faced Dixon.

"Ragmon." Dixon's teeth glittered as he yelled. "Everyone along North Street near the river calls him TB—two bellies."

Deet grinned and nodded as he watched the chubby detective strut down the main aisle with Harley Kershaw.

"Well, well, how are you Dixon?" A glint of light twinkled off a tiny stretch of one of the detective's blue eyes as it escaped the heavy folds of his eyelids. "How are things along North Street?" Ragmon's entire face squinted into pinched rolls as he raised his voice to challenge the machinery.

"Just fine, Detective, just fine." Dixon wiped his hands with a clean rag. "What brings—"

"The detective needs to speak to Jenkins here about a police matter . . . in private." Kershaw stamped his arrogance on the brief conversation with an exaggerated wink.

"Yes, hello again, Mister Jenkins. Deet, right?" By now, the volume of the detective's voice accounted for his surroundings.

Deet nodded.

"Yes, I've got some news regarding that assault on your home a couple months back."

"You're working kind of late, Detective, aren't you?" Dixon asked.

"Started night shift couple weeks ago but still serving the public."

"Alright, back to work, Dixon," Kershaw growled.

Deet and Ragmon started down the aisle towards Kershaw's tiny office.

"I hear your father finally snapped out of his coma." Ragmon shouted some chit-chat as if he'd known the family for years. "I trust he's recovering. Oh, by the way," the detective stopped in the middle of the aisle and faced Deet, "Kelly and I checked into what happened to your dad here at the plant. Turns out, nobody saw anything, and as far as we know, he just fainted."

The two continued toward the exit with Deet less than impressed with Ragmon's meaningless update. The doc covered all that weeks ago. Right now, he felt as if the floor had been thrown into pitch darkness with a lone spotlight marking each one of his steps as Chaw Nelson, Mike Kobenko, and others stared at him.

Once Ragmon shut the metal door leading out of the milling area to other parts of the plant, his act ended. "Damn! You can go deaf in there." He put a hand on his ear and shook his head. "Alright, kid, I don't need to talk to you, but someone very important does. We need to go upstairs to Benson's office right now."

Confused, Deet followed in Ragmon's footsteps.

Ragmon led Deet into night shift manager Nate Benson's office where the white-shirted Benson sat behind his desk while another man sat in front of it. Deet had seen Benson on occasion, wrapped in a mechanic's coat, inspecting various machines on the first floor, but he'd not said a word to him since that first night's accident that crippled Simpkins. A hollow feeling came over the nineteen-year-old at that moment.

A cop, the night shift's boss, and a stranger—what have I done?

"Hello, Deet." Benson stood up and extended his hand. His wide smile perked up the graying strands of otherwise brown hair near his temples. "Have a seat."

"Hello, Mister Benson." Deet wiped his hand off on the cleanest spot left on his shirt before shaking the boss's hand and sat down on a plain wooden chair, relieved the meeting seemed cordial.

"This is Special Agent Burt Smith." Benson used his opened palm to point in the direction of the seated gentleman in a navy suit and tie with a trench coat draped over his crossed knee, topped with a brown fedora. "Agent Smith is with the Federal Bureau of Investigation."

A G-man! Holy shit!

Deet's armpits warmed, and his mouth dried.

"Hello," Smith said as he reached his hand across to Deet.

"Hi." Deet could only offer a limp fish of a shake.

"I apologize for the drama with Detective Ragmon." Smith spoke softly with no hand gestures and not even a twitch on his handsome face. "We wanted the pretense of the attack on your home to cover for my real reason to question you."

"Question me? About what?" Deet couldn't size up this G-man. Certainly, no Jimmy Cagney tough guy. With his wavy, combed-back, brown hair, he looked more like a college professor with a poker face, who could double his salary with a deck of cards on the weekends.

"The Bureau has been concerned about communist activity in the northern part of Ohio, and it's been noted that on at least one occasion a communist activist, Jimmy Bryant, solicited you for conversation in the breakroom." Smith's calm, steady demeanor reminded Deet of a pendulum—his lips moved with precision and no wasted energy. "Is that correct?"

"Yeah, but that was a while back . . . more than . . . no, that's been months ago, I think."

"What did he share with you, Deet? Please think hard and remember whatever you can."

Deet rubbed his forehead with his fingers and closed his eyes. "It was hot outside. I mean it was muggy and uncomfortable outside at midnight, so it was probably August. He came in from out of the blue during lunch break and sat across from me." He exhaled as if he'd come up for air after being underwater for a minute or two. "Asked me about concerns in the milling room, and I mentioned safety concerns. He said the company union was bad and the URW wasn't good enough . . . that's it!" Deet's eyes and mouth opened. "He said workers have to control the government in order to make things better."

"Did he give you any literature, leaflet or something?"

"Yeah, but I tore it up once I saw the hammer and sickle emblem. The men down here don't care much for commies. They were happy I pitched the paper."

"The mill workers don't like communists?" Uninvited, Benson jumped into the conversation.

"As far as I can tell, no they don't. They told me not to get too close to Bryant, and I haven't."

"That's very good to know, Deet." Benson gave out a nervous giggle.

"Anything else you can remember from Jimmy Bryant or any other communist subversive who might have crossed your path?" Smith placed his fingertips on the top of his hat as it rested on his coat.

Deet drew his lips in and ran his tongue across the inside of his mouth before he turned toward Ragmon standing against the far wall like a third wheel. "No, but you and Detective Ragmon might be interested in knowing about a vigilante group known as the Brigade hanging around Akron. Came from Toledo and apparently like to roust union members and foreigners. Sound like some likely brick throwers. What do you say, Detective?"

"We're working on any lead we get, son."

"Well, here's one—Duke's Billiard Hall in downtown, there's an employee, Pike's his name . . . works the back room . . . he's got a tattoo labeled *Brigade* on his forearm . . . black hair *and blue eyes*." Deet turned back to Smith. "No disrespect Agent Smith, but rubber workers are probably more concerned about those hoodlums than some isolated commies here or there."

"No disrespect taken, Deet." Smith allowed a shallow smile to ebb across his face. "Thanks for your time."

Chapter 15

Akron

December 1937

How would you like your job back? Join the Brigade.

Ricky stared down at the leaflet with a simple message placed over a symbol of two crossed lightning bolts and wondered why he let Bill Mowery talk him into coming to this place. He stuffed the paper into his coat pocket and surveyed the gathering of several dozen men shuffling about in the abandoned warehouse on the east side of Akron near the Little Cuyahoga River. Their thin jackets, tattered coats, and flat caps seemed incapable of fending off the bitter cold of the mid-December evening. As a few more drifted in through a rusted service door, a man wearing a dented, black top hat and sporting a flowing beard—someone who looked more suited to the previous century than the present—arranged several wooden crates into a makeshift stage at one end of the building. An American flag hung suspended from a steel girder above the speaker.

"My name is Phineas Jones, and I hope to help you get your jobs back." With grayish-black hair sticking out underneath the dilapidated hat, the bearded speaker brought his meeting to order with a coarse voice, which seemed funneled through an ash-lined throat. He stood tall on top of a crate with his arms stretched toward the corrugated metal ceiling. The tip of his salt and pepper beard tickled the wide belt exposed by his unbuttoned coat with a sheep's wool lining. It made his height even more imposing. "How many of you have been laid off in the past two years?"

Everyone raised his hand, prompting Ricky to raise his.

"First, you must understand a bitter truth of life. Fairness for everyone . . . fairness for everyone is a crock of malarkey!" Phineas Jones bellowed the last half of that sentence, seizing the full attention of the men as he plunged forward with his speech. "You need something to survive; you must take it!" His voice was a crack of thunder on the heels of a lightning bolt before fading off into a low rumble. "Since when has life been fair. There are labor unions wooing workers in this town and across the nation with a siren's song of fairness in the workplace when, in fact, they are the wolves in sheep's clothing. How can this be?" The speaker raised a clenched fist. "Unions are designed to beguile you because they are the precursor for the red hoards . . . of communism! They will gut your will to do a decent day's work and feed you the illusion that workers will rule the nation." Then he pointed upward toward the Stars and Stripes. "They will be the ruin of our great nation unless we, The Brigade, stop them!"

Boisterous mumblings and head bobbing sprung up throughout the crowd of scruffy-looking men wearing second-hand clothing.

Ricky immediately thought of his bedridden father, who'd championed the need for a union inside the Consolidated factory. In the back row of the crowd, Ricky nudged Mowrey. "Bill, what are we doing here?"

"We're here to listen to some good sense. Now shush."

Fumes from a half-dozen kerosene lanterns, which barely illuminated the building's cavernous interior, drifted in and out of Ricky's nose as the speaker continued. "Not only will unions dull your pride in your work, but their communist overlords, who . . . by the way, take their orders from the occupant of the White House, will also take God away from you when they impale you on the altar of atheism."

A baritone wave of grumbling spread over the downtrodden gathering.

"Unfortunately, there's another menace among us here in Akron, a danger especially aimed at you, the downtrodden *unemployed American* worker." The leader raised an index finger before softening his voice. "You know who you can also thank for your predicament?"

Ricky looked around to see most of the fifty or so heads in the crowd uplifted, eager for an answer.

Jones answered in a feverish pitch. "Foreign interlopers have come into Akron with their babbling tongues and stolen your jobs . . .

jobs that rightfully belong to you!" He pointed a damning finger at the crowd.

What had earlier been low murmuring and grumbling now erupted into shouting.

"He's right!"

"Damn Polaks!"

"Stupid garlic-eaters!"

Jones' hands grabbed hold of the thick lapels of his coat while his face presented a smirk of self-assuredness. "You know that while you suffer . . . and your family suffers . . . and your personal sense of worth is broken on a daily basis, these lesser men *and women* have stolen your God-given right to work in the rubber mills and beyond." He dropped his hands before extending a wagging finger at the crowd and shouting, "The question is *what are you going to do about it?*"

The agitated crowd squirmed, ranted, and divided into smaller groups while manufacturing a collective uproar. To Ricky, it was like watching a number of junk yard dogs testing the limits of their thick, leather collars. He thought of Maria and how she lost her waitressing job at Bob's Diner.

Would this crowd tear into her?

He began to drift back into one of the sporadic patches of shadows. In a cube of silence, he watched as Bill's blond head stood over two older men as the trio pumped their fists while shouting with twisted faces.

"Alright, alright," the speaker yelled, raising his hands. Once the frothing mob quieted down, he continued. "I can see I touched a nerve that needs tending. If you're interested in taking action to stop the commie unionists and remove the foreign menace from our fair community, talk to the sponsor who brought you to tonight's Brigade meeting. They'll have membership forms for you to complete, and there will be a three-dollar membership fee. That will help to rent better accommodations for our meetings. Thank you for your interest. It's time to take back Akron!"

In the roar of the cobbled together pack, a hollowness began to consume Ricky from the inside out.

****

"From what I've seen in there," Louie whispered as he pitched a thumb over his shoulder in the direction of the dining room, "I think your mother is going to start drinking just like me."

Close enough to his uncle to get a whiff of cheap whiskey, Deet dodged the leftover mess on the extended kitchen table in order to put a dirtied plate into the sink. "Ever since he's been back from the hospital, he blows his wig at times and gets whacky. I think she can handle it. I'm more concerned about Ricky . . . he's done nothing but mope all evening. Hell, Dad's home, and it's Christmas Eve." Deet shook his head. "Something's eating him up on the inside."

"Yeah . . . agh-h-h." Louie sounded like he hacked up some disgusting phlegm. "I wondered myself what crawled up his ass and died." He dropped the butt of his spent cigarette into a cup, extinguishing it with a sizzle in a remnant of coffee.

The two worked their way back into his parent's makeshift bedroom via the foyer and living room, passing between the oversized Christmas tree and a sulking Ricky in his father's upholstered chair along the way. The aromatic spruce, a two-dollar tribute to holiday normalcy, liberated Deet's nose from his uncle's walking distillery.

Arch sat smiling on the bed with a pillow cushioning his back from the high oak headboard as torn newspaper wrapping paper created a secondary blanket. The boys had moved their parents' bed and nightstands into the dining room when Arch came home from the hospital in the middle of the month. Doctor Salter suggested it since he believed their father would suffer debilitating spasms in his limbs as an after effect of the long bout with encephalitis.

Arch's yellowed teeth showed through as he held a pair of cream-colored, woolen socks in his hand. "Thank you, Lacey, for such a thoughtful gift. Nothing like wool to keep one's feet warm." He turned toward his right but grimaced when his arm wouldn't respond to an attempt to lift it, remaining limp at his side. "Damnit. Sometimes it works and sometimes it doesn't."

Sitting on a kitchen chair next to Arch, Lacey took the initiative to pat Deet's father on the shoulder. "No problem, Arch. I know you appreciate them. I could read it on your face."

"You know, Archie, the doctor said the medicine would need weeks to really kick in to help your muscles move like they used to," Trudi said, sitting on the opposite side of the bed from Lacey.

"I know, I know." Arch's face rounded into a more somber form as he grabbed his wife's wrist with his left hand. "This Parkinson's, or whatever they call it, has me down for the moment . . . but I'll bounce back." He exhaled.

"Here, Dad, this is from Ricky and me." Deet handed his father a long, narrow, wrapped gift.

"What the hell," Arch scoffed. "You think I need a baseball bat." He let out a nervous chuckle before holding up his left hand to stop Trudi from helping him. Even though the disease limited him to sporadic use of either arm, he ripped the paper off with one hand, exposing a polished wooden cane. Emotionless, he stared at the stick as he held it out over his waist with his one functioning hand. "I hope I can use it."

"I told you it was a stupid idea." Ricky's whisper crept out of the living room, loud enough for all to hear.

Deet held out an arm to his side as if to keep his brother at bay but didn't address him. "It could help you get around the house, Pop."

"Yeah, perhaps it could." Arch still stared at the clenched cane in his left hand. "These seizures in my arms come unexpectedly, so I hope to God the medicine controls them. If so, I expect to be back at Consolidated within a month. If not, I'll fall on my ass with or without a cane."

Deet's eyes flashed from his mother's to his uncle's and over to Lacey.

"A-hem." Louie cleared his throat. "Don't go rushing back into it, Arch. You've been knocked off your feet for quite some time. You have to ease back into the saddle."

"You know the doctor told you it would be months—" Trudi didn't get a chance to finish.

"The doctor this! The doctor that! Damn it! Damn it! Damn it! I know what he said, and I don't give a shit!" With his one good arm, he raked it back and forth across his sheets, sending torn newsprint paper and the cane flying through his tornadic rage.

"I can't take this. I told you the cane was a dumb idea." Ricky stormed out of the room and tromped up the stairs to his room.

Trudi fended off the airborne stick with her arms before pleading for peace. "Archie . . . Archie, don't let this ruin Christmas." With deep lines of desperation etched around her eyes and mouth, she looked at Deet and gave a head nod upward as a signal to go after his brother.

With one eye on his father's beet red face, Deet acknowledged his mother's signal with a quick nod of his own and a raised right hand. "Dad, no one knows the future. Try to focus on one day at a time. Besides, Mom's right—today's Christmas. Let's enjoy it for all it's worth just because we're all together, and we're lucky to have each other."

Arch exhaled several times and bobbed his head. "I'm sorry, you're right. I have all of you here to support me, and for once I don't have Fred Geller around trying to convince me Hitler is Father Christmas."

The sound of his father chuckling sent Deet upstairs to check on the family's other dejected soul. The crunching of paper under his feet as he entered his brother's room accompanied an orchestral rendition of *Silent Night* streaming out of an old Philco radio cabinet. The radio had been salvaged by Louie and repaired by his uncle and father, who gave it to him as this past year's birthday present. Out of frustration, Deet swept a trail through the paper mess with his feet with some unidentified scraps shooting out into the hallway.

The Christmas music softened Deet's irritation. "What the hell is wrong with you?" he whispered as he slowly closed the door to Ricky's room, pushing paper aside like a road grader.

"Just leave me alone." Ricky lay on his bed with his hands locked behind his head. The faint light of a wall lamp highlighted half of his freckled face as a Saint Nicholas Christmas card looked down on him from the top of the radio's cabinet. The younger brother stared into the obscurity of the plastered ceiling surrounded by the clutter of cast-off clothing on his bed.

"I know something's eating at you . . . something more than the thought Dad might not be able to use the cane we got him." Deet sat down on a surprisingly vacant t-backed chair.

"Well, that didn't turn out so well, now did it, genius?" Ricky blinked for the first time since Deet entered the room.

"Time and medicine will tell about the cane's usefulness, but you were brooding during the meal and while we opened presents. What gives?"

"Nothing."

"Whatever it is, snap out of it, you've got Mom all worked up, and she's got enough on her plate." Deet rose from the chair. "I'm not here to become a stool pigeon about your problem. I just want to help you."

The way Deet viewed it, he'd done his duty, but he realized he wasn't going to pry open this clam. He opened the door, and the hall light illuminated the paper garbage which had overflowed from his entry into Ricky's room—crumpled balls of notebook paper, random scraps of wrapping paper, and a wrinkled white sheet folded in a triangular shape. Although scuffed, the word *Brigade* was legible as he closed the door behind him. He picked up the paper and unfolded it, discovering its simple message.

How would you like your job back? Join the Brigade.

Deet shivered at the sight of the crossed lightning bolt symbols and then exhaled. He went back into his brother's room with the paper in his hand and heaved words in a heavy whisper as if he'd just run a mile. "Where . . . did you . . . pick up this . . . shit ?"

Ricky's stone face retreated into guilt.

"This is what's eating at you, isn't it." Deet strained to keep his tone to just above a murmur. He had to handle this, not his mother, uncle, and surely not his father.

Ricky gave a weak nod and sat up against the headboard. "Mowery took me to one of their meetings and wants me to join."

"Are you kidding me?" Although muted, Deet's words shot out from gritted teeth as he balled his fists. "You know what these assholes are all about? More than likely, they're the ones who attacked Mom and Dad. You tell that bastard that you want nothing to do with them." He relaxed his mouth enough to inhale and released his fingers. "Got it?"

"Yeah."

"If he doesn't let up, you tell him I'll beat the shit out of him." Deet thrust out a forefinger like it was a javelin.

Ricky put up a hand. "Alright, alright. I knew at that meeting I wasn't joining those creeps. Trust me, I'll take care of this."

Chapter 16

Akron

February 1938

Taken aback by Lacey ignoring his attempt at a kiss upon his arrival, Deet took off his worn flat cap and followed her into her apartment on a Sunday afternoon. There he found a thin, middle-aged man sitting on her green sofa fingering the bill of a dark brown fedora as he held the hat in his hands.

"Hello." The nineteen-year-old looked down on a short man with greased-back brown hair.

"Hello." The man bobbed his head several times with a modest smile while his fedora featured a permanent fold on its bill. "I'm—"

"This is my father, Gene Frazier," Lacey interrupted with all the enthusiasm of biting into an onion. "This is Deet Jenkins."

Lacey's father stood up and shook Deet's hand. At least a head shorter and dressed in a white shirt with brown trousers, Gene offered a surprisingly firm hand. Standing a mere yard apart, his greenish amber eyes remained pinned on Deet during the greeting.

This shrimp beat up Lace's mother?

In the past couple months, Lacey had opened up more to Deet about moving out of her parents' home because of her father's drinking and abusive behavior. It made him wonder if Louie had been violent with his aunt before she left him, or if she just couldn't tolerate the recurring wartime nightmares. Despite Lacey's holiday anecdote about her father's attempts at sobriety, his presence today was unexpected.

"So, you're the gummer I heard about back at Christmas." Gene's face lit up as if he'd just found religion and treated Deet's hand like a pump handle. "From what I understand, Lacey's taken a real shine to you." He let go and sat down at one end of the sofa.

"I guess the feeling's mutual." Deet tossed his cap and coat on a wooden t-back chair and sat at the opposite end of the couch, shooting Lacey a curled smile. He didn't exactly know how to navigate the conversation with the black sheep of her family. *I hear you dropped the boozin'* wouldn't be the most appropriate response. His gears spun in his head when their teeth finally engaged. "What line of work might you be in, Mister Frazier?"

"I used to work in a machine shop, a small tool and dye outfit on the east side . . . close to Mogadore. That is before my illness took over my life."

Deet nodded but wondered how drunkenness could be in the same lineup as tuberculosis, cancer, measles, or influenza. He hoped he hadn't opened a can of worms.

"But now, I'm better, and I'm a barber, working in a three-man shop on West Market. I'm keeping myself clean, and things are looking up." Gene smacked his thighs with his flattened palms as he gave a clenched grin toward his daughter across the room.

"You're probably surprised by my being here, Deet." Frazier's face drooped. "Since you mean a lot to my daughter, I think you have a right to know that reliance on alcohol helped make a mess of my life. Through the help of some fine folks, I've come to see that alcohol ruled me and not the other way around. I've learned to put my life into the hands of God and lean onto his mercy to remove the defects of my character that lead me to drink and destruction."

To Deet, Frazier's speech reminded him of a stiff grade schooler reciting the Gettysburg Address, hoping to get each sentence in proper order.

Frazier paused, exhaled, and looked at Lacey. "I'm on the path to recovery, a path of numerous steps . . . twelve steps to be precise.

"One of those steps brought me here today. Lacey, you are one of many individuals that I have hurt with my drinking. I've come here to today to ask your forgiveness and to assure you that I will be here to help you in whatever way you need it in the future."

"That's quite a statement, Gene, based on what you've put Mom and me through in the past decade. As it is right now, having seen you sober once at Christmas and now today, it could still be just so much bullshit." Sitting in a burgundy upholstered chair with threadbare arm rests, she took out a Lucky Strike from a crumpled pack in her purse. After lighting it, she sent a plume of smoke rushing out of her nose. "For all I know, you'll get stewed tonight. It's going to take time and honest action on your part for me to really accept you. You talk about your steps to recovery, but I think it will be a step-by-step process for me and Mom to allow you to reenter our lives."

Deet felt like he was sitting on a cactus.

Gene stood up with a smile on his face. "I completely understand. With so much wreckage in my wake, it will be a long road back to acceptance and love. I just wanted to stop by today to let you know that I still love you, and I am working hard to get back into your good graces. It's been sixty days without a drop, and with the support I now have, I hope someday to help others regain their sobriety and dignity as well. So, for now, good-bye, my precious daughter."

Except for another puff on her cigarette, Lacey sat motionless. "You can show yourself out."

Once he heard the door close and Gene's feet pounding the steel fire escape, Deet repositioned himself in the middle of the sofa. "Whoa, what was that all about?"

"Some part of my life I'd rather forget." Lacey crushed the half-finished smoke in a metal ashtray, walked over, and straddled her groin atop Deet's waist. Smiling, she kissed him lightly several times. With each successive honey cooler, her passion ignited more of his body heat as she dug her limbs into his body.

Deet doused the fire as his curiosity outran his libido. He rolled her over, so they lay side by side, no longer entwined at the waist. "How do you forget your dad?" He sat up and scratched his blond curls. The Gene Frazier he'd just met seemed sincere and clean. Images of a soused Louie faded in and out of his thoughts.

"Easy." Lacey exhaled a deep breath of frustration and also sat up, staring at the ceiling. "Year after year of watching my father drown his disappointments in beer and liquor a couple times each week did it to me. Oh, you remember my telling you that he hit my mom." Her eyes turned toward Deet. "He did more than that. He'd take his belt to her back as if he was trying to break a horse. He'd punch her arms and drag her around the apartment by the wrists from room to room. My mother never wore a short-sleeved dress or blouse during those years. He took out his inadequacies on her, one beating at a time. Once I was out of school, I moved out."

Tears began to trinkle down Lacey's cheeks. "According to my mom," she began to heave. "One night after I left, he was so drunk . . . he took to hitting her out into the apartment hall. Some . . . some new neighbors didn't like what they saw, and the husband, a burly-looking guy, caved my dad's face with one punch. They called the police on him. The cops arrested my dad, and my mom took the opening to divorce the piece of shit." She collapsed into Deet's arms, sobbing.

"Hey, it's over. Everything's alright." Deet nuzzled in her ears. "You're with me, you're safe."

"That's it." She broke from him and gazed at him with reddened eyes and moistened strands of tawny hair. "*I* was safe."

Deet twitched his head a bit with uncertainty.

"I abandoned her, Deet!" Lacey wailed again in his arms. "I should have stayed and beat the shit out of that runt of a man. I should have stayed." Her tears flowed enough to soak the upper arm of his shirt.

Deet thought about Lacey's athletic ability and the puny stature of her father. He dared not utter what he was thinking.

You could have beaten the shit out of him.

"Why did you leave, Babydoll?"

Having ratcheted down her grief to sniffling, Lacey wiped tears from her face with Deet's shirt. "Part of me just wanted out, but a good part of me thought I was to blame. I mean when I was a little kid, my father treated me like a boy . . . the boy he never had. Birthday and Christmas presents always included balls, bats, and gloves. All through elementary school, he played catch with me, and we'd have batting practice at the park's diamond, just him and me. He took me to the billiards hall, and that's where I learned the game."

She pushed herself off of his shoulder for a moment, so she could face her boyfriend. "You don't think I picked it up out of thin air, now do you?"

Lacey snuggled her way back into Deet's shoulder. "The boys back then loved to have me on their team at recess. As I got into junior high and high school and my body matured, my love for sports still stayed strong. But the boys began to look at me as if I was whacko. I accepted that I was a tomboy long past the stage when a girl being a tomboy was considered *cute*. Even though I knew I had girl urges on the inside, the guys and gals at Central didn't know what to make of me. I got used to being a loner. I got used to hearing *that name* behind my back in the halls. That's why I guessed my dad was secretly angry at me, thinking I was something that I wasn't. I just figured because of that and problems at work, he took it out on Mom as if it was her fault."

Words spewed from Deet's mouth without any hesitation. "That name? You thought your dad thought you were a . . . a les—?"

Lacey raised her head from his shoulder, looked with sullen brown eyes, big as chocolate drops, and nodded.

"Well, if he ever had doubts, I could certainly set him straight on that." He brought his lips to hers, and the two spent the next half hour attesting to their attraction to the opposite sex.

Half naked, Deet came up for air shortly after he realized his head was on the floor. After his feet joined the same plane as his noggin, he picked himself up and sat in the burgundy chair. "You told me you saw your dad at Christmas, and he looked sober?"

"Yeah, he was." Lacy said as she wrestled her bra back into position. "And he certainly was sober just now, but he left scars on my mom and on the inside of me."

"So, you don't think he's changed?"

"He says he's been off the sauce for two months. I'm not sure if I'm buying that. You know what they say, 'Once a drunk, always a drunk.'"

Deet couldn't get his uncle separated from Lacey's father, and right now, his hope for Louie lay in the transformation of Gene

Frazier. "Well, what if he *really* has been sober for two months? Wouldn't that count for something?"

"Well, I'll give him credit for one thing—he wasn't begging. After slappin' Mom around at night and having slept it off, the next morning he'd always beg for her forgiveness. 'It'll never happen again. I'm so sorry.' There wasn't any of that today."

"Yeah, he fessed up to what he'd done and said how *he* was going to be taking responsibility." Deet picked up his undershirt from the floor and put it back on.

"Don't forget that he threw in *God* a couple times as well." Lacey opened the palm of her hands with an exaggerated widening of her eyes and opening of her mouth as she picked up her pink blouse.

"God certainly can't hurt. I mean when you hit rock bottom, who else do you turn to?" Deet's eyes sparked at Lacey's partially nude figure, but he was able to resist further urges and buttoned up his flannel shirt. "Didn't he mention some people supporting . . . helping him?"

"Yeah, back at Christmas he told Mom and me that the cops picked him up out of the gutter around Thanksgiving, and a judge suspended his sentence on the condition he get some sort of treatment at City Hospital. A doc there told him to come to his house on Ardmore, off of Exchange. I guess the doc and some businessman, who used to be a drunk, try to talk things out with alkies. Anyway, seeing is believing, and I haven't seen enough as of yet."

"Ardmore off Exchange . . . City Hospital."

"What?" Lacey's face rumpled with curiosity after she pulled her sweater over her head..

"Nothing," Deet said. "Just thinking out loud. What would you have to see to make you believe there's been some real change?"

"Well, he looked better today than at Christmas, and certainly better than when he was living with us—kempt hair, clean-shaven, clean clothes, and no hint of booze. I guess if he keeps that up and can keep that barbering job that would be a good start. If he does more giving than taking, that would even be a bigger step in the right direction." She walked within kissing distance of Deet and wrapped her hands around his neck.

"I guess that would be one of those steps that he was talking about." He kissed her and let his arms proclaim her security with him.

****

The following Sunday, Deet and hundreds of his fellow United Rubber Workers union members, who worked at Consolidated, funneled in and out of the union hall at various times. Meeting in smaller groups, they voiced concerns and heard updates from union officials about previous complaints. Jake Carver tagged along, and the two sat through an hour-long session before stopping at the hall's cafeteria to get a cheap meal.

"So, if I understand this right, the company said it wanted a seniority system. Right?" Jake slid his tray down the serving line towards the cashier. After showing the cashier his union card and paying a dime, he waited on Deet.

Deet gave a thumbs up sign to his friend before leading them to an open space at one of many crude, wooden tables where they sat on benches across from a stranger, who was finishing his meal. Deet took a drink of milk and dug into his meat loaf before finally responding to Jake's comment. "As I understand it, the union wanted one too. But the company's idea of seniority doesn't line up with that of the union." He stuffed some potato salad into his mouth. "I'm just not sure I got the particulars."

The grizzle-faced man across from them gripped a fork with callused hands and bald fingertips just like Deet's father's and took the last bite of his spaghetti before licking his thumb. "You youngins . . . let me make it as simple as possible, if I may." He looked them in the eye and jerked his head towards Deet before pulling it back toward Jake for their approval.

"Sure," Deet topped his meat loaf with baked beans before shoveling the top of the mound into his mouth.

"Which department you guys work?" The man, whose curly, black hair was edged in gray along the side of his head, just like his words were sprinkled with an Italian accent, wagged a forefinger back and forth.

"Milling."

"How long you employed by the Big C?" The man wiped his hands with a paper napkin.

"A year." Carver answered

Deet looked up, working the math in his head. "A bit over eight months."

"Alright, now . . . say Consolidated wants to lay off thirty men in milling." He wiggled his finger some more. "The Big C told us almost two years ago, after the big strike, that they would use strict seniority. In this case the thirty men with least time in the company." The whites around his dark eyes swelled, and he sucked in his lips. "That could very well be you. But what-a they doing now is making a list of workers they want to keep, and then they pretend the seniority list only applies to everyone else. So, if your names . . ." The man paused and pointed at the two younger men. ". . . what-a your names?"

"Jake Carver."

"Deet Jenkins."

"Well, let's say your names are on the list, the Big C is protecting you, but I—Vinni Giloto—could possibly be laid off even with many more years here than you."

Deet stopped chewing and nodded.

"The union says *bullshit* to that. It say no senior worker should be laid off only to be replaced by someone with lesser seniority."

Another man sat down next to Giloto as they absorbed the explanation. Sandy-haired with an open flannel shirt, he attacked his plate of food, smacking his lips and letting loose with occasional snorts and sniffles.

"So," Jake took a bite of corn bread after he dipped it in his chili, "basically the union wants to protect seniority based on time worked in the plant, and Consolidated likes to grease the rules."

Giloto's head bobbed up and down.

"Thanks, Mister Giloto for the explanation."

"Hey, you-a Arch's boy?" Giloto cocked his head toward Deet.

The teen offered a sheepish smile and nodded.

"Arch a good man, a good tire builder." Deet saw Giloto's brown eyes soften. "How's he doing?"

Deet shared about the coma and the disease and how his father was making slow progress in regaining the use of his limbs, especially his arms.

"You tella him, Vinnie Giloto wishes him everything good, okay?" Giloto stood up with tray in hand.

"I will, Mister Giloto."

As Vinnie Giloto left, a loud belch by the man who had sat down next to him sent an invisible cloud of stink towards Deet, causing him to abandon the dinner roll he had hoped to save for last.

"Youins know the wop was right about seniority," the man with manners of a pig blurted out with a West Virginia accent. "But youins also got to watch your paychecks."

"What do you mean?" Jake asked as Deet covered his nose with a paper napkin, pretending to wipe his mouth.

"They've been chiselin' people by delayin' pay upgrades once you reach certain time- served ana-ana-anniversaries." He cut off the lower half of his piece of apple pie with a fork and shoved it into his mouth. But he didn't stop talking. "Things are headed to where . . . where we were two years ago when we had a big strike."

He paused for a while to swallow, causing Deet to worry the man would choke to death in front of him. Another belch wiped away that concern, and the man continued. "They thought they could get company thugs, cops, and vigilantes to root us out and break us. Hah! We took 'em on in the streets." He ran his shirt sleeve over his pastry-crusted lips. "I was in the Klan long time before they even got out of bed. I'll be damned if I let them try it again."

Deet and Jake went their separate ways as they walked toward trash barrels at either end of the cafeteria's serving line. As Deet turned away after dropping off his tray, he stepped into the path of a woman in a plain gray dress, causing her to spill the dish, silverware, and paper trash on her tray.

"I'm so sorry, ma'am." Without so much of a glance, Deet bent down and began picking up the trail of litter he created.

It wasn't until he got up with a plate in hand that he noticed the curly, black-haired beauty he'd seen at the dance months earlier standing in front of him, smiling. He couldn't take his gaze off of her as his arm reached out and dropped the plate in the dishwater tub.

"No need for such formalities." With her holding the tray under the shapely contours of her breasts, she waited for him to return the plate as her eyes drifted from his muscular shoulders downward. "I'm not a ma'am. I'm a miss . . . Sophie Getz." The tip of her tongue snuck out between her lips like some sort of worm, and she let it crawl from one side of her mouth to the other. "What's yours?"

Deet felt his blood rush to his groin as his knees weakened.

Chapter 17

Cleveland

February 1938

As Hugo walked down the East Ninth Street pier toward the ship, its ruddy hull blended into the pinkish purple sunset on a wide-open Lake Erie. Only its bridge stood silhouetted against the dappled sky. As he approached the boarding ramp, the sound of running water diverted his attention to a mini waterfall cascading out of the hole from which suspended the anchor chain. Despite the abnormally warm weather, his hands tingled, and he shivered on the inside as he approached a sailor smoking a cigar.

"Zweiback." Hugo mustered a commanding voice to disguise his anxiety, addressing the hulking sailor with the simple word meaning *hard toast*. It seemed so ludicrous, even idiotic. However, he followed *Herr* Schmidt's order precisely. The Cleveland German American Bund leader's fear of being surveilled by American agents promoted the young Geller into a new role of intrigue. Now, he hoped that the man under a knitted cap at the end of the gangway with a lit cigar stuck in his mouth was the sailor who was supposed to receive the message.

The blond-haired man wearing a striped shirt partially covered by an unbuttoned, olive pea coat stared at the teen. His leathery face gave away his years on the sea, but not his thoughts as he sized up Hugo. After countless seconds, he muttered, "Orange marmalade is good."

Hugo exhaled and followed the sailor up the ramp to board the freighter *John R. Austin*, which had docked earlier that afternoon from Buffalo. Hugo stopped at the top of the ramp and pointed to the water pouring out of the chain's hole.

"Bilge pump." Blowing out acrid cigar smoke, the sailor offered limited explanation and led Hugo to a cabin not far from the gangway. A number of stacked boxes covered one corner of the room. The sailor helped him make several trips up and down the gangway to the

1930 Dodge sedan *Herr* Schmidt lent Hugo, loading its trunk and back seat. One box marked *Fleischer* was for a special delivery. The others were to be dropped off at the German American consulate, several blocks south of the pier. Already crammed to the ceiling, the back seat rejected Hugo's last box. It tipped over, and a stack of Nazi magazines spilled over the door sill onto the pavement. By the glow of a flashlight, the teen caught its headline, *Der verdammte Jude*— The Damned Jew.

After tidying up the mess, Geller walked back into the dim light under a lamp post near the gangway where the sailor needed a signature. Hugo scrawled *H. Geller* on the paper and returned to the black sedan that fused the onset of night with the darkened macadam surface of the pier. Its silver-painted wheel spokes and chrome bumpers were its only markers.

Somewhat exhilarated at his first successful mission for the Bund, he stripped second gear as he tried to reach third with the floor stick. His imitation of the Indianapolis 500 was short-lived as less than a half mile up the street from the pier, he parked in front of a limestone-walled building. He delivered all but one of the boxes with the assistance of a wheeled cart. Before he left, a small pamphlet in the lobby, entitled *Rueckwanderer,* grabbed his attention, and he took it.

His last stop was at the Caxton Building on Huron Avenue. An eight-story brick building with various offices on the upper floors, the Caxton featured several street level shops, including The Magical Book Shop. A sign over the bookstore—*Don't Commit Suicide Until You've Visited the Magical Book Shop*—left Hugo wondering.

Hugo carried the box labeled *Fleischer* into the bookstore, where another prominent sign hung on the back wall, centered under a picture of Christ—*Don't Die Dumb*. Focused on the sign, he almost stumbled over the lip of a carpet runner as he approached the counter. Flushed, but upright, he met an elderly gentleman with strands of wispy, white hair combed sideways over a bald head. "Hello, I have a box for a Mister Fleischer from the Bund."

"*Ja,* that is me." A German accent caked the few words. "Just put it on the counter, young man, would you please?"

As Hugo lifted the box, he asked the owner about the strange sign outside his shop.

"Ha," the old man chuckled. "It does get one's attention now doesn't it? Besides, in all sincerity, *we* shouldn't die dumb." He wagged his index finger towards the back wall.

Hugo nodded and then noticed a number of folded pamphlets on the counter, including *Rueckwanderer.* Shadow images of people walking into Germany, represented by a map, made up the cover on the front fold. After setting the box in place, the teen opened the trifold and scanned its contents.

"That one, *Coming Home,* has drawn some interest of late." The old man used a penknife to slice the box's wrapping tape an inch at a time. "The Fuehrer wants ethnic Germans to come back and defend the Fatherland if necessary."

"From what?"

"Not what," Fleischer spoke with his eyes concentrating on the knife, "but *who?* The communists and Jews, of course."

"Of course."

"Does that interest you?" With the center line of tape cut, the bookstore owner began an incision on one of the side edges.

Hugo looked across at Fleisher as the old man continued slicing with surgical precision. "Yes, *Herr* Fleisher, it does. I really would like to fight for *Herr* Hitler."

"How old are you?" The elderly man finished the cut on one side and turned his attention to the last line of tape on the other.

"Eighteen next month."

"Then you will have to talk it over with your parents. You still have a few more years to go before you can wander off on your own." A slight grin spread across his wrinkled face as he folded the knife and put it in his pocket. "I wish I could, but age has overtaken me, so I do my part by feeding the locals the truth about the Jews." He grabbed a handful of small posters from the box and put them on the counter.

"Yes, the communists must never rise here and especially never in the Fatherland." The conversation energized Hugo, bolstering the legitimacy of his thinking.

"True, but the Jews are behind it all." The store owner put another handful of flyers on the counter. "They want to annihilate Christians like me and you. Did you know *Der Jude* poisons vitamins and health foods they sell to Christians?

"Oh yes," Fleischer said, walking to the end of the counter and picking up another paper. "It's all right here. Mister Pelley, from the Silver Shirts organization has documented it here." He handed the flyer to the boy. "Good people those Silver Shirts. You won't find a Jew or a colored anywhere in their group."

Hugo picked up a small poster the owner had just removed from the box and read the text accompanied by a picture of Benjamin Franklin. "So, even Benjamin Franklin knew the Jews were corrupt?"

"Maybe yes, maybe no," the elderly man said hunched over another stack of posters. "The truth is the average American is ignorant of such things and is easily convinced by our positions. In fact, many don't need much prodding at all, just look at Lindbergh, America's greatest hero. He admires *Der Fuehrer* almost as much as we do." The old man's smile revealed a near complete set of yellowed teeth.

Hugo scanned another poster with a letter written by a German Jew to his son in America explaining how news reports of the persecution of Jews were *made up stories* created by rich American Jews who owned newspapers and wanted to make more money.

"Young man, let me show you something." Fleischer came out from behind the counter and beckoned Hugo with a curled forefinger. "I want to show you my news station." He shuffled to the back room behind a fabric curtain.

An oblong radio rested on a side table against a wall. A large circular antenna, almost the diameter of an automobile tire sat perched atop of the radio. Fleisher put on a pair of headphones and then tuned the radio, using either one of two dials. Satisfied with whatever he selected, he took off the headphones and handed them to the youthful Geller. "Here, it's the midnight news . . . from Berlin."

After he put on the headphones, Hugo's mouth opened, and he felt his eyes widen. "It is! This is fantastic!"

"I don't rely on Jewish lies in American papers. I get my truth direct from *Herr* Hitler."

****

Akron

February 1938

Deet blew a smoke ring into the air and watched it vanish into the murky atmosphere of a cheap hotel room. For an instant, the herringbone-patterned wallpaper captured his attention. The repetitive, horizontal right angles massaged the roiling emotions of this evening. This wasn't what he had planned, but spontaneous lust took over. Lying on a bed, whose springs bounced only minutes earlier with a racket standard in such an establishment, he held onto the cusp of a supple shoulder with his right hand while a pillow of brunette curls cushioned his arm.

It began when he gave Sophie Getz his phone number in the union hall cafeteria the previous Sunday. This particular evening started out with the two sharing an innocent beer at Wiley's, a local bar on a side street off of East Market, where lots of gummers went. Although excited at spending some time with the daring broad, who wore a satiny blouse and pants, he approached it as mere union work. She'd explained she wanted a mill worker's opinion on a certain issue.

Indeed, that's what happened. Over a couple low power brews, she asked Deet his opinion on letting Blacks into the URW. The former nationwide organization representing the gummers in Washington balked at the idea. Then again, that outfit failed them miserably, caving in to the big corporations. A new national union organization thought it might be time to build a bigger tent.

Deet told her he wouldn't be opposed, especially since Dixon's friends helped save his job. Yet, he couldn't speak for everyone in the milling department. Sophie smiled at him and then shared how ten years earlier, at nineteen, she took matters into her own hands in the garment sweatshops of Lower Manhattan and organized the first garment workers union. She was convinced unions needed to make connections like Deet must have made with his fellow workers of color. He collapsed under her forceful presence and couldn't resist when she invited him to her room less than a block away.

The strapping teen stared at the ceiling, acknowledging Sophie had been the conductor of their duet. He tried to wrap his mind around what had happened in the past few hours just as her body had wrapped around his as if they were shared halves of the same mold. But they weren't.

Sophie slid out of bed and draped a robe around her naked body. Drawn by the memory of what he'd just experienced, a nude Deet clung to her as they both stood by the bed. She kissed him on the cheek like a mother would a child. "I've got to meet some staff soon to go over strategies, so the Consolidated situation doesn't boil over like it did in '36," she said, patting his hand. "Besides, you need to get ready for work pretty soon."

Aroused, Deet worked a hand inside her robe and began exploring with the lightest touch.

Sophie clamped a hand on his invasive wrist and evicted it from her person. "Listen," her dark eyes projected a hollow look, "this was nice, but you know what they say about a rolling stone."

By now, Deet's body had cooled, and he shot a scowl toward her. "What?" By now, he realized the party was over, and he donned his underwear.

"Look Darling, I live life by my own rules, and I get my *sweets* from different sources. I'm not going to be tied down." She walked to the dresser and stood in front of the mirror as she put on her undergarments. "Think of this as a pleasant memory. I carry mine with me wherever I go, and they don't interrupt my work. They help keep me warm in Buffalo and cool me in Miami. They even overcome the stench of Akron." She spritzed a bit of perfume under her neck and dug out another dress from her suitcase.

I'm one of her sweets?

He shook his head as he pulled his shirt down over his head.

The term must have been some New York slang. Deet had never heard it used that way before. Things began to sink in for him. This wasn't the beginning of something wonderful but the end of a momentary illusion. This wasn't how these things were supposed to work, at least that's not what he'd heard from his pals, nor when he was younger eavesdropping on his father and uncle reminiscing about 'the good old days'. He'd even pulled it off once before himself when Betty Fingerhoffen offered herself in the back seat of the Pontiac. For the following few weeks at Central, he gave her the cold shoulder until the freeze numbed her amorous ambitions. Now, the shoe was on the other foot, although it certainly didn't take as long to get Sophie's message. He exhaled his frustration as he pulled up his trousers.

I'm such a dumb ass—

A knock on the door interrupted his epiphany, as he looked back toward Sophie while he finished buckling his belt.

"Open the door will ya," Sophie pleaded as she struggled to bring the dress over her head.

Deet swung open the door after a second knock and a young woman, perhaps in her early twenties, waited with a smile and her hand leaning against the door casing. The dingy lighting made details difficult, but she wore a bucket hat and enough cosmetics to make a clown jealous.

She slung a feather wrap around her neck barely covering her low-cut dress. "Is Sophie ready, Honey Bun?"

"Ah . . . eh," Deet didn't know what to say.

"Yes, I am, Lilly. I'll be right with ya. Come on in."

The scent of lavender oil invaded Deet's space, and he felt Sophie's dress brush against him from behind. She patted him on his shoulder and pecked his cheek. "Be a good boy, Darling, I'll see you around." Like a kindergartener, he'd been sent on his way home.

Behind the door Sophie had closed with finality, the two women giggled like high school girls back at Central flirting with the guys on the football team. Meanwhile, Deet stood in the dimly lit hall, looking at his watch. His shift started in less than an hour. As he looked up, he noticed a fedora-topped head poking its way out at the end of the corridor at the top of the stairway. He stared at the shadowed face for several seconds before it vanished. Deet took little notice of the man as he began his walk of shame.

Chapter 18

Akron

March 1938

6 6 She's killing the children! She's killing the children!"
Arch's cries brought Trudi rushing downstairs as well as rousting Deet and Louie from the basement. They found him, arms flailing upward, circling the center of the living room in his pajamas.

"He's hallucinating again." Standing in the foyer, Trudi dug what was left of her nails into Deet's bicep. "That's all the neighbors need to hear—him screaming bloody murder."

Arch stopped his orbit, dropped his arms, and stared at the trio with wide-eyed panic. "We must hurry. We *must* hurry!"

"To where, Arch?" Louie broke an uncomfortable silence with a soothing voice. Deet couldn't help but notice his uncle's hand twitching as it was attached to his trousers on the hip.

Arch's face froze.

"You drunken monkey!" Trudi turned on Louie, slapping his shoulder. "What kind of a question is that? He needs to go back to bed."

Before Trudi took a step, Arch broke out of his catatonic spell. "We have to go to Burluk. Burluk! Quickly, come!" He resumed his rotating walk.

Deet looked at Louie for some direction. There was something different about him today. Side by side, the two of them had just spent close to an hour fixing a plumbing issue. His mother's pointed insult to her brother-in-law awakened Deet to the fact he'd not smelled any alcohol on Louie the entire time in the basement.

"Burluk?" Louie turned toward his nephew. "I've heard that name before."

As Arch continued his hysterical walk, Louie challenged Trudi. "Trudi, let me try to make some sense of this. I promise my goal will be to get him back to bed."

Deet looked at his mother. Beaten down by several months of his father's cycle of tremors, rage, intermittent delusions, and self-pity, she exhaled and nodded.

"What's going on in Burluk?" Louie walked into the living room a few feet from the perimeter of Arch's circle.

Arch stopped as strands of his blond hair drooped over his sweat-dotted face. "The old woman is trying to kill her grandchildren. She started a fire in the hearth and closed the damper to the chimney." He resumed his walk. "She's going to suffocate them and her. She will suffocate them all!"

Louie looked back at Trudi and Deet, compressing his lips and raising his eyes. Then he tried to learn more. "Why would the old woman want to kill her grandchildren, Arch?"

Arch stopped again. "There's very little to eat in Burluk, and the children keep crying out, 'I'm hungry! I'm hungry!'" Arch grabbed Louie's arm. "She can't take it anymore."

"Arch," Louie spoke with the calmness of a pastor handing out communion, "if I promise you we'll rescue those children and feed the family will you go back to bed?"

"Back to bed?" Arch's one arm trembled.

Louie nodded as he took off his spectacles and wiped them with a handkerchief.

"You'll be sure to save them? Feed them?"

After he put his glasses on, Louie gently took his brother by the arm. "Absolutely, Arch."

"Back to bed," Deet's father muttered as Louie led him into the reconfigured dining room.

Deet's uncle sat on the edge of the bed as his brother stretched himself out. Within seconds, Arch was fast asleep.

Deet joined his mother and uncle in the kitchen, where Trudi made some coffee.

"How long has he been having hallucinations?" Louie asked of no one in particular as he sat emotionless, his eyes swelled through the lenses of his spectacles.

"Probably the last month," Deet offered. "Right Mom?" He gathered the cups and saucers from a cupboard.

"*Ja,*" Trudi reverted to a bit of German as she put the coffee pot on the gas burner. "It shocked me at first even though the doctor said it could happen with Parkinson's. Now it occurs several times a week."

Louie inhaled and propped his head with a hand supported by an elbow on the table. "Has the medicine helped at all?"

"Perhaps, there are some days where Archie says he feels fine . . . the arm, hand tremors are barely noticeable. He dresses himself and walks around the kitchen and living room." She poured coffee into each of their cups. "Even those days can be difficult. He's so bull-headed, he insists on going into the basement or upstairs to check things out. If not, he raves about going out of his mind if he can't go back to work." She sat and took a sip from her cup. "Then again, there are enough days like today to make life discouraging."

"What was all that about Burluk and the old woman wanting to kill her grandchildren?" Deet offered the sugar jar to any takers of which there were none but himself.

"I can't tell you much, but the word *Burluk* did bring up a memory." Louie used both hands to pick up his cup and take a sip. "Pops came from the old country—Ukraine—around 1880. His last name was Jenkevko. At some point, he changed it to Jenkins in order to better fit into his new surroundings. He met our mother over here, and off and on he'd talk about Burluk, his hometown." Again, with both hands, he put down the white cup with a red line bordering its lip.

Deet watched Louie, his thick lenses glued to his cup, mindlessly stir his spoon in the pitch-dark java with one hand while the fingers of the other fluttered just above the tablecloth. "It wasn't very big. It was rural . . . a wheat growing region, sort of like Kansas is over here. Well, that's as much as I remember."

"What about the old woman?" The heat of the coffee caused Deet to clench his teeth, forcing his cheeks out.

"I haven't the faintest idea where that came from. I guess that's why it's called a hallucination." Again, Deet's uncle cradled the coffee to his mouth with both hands.

"I'm going to lay down for a bit. I'm exhausted." Wisps of dark brown hair dangled in front of Trudi's baggy eyes. After she got up, she put her hand on Louie's arm. "Thank you, Louie, for talking Archie out of whatever world he was in. I'm sorry for what I said."

Louie looked up, patted her hand, and nodded as Trudi went into the bedroom, closing the door behind her.

Deet's uncle downed what was left of his coffee. "Well, I need to get a tune-up done." His ass had just left its seat when his nephew stopped him with a simple question.

"How long have you been sober?"

Louie settled back down on the chair and looked at his nephew. "It's fairly obvious, isn't it?" Louie paused, biting on his lower lip. "Two days."

Deet drummed his fingertips on the table.

"Got something to say, Deet?" Louie's pointed question wasn't rude. "If not, I need to go."

While Deet had dreaded the thought of this moment, he also welcomed it. Knowing there were no guarantees how Louie would react, he decided to probe a bit. "What made you decide to stop?"

Louie turned his head toward the dining room door. "Twenty years of living in the trenches is way too long. I lost my wife because the booze was a worthless crutch. Now the only family I have left needs some help."

The water seemed deep enough to take the dive. "Would you care to have some real professional help? People who know what you've gone through."

Louie's exaggerated eyes narrowed. "Professional help?" He shook his head with a wry smile stretched across his clean-shaven face. "I can't afford—"

"No, no. Let me explain."

****

Deet walked with Dixon down the aisle after the bell alarm announced the mealtime. "Hey, I wanted to let you know the new national group that wants to cover the URW is thinking about letting Blacks in the union."

"Really?" Dixon offered a look of mock surprise. "What group?"

"I'm not sure." Deet still hoped his mill mate would take him seriously. "I can't remember the exact name, but its initials are C.I.O."

Dixon stopped at a rusting, steel I-beam support and folded his arms across his chest. "And who might be feeding you this line of bullshit?"

Deet wished he'd never broached the subject. "That good-looking union woman from New York, Sophie Getz."

"Getz? I've heard through the grapevine that that woman creates a lot of heat. From what I've heard she's a crumb . . . maybe worse." Dixon resumed his walk to the breakroom.

"What do you mean?" Deet followed in his wake.

"A Red." The Negro looked back at Deet. "I'd avoid her like the plague. Besides," Dixon stopped just inside the entrance to the large breakroom, where he pointed as Blacks went left into their dimly lit cavern while whites passed to the open expanse of tables and chairs on the right, "does this group look like they're ready for that?" Dixon left Deet pondering to eat with the rest of the coloreds.

A copy of the local paper's morning edition drew the younger Jenkins to a table, where only Big Mike sat with a half-empty canning jar of beets. The bold headline grabbed Deet's attention as he put down his bottle of milk and sack lunch.

North Hill Home Torched by Arsonists

"Is this yours, Mike?" Deet asked as he sat down.

"No. You can read." The words worked their way through a mouthful of sliced beets with a few slivers hanging on for dear life on his beard. "It was here when we come in."

Deet took out a bologna sandwich from his bag and unfolded the paper to its full front page. He froze as he saw Maria Rossi—a school photo of her—towards the bottom of the page, accompanying the story. Deet bit into his sandwich but never tasted that first bite as the newspaper account sucked him into the page.

A house on Alfaretta Avenue in the city's North Hill district was severely damaged by fire, apparently started by a group of disguised arsonists. Residents of the home, the Enrico Rossi family, suffered injuries ranging from burns to smoke inhalation. None are considered life threatening, although 19-year-old Maria Rossi was taken to Akron City Hospital with second degree burns.

According to neighborhood witnesses, a band of men dressed in black with blackened faces, perhaps smudged with shoe polish, drove up to the home around 10 P.M. Climbing out of the back of an older model Ford pick-up truck, the men lit torches, which they threw into the house after breaking ground floor windows. In addition, some form of accelerant was poured on the front porch before being ignited. Police said they found an undisclosed message in a bottle on the front yard of the Rossi property, which is being investigated.

Council President Jack Acker was at the scene as firemen were dousing the last flickering flames of the blaze. He commented, "This sort of crime will not be tolerated in our community."

Further updates will be given in upcoming editions.

"Did you see this, Mike?" Deet asked before taking a second bite of his sandwich.

With a mouthful of food, Kobenko nodded.

"Listen up, everyone." Chaw Nelson held up another copy of the morning edition. "We'd been warned this might happen, and it has. Rico's a tire builder upstairs, and his daughter, Maria, works in the flipper department. She's in the hospital.

"Police aren't saying what's in the note they found in the front yard, but this looks like the work of the Brigade. Keep an eye out for these bastards. By tomorrow, the union's going to start a benevolent fund to help the family get back on their feet. Stay sharp."

"Dat is why I live in the country. Too many rats in city." Mike closed his beet jar and put it and his fork into his lunch pail.

Deet knew he and Lacey had to go see Maria.

Why would anyone be so cruel? Was it because they were Italian, or because they're union members? Are you going to burn out half of Akron because they came from other places? Who's next . . . Germans? Hillbillies?

The bell ending the meal break sent Deet scurrying to clean up and catch up with Big Mike. "Mike, I hope you don't mind my asking, but where are you from originally?"

"Ukraine."

Chapter 19

Akron

March 1938

❝ I am very lucky to be alive." Dressed in a pale green hospital gown, Maria Rossi lay on her bed with a blanket drawn up to her waist. "I sleep . . . so deep I not hear the glass break when the fire start."

Deet looked down at her from one side of the bed, anger blistering inside as he focused on her bandaged arm.

I wish I could get my hands on the son-of-a-bitch who did this.

Lacey, seated by her side opposite Deet, stroked the understated curls of Maria's raven-colored hair from the part in the middle of her head to where they flattened at the top of the shoulder. "Maria, we're so sorry you and your family had to go through such a hellish experience." Careful not to disturb her friend's wrapped right arm as she caressed her hair, she glared across the bed at Deet, who seemed distracted. "Wasn't that awful, Deet?"

Moans from patients in an adjoining ward diverted Deet's genuine pity for Maria and her family and inner rage against the perpetrator, putting him on edge. He turned back toward Maria. "Ah, absolutely. How long before they release—"

A scream from the adjacent room sent an uncomfortable wave from Deet's stomach up to his throat, causing him to grimace.

Maria's dark brown eyes pivoted up toward Lacey's boyfriend. She lifted her left arm and pointed a finger in the direction of the cries. "Those people are burned badly."

Deet nodded, grabbed a nearby folding chair, and sat down. "How long before the doctor releases you?"

"The doctor says maybe tomorrow . . . for sure the day after tomorrow."

"Maria, if you were sound asleep, how did you get out?" By now, Lacey had stopped grooming Maria's hair.

Maria's eyes welled. "My brother . . ." Tears began to stream down her cheeks.

"Here." Lacey pulled out a paper tissue from its dispenser on a side table and handed it to Maria.

"*Grazie*." Maria dabbed her eyes. "Gino, my brother, run into my room. I wake up when I feel a blanket hit my face. Gino put out fire with a blanket, and he take me out of the house."

"Where's your family staying?" Lacey asked.

"Momma and little Sophia stay YWCA. Papa and Gino go to YMCA." She closed her eyes. "I miss them."

Lacey began to stroke Maria's hair again.

Deet cleared his throat. "Have you heard anything from the police . . . I mean about the bastards who did this?"

"May I have water?" Maria turned her head to one side as Deet poured water from a silver pitcher into a waiting glass. "*Grazie*. Police not sure, but tink a neighbor, Toog . . . don't know last name, might be part of the group."

"Toog?" Deet's forehead crinkled like a rug pushed forward on a polished wood floor. "Was that his first name or last?"

"First name, I tink."

"Did you say he was a neighbor?" Lacey moved her hand from Maria's hair and cupped the knob of her shoulder.

"*Si*. I don't know him much. I talk to him once. He seemed friendly. Papa said he help get car started once."

"Toog?" Deet shook his head. "You never know about people, do you?"

"Deet, I think we need to let Maria rest. When do you think you'll make it back to work?"

"Doctor says at least one week, maybe two. He say I was lucky."

"Considering what could have happened, you probably were lucky." Deet stood up. "Don't worry too much. The union guys and gals are raising money for you and your family. We won't forget you."

"*Grazie, grazie, grazie.*" Maria lifted her left arm to clasp Deet's hand.

Walking down the hospital corridor, Lacey turned to Deet. "Can you imagine someone you thought of as a friend and that you could trust doing that type of shit to you and your family?"

A switch turned on in Deet's head, playing a movie in which he starred. The camera is pointed down on the bed he and Sophie Getz shared in that low rent hotel. But this time Lacey co-starred instead of the union organizer and there was no heat of passion as she turned into a block of ice.

She'll never know. Sophie won't broadcast it. It meant nothing to her. What kind of fool was I?

"Hey, Deet, where are you going?" Lacey called out, having turned left at an intersecting corridor while Deet continued straight for at least fifteen feet.

As the two reconnected in the center of the corridors' square, Deet wiped a couple tears off his cheeks.

"What's wrong, Deet?" Lacey grabbed both his hands. "Is it Maria and her family?"

Deet coughed up a sheepish nod.

She drew him close and wrapped an arm around his waist, leading both of them in the proper direction. "They'll make it through this, Babydoll. With our help they will."

****

"Wait here." The handsome stranger got out of his Chevy sedan wearing a flat cap and a gray overcoat as the clouds were being put to bed on this overcast March evening. Ricky Jenkins and Bill Mowery remained in the front seat, totally subservient to the twenty-five-year-old who'd been put in charge by Mowery's mysterious female boss.

Before entering the back entrance of one of the largest pawn shops in town, he turned back and stuck his head through the lowered front passenger window, where his aftershave fought off the Akron industrial stink. "I'm going in to make sure everything's set as it's supposed to be. Mowery, keep an eye on your watch. If you don't hear anything, after two minutes you come in to help take out the loot. Kid," he looked at a petrified Ricky, "if you see anyone suspicious while we're in there, hit that horn twice. Got it!"

Ricky nodded, his legs and feet stiffened against the floorboard hoping to contain the tremble in his chest. "Two horns, right."

"Why do you keep calling me at home?" Ricky turned on Bill Mowery as soon as the new guy vanished into the store. "You know how many busybodies can listen in?"

"When the boss says you're working with Tug McGirt, you don't question it, you do it. Besides, you know you owe me. If it weren't for me convincing people you weren't right for the Brigade, you might have been part of that torching on North Hill a couple days ago." Mowery looked at his watch. "Another minute. I've been watching out for you, Ricky, and you've made some good dough, so shut your lip. Everything's just fine."

Mowery left the sedan, closing the door with a gentle touch. He hadn't been inside the shop for ten seconds when . . . *Pop! Pop!*

Mowery rushed out of the shop with McGirt on his heels, holding a pistol in one hand with a wad of cash in the other. Mowery slammed the passenger door shut as McGirt raced around the back of the Chevy and threw himself into the driver's seat.

Ricky, stuck in between the two, rolled his tongue to moisten an arid mouth, but it was no use. "W-h-hat happened?"

"Why the hell did you shoot the guy, Tug?" Bill's voice squeaked in a manner Ricky had never heard.

"He was playin' a double-cross." Tug engaged the clutch, floored the gas pedal, and shot down the alley, side-swiping several trash cans along the way. "He changed his mind about the insurance scam and picked up the phone to call the police when I leaned on him. What was I supposed to do? Let him turn us in?" He barely stopped when the alley emptied onto a side street before tearing down West Market. "I left the ice and watches and took all the cash in his register. Leastways, that can't be connected to us.

With his feet once again pressed against the floorboard, Ricky struggled to stay calm on the outside while his stomach somersaulted.

Us?

"How about this guy?" Tug shot an elbow into Ricky. "What'll keep him from spillin' the beans?"

"I'm no stoolie!" Ricky mustered all the confidence left in him to at least sound loyal.

"I'll vouch for him, Tug. Besides, he's as deep into this shit as we are . . . and he knows it." Now it was Mowery's turn to stick an elbow into Ricky. "Don't ya?"

"Yeah, I know." Ricky's growl disguised his panic as he could feel his feet pushing for the pavement.

Chapter 20

Akron

April 1938

Even though the early spring sun sparkled in a cloudless, blue sky, Detective Gerald Ragmon shivered a bit in the sixty-degree weather. A stiff northerly breeze chopped the water of the Beaver Street clay pit pond as it punished him for leaving his suit coat in the car.

Damn coat can't be buttoned anyway.

He walked the perimeter of the abandoned nine-acre site to meet up with his partner, Abe Kelly. "What'd we got, Abe?" The sound of lapping water provided the backdrop as Kelly knelt his tall frame over a blanket-covered mound. Ragmon knew it was a dead body, but it was the particulars that interested him.

"Middle-aged Jane Doe, shot in the back of the head." Kelly pulled back the olive blanket far enough to display the head and shoulders, which were clad in a floral-print dress or blouse.

"Messy business," muttered Ragmon as he rambled on with his first impressions. He'd seen dozens of murder victims in his decade as a detective, so much so, the ghastly remains prompted analysis more than pity. "Possible .38 to the back of the head. Execution . . . maybe, but I doubt it . . . no wound to face. Bullet probably still lodged in the brain. Looks like she's been in the water for some time."

"Oh, yeah," Kelly chirped. "Look at this, Jerry." He pulled back enough of the blanket to expose a sodden, six-foot rope tied to the victim's wrist. "Whoever rushed to weigh her down with a block or whatever did a bum job of tying off the weight. That's why she surfaced."

"Any ID?"

Kelly shook his head and whispered an unintelligible profanity as he stood up and realized the moistened grass stain on the knee of his pants.

"Who found her?"

"A group of kids, skipping stones." Kelly brushed the stain with his hand in a fruitless attempt at impromptu dry-cleaning.

"Ah, Jee-sus!"

"Yeah, according to the parent that called, the kids were on their way home from the nearby elementary school, and they were pretty shook up."

"Anyone talk to them yet?" Ragmon shielded his eyes from the sun with his hand as he scanned the neighborhood behind the tree line.

"I sent a patrol over to their neighborhood to get statements."

"This is a great place to dump a body and a deadly place for kids to play."

Kelly's head flinched to one side, and his face squeezed together from forehead to chin. "What do you mean?"

"They dug clay out of here years ago, and when they were done, they just left this gigantic ten-acre hole to be filled with runoff. Chances are there's a twenty to thirty-foot drop just ten feet behind you, Abe."

The tall detective turned around and gazed at the heaving, grayish-brown water that not even the clear sky could mask its murkiness. "It doesn't look that deep."

"That's the point! I bet you that there's been at least a half-dozen kids drown in this over-sized mud puddle in the past decade." Jerry Ragmon's eyelids opened to a point he had to use a hand as a visor once more. "People in this neighborhood have been bitching for years for the city do something about it, but *good people* like Jack Acker keep putting it off. Now, kids have to look at this!" He pointed to the covered corpse. "The world's going to hell in a handbasket, Abe, and we're its chaperones."

The sound of a siren announced the arrival of the meat wagon some hundred yards across the pond, near where Ragmon parked his car.

"Alright, the boys are here to take her to the morgue. The cold water left her in pretty good condition, but the faster they get her into the cooler, the better it'll be for our evidence." Ragmon dug out a pack of chewing gum from a pocket and put a stick in his mouth. "Coroner should give us an idea how long she's been in the water and that slug."

"I'll start with a guess of about a week and check out any missing persons reports." Kelly cringed at his partner's gum smacking as he made a note on a paper pad.

"Once the boys take her out, we need to do a walk around the pond. Let's see if there's anything obvious laying around. Who knows? There might be a shell casing or piece of clothing."

"Best clue will be her clothes and the slug."

"You know, Abe, she was shot from the back, so I don't see this as a lover's revenge. If so, he'd take her out face-to-face." Ragmon picked the wad of gum out of his mouth and pitched it into the pond and looked out over its restless water. "This could be a gang shooting . . . business deal gone wrong . . . but it wasn't close range." He turned back toward Kelly and let his blue eyes sparkle. "Who knows how many stiffs might be in the bottom of this pit?"

****

Ragmon and Kelly's search around the pond came up empty. Shortly after he returned to the station, Ragmon munched on a bologna sandwich, filling out forms from other cases, as he waited for the coroner to provide vital information on the murder victim. Of course, his phone would ring when he'd just stuffed the last third of his sandwich into his mouth.   "Detective . . . Sergeant . . . Ragmon." The words barely navigated through the mush in his mouth before an elderly voice imitating a door hinge in need of oiling spoke over him.

162

"This is Ma-bel Din-gus on Laird Street, and I need to re-port some mis-chief."

Why do I get all the screwballs?

"What is it that's so concerning, Missus Dingus?" By now, Ragmon had swallowed his food and anticipated heartburn if not from the bologna then from the old lady.

"My phone is on a par-ty line, and eve-ry time I call my sis-ter—I u-su-al-ly call before sev-en in the e-ven-ing—"

"Yes, yes, Missus Dingus, just what is the problem?" Ragmon stood up only to park his ass on the edge of his desk.

"I'm try-ing to tell you if you wouldn't be so rude. I have to call be-fore sev-en be-cause she goes to bed ear-ly. On sev-er-al oc-ca-sions I've had to wait be-cause two young scal-ly-wags are talk-ing, and from the sounds of their con-ver-sa-tion, they're up to no good."

"How do you know they're up to no good?" By now, Ragmon inhaled and exhaled like a corralled bull.

"One of them men-tions mo-ving goods in the mid-dle of the night. What re-spect-a-ble per-son moves things at such an hour?"

"Well, Missus Dingus, it's no telling what hours some folks work." Standing up, the detective readied his cut-off line. "Thank you, Missus Dingus, I think—"

"To be quite hon-est, I don't trust that young-est Jen-kins boy. What's a sixteen-year-old boy doing run-ning a-round town at all hours of the—"

"Jenkins? Deet Jenkins? Arch Jenkins' boy?" Ragmon sat down in his oak swivel chair. While his breathing was no longer exaggerated, his heart beat a bit faster.

"No, it's the young-est boy, Ricky."

"Now, about how often do you end up listening to Ricky Jenkins and this other boy?" Ragmon picked up a pencil and note pad.

"W-wel-l, at least once a week, some-times twice."

"You said this was in the evening, right? At five? Six? Seven?"

"U-su-al-ly between six and seven. My sis-ter, Ma-til-da, goes to bed ear-ly."

"Did you ever hear the name of the other boy or man talking to Ricky?"

"Once. Rick-y cal-led him Bill." Missus Dingus coughed. "Ex-cuse me."

Ragmon never noticed her discomfort. "Did either one ever mention a business involved with whatever they were moving?

"Yes and no." She paused, prompting a heavy sigh from the detective. "No ac-tu-al busi-ness name was e-ver men-tioned. But that Bill fel-low re-fer-red to a tire ware-house, a pawn shop, and a jew-el-ry store."

"Really!" Ragmon felt like he'd drawn two kings to accompany three aces. He jotted down the types of businesses Missus Dingus listed.

"Are you still there, De-tec-tive?"

"Yes, yes I am, Missus Dingus." Ragmon put the finishing touches on his notes.

"Do you think you can use this in-for-ma-tion?"

"I do believe so. Now, in the future, if you happen to listen in to another one of their conversations, please be careful and hang up your receiver very gently, so they're not aware of your presence."

"You mean I shouldn't lis-ten in any-more?"

"No." Ragmon's voice lightened. "What I mean, Missus Dingus, is that you shouldn't listen anymore because it might make them suspicious."

"I be-lieve Rick-y may al-read-y be sus-pi-cious. He gets an-gry at Bill for call-ing on the phone."

"Rest assured, Missus Dingus, you've done your duty as a law-abiding citizen, and we'll most certainly take it from here."

"Glad to be of ser-vice, De-tec-tive. Good-bye."

"Good-bye, Missus Dingus." No sooner had Ragmon hung up his phone, than his index finger spun the rotary dial once. "Yes, Captain

Clark, Ragmon here. I'd like to request a phone tap. I've got a credible lead on these midnight burglaries."

****

The phone rang on the side table in the Jenkins' foyer. With his mother tending to his father and his brother not yet home from work, Ricky didn't have to race to pick up the receiver. "Hello."

"Hey, it's been awhile. Listen, we got a new boss, and we got another delivery for tomorrow night." The recognizable voice on the other end of the line oozed enthusiasm.

"What? Who the hell are you?" Ricky played opossum.

"Come on. It's Bill Mow—"

Click.

Weeks after the botched pick-up at the pawn shop, Ricky hoped everything, everyone, had just gone away. He wanted to lay so low that grass might even sprout on his clothing. He wished he'd never met Bill Mowery. Worse, he wished he'd listened to Deet. How could he tell his brother, let alone his parents, he'd been involved in a murder? He just wanted to return to the anonymity of everyday life at Central High.

"Who was that, Ricky?" His mother asked as she came out of the former dining room after having tended to his father.

"Just a wrong number . . . a wrong number."

Chapter 21

Akron

May 1938

Deet sat next to Lacey in the third row of folding wooden chairs in front of the stage in the union hall's auditorium. Industrial-sized fans, positioned on the floor on either side of the stage, manufactured a breeze on this sultry, late spring day. He longed for a breeze that could cleanse his spirit. For the past couple months, his soul vacillated between caged guilt and the cold, hard rationale of his own creation.

Each outing with Lacey became an exercise in mining the tell-tale signs that she'd discovered his indiscretion—an icy stare, an unprovoked flash of anger, or worse yet, a prolonged malaise of apathy. There'd been nothing of that nature, only her continual love, admiration, and companionship. That only created more self-loathing within him. Even now, with labor strife on the horizon, he felt her hand clamp onto his as if he were the life preserver which would keep her afloat in these turbulent waters. For his part, he could always assuage his guilt for a time with the masculine stand-by—*Hey, we're not married, why would it matter anyway? All's fair in love and war, right?* In this moment, surrounded by some five-hundred co-workers, their teeth glistened, and eyes sparkled as they adored each other.

"Can't hear!" Several rough voices called out from Deet's and Lacey's row as a ripple of agitation flowed in the rows behind them.

A short, barrel-chested man, wearing a gray short-sleeved shirt and blue jeans, tapped the cylindrical microphone atop a metal stand in the center of the stage. Deet watched him lower the mic at an acute angle from the vertical pole to which it was attached. After a high-pitched squeal from both speakers at either side of the stage, the man's baritone voice rang true. "Can you hear me now?"

The restlessness of the crowd subsided, and the speaker took charge. "For those of you who don't know me, I'm Gene Shaw, president of your Consolidated URW union." Square-jawed, with deep-set eyes, Shaw held a couple pieces of paper in his hands.

Deet thought the man was ready to put the hall to sleep with a long-winded speech. Shaw surprised him.

"Hard working men and women of the Consolidated URW, I had a speech prepared for this afternoon." Shaw held up the papers, crumpled them into a tight wad, and tossed it over his shoulder with his eyes focused on his audience. He walked out from behind the podium to the front edge of the stage. His unamplified voice boomed towards the far corners in the rear of the hall. "I don't need to read anything. I'll give it to you straight."

Deet sat upright at the union leader's forcefulness as he even released his grip on Lacey's hand.

The entire hall fell silent as if a minister left the security of his pulpit near the altar to deliver his message below, among the pews.

"Regarding the ongoing complaints concerning strict seniority among transfers," Shaw resumed his message, "Consolidated isn't interested in our concerns."

"Boo!" Several audience members echoed their displeasure.

"Regarding layoffs based upon seniority," Shaw paused. "Consolidated isn't interested in our concerns."

"Boo!" This time, a greater number of members sounded off.

"Regarding the limited use of overtime based upon a union steward's approval or the approval of a joint labor/management committee," the union president halted again as his dark eyes roved the hall. "Consolidated isn't interested in our position."

Deet felt his seat vibrate as a number of people around him stood up and roared their disapproval. The hall had settled before it dawned on Deet that there were people in attendance who had sat down for a day in order to get his job back for him. Why hadn't he stood up? He felt shallow, just as shallow as in his betrayal of Lacey.

"Regarding wage adjustments for those transferring to new jobs being set by a joint committee of labor and management," Shaw raised his right hand and shook it, "*Consolidated isn't interested in us!*"

Deet flew up from his seat, lifting Lacey with his right hand, as the entire hall erupted. Fists shook and faces curled in anger as *Boos* were replaced by cries of *Bastards! Assholes! Sons-of-bitches!* Pumping his left fist, he caught his first glimpse of a table near the right side of the stage. Partially hidden by the numerous curtain folds, four people sat there, including Sophie, who had a white cardboard box in front of her. Deet locked eyes with the female unionist, and she smiled.

Sophie's subtle pink lips, arching over and under gleaming teeth, proved too much of a personal indictment. Deet looked away just as Lacey squeezed his hand. Her touch drew his eyes into hers.

Does she know?

"Hey, either take it outside or sit down." A smoker's voice complained from behind them.

By now, the agitated assembly had calmed down and returned to their seats. Deet and Lacey plopped themselves into their seats and returned their focus to Gene Shaw.

"It looks like we may well be headed toward another strike—a big one—just like back in '36. We're going to need help, and with that, I'd like to introduce a few folks from the C.I.O., the Congress of Industrial Organizations. They have some ideas on how to get us prepared and stay safe if this thing goes south.

"First, I'd like to introduce Miss Sophie Getz."

Sophie walked across the stage with her hands supporting the cardboard box at the bottom. Dressed in gray work pants and a pale blue shirt, she attracted a number of cat calls and whistles as her dark curls bounced with each step.

Shaw waited for her at the microphone. "If you guys would get your mind out of the gutter for a few minutes, I'd like to let you know that Miss Getz started *and headed* the first women's garment makers union in Manhattan when she was just nineteen years old. Don't let that pretty face fool you, she's proved she's got gravel in her guts and a solid backbone." He made way for Sophie, who put the box down on the floor.

Sophie made a minor adjustment to the microphone's angle. "Thank you, Gene. Ladies and gentlemen." She stared momentarily toward the back of the hall. "And that includes the clown in the back making obscene gestures at me at this moment." She stepped to the side of the microphone stand and pointed at some red-faced Joe whose belt sagged under the strain of his bloated stomach.

All the gummers turned a hundred-and-eighty degrees and ridiculed the jerk into an invisible hole of his own creation.

Sophie returned to behind the mic. "This is serious business we're about, so enough of the nonsense. The most important lesson I learned from organizing garment workers a decade ago is this—*stand together or you'll be broken one by one.*

"Companies are in business to make money, and there's absolutely nothing wrong with that idea. Capitalism is good. In fact, it's the best economic system humanity has ever created . . . as long as workers are seen as human beings who benefit the company and *not as tools to be used by the company.*"

The gathering thundered its approval with shouts and clapping while Sophie bent down and picked up what appeared to be a narrow stick from the box.

"One of my grandparents was a full-blooded Iroquois, and she taught me a unique lesson about strength in numbers. See this dowel?" She held up the wooden piece, which looked to be about two feet long. "This dowel is a quarter inch in diameter, roughly the thickness and length of an arrow."

Sophie stepped to one side of the microphone and proceeded to snap the dowel over her knee. Then she picked up four more sticks out of the box and bundled them, but she couldn't break them on a successive attempt. "Could I get one of you strong men to volunteer to break this bundle of four dowels?"

"Why don't you go up?" Lacey nudged Deet, and before he could react, she waved her arm and attracted Sophie's attention.

Deet hung his head as if he'd vomit.

Thanks to Lacey's excitement, Sophie didn't need another volunteer. "Looks like we may have one brave young man in the third row. Let's give him some encouragement." She stepped back from the mic and clapped as the audience joined in putting a spotlight on him.

With his ears feverish, Deet sheepishly stood up, worked his way down his row, and walked up the three steps to the stage floor. He felt no qualms about busting several round sticks over his knee. He trembled at the thought that Sophie might reveal a past relationship with him—a relationship of any kind—by addressing him by his name. The sweet illusion of an eternal secret could go up in a puff of smoke in seconds. As he crossed the stage, his mind already worked a legitimate excuse should Lacey question him.

Oh, yeah, she'd surveyed me about some ideas the C.I.O. had for union membership.

"Hello!" Sophie poked his shoulder several times. "Hello, young man, what might be your name?"

The tall youth, whose chest had broadened in the past year, stared into a mass of warped faces, laughing their asses off. The reality of his situation sank in, and he responded, "D-d-deet, Deet Jen-kins."

She acted like she didn't know me! Thank God!

Whether it was her lilac perfume or her tact in not admitting that she already knew him, Deet never heard the renewed laughter of the crowd as he'd almost bit into the mic, causing it to squeal.

"Not so close, Deet." Sophie smiled as she pulled him back from the microphone. "Here are the four dowels. Do your best."

With the weight of possible explanations to Lacey removed, Deet snapped the bundle of four sticks with ease.

"How about eight?" Sophie dug out more dowels from the box.

With a bit more effort, Deet snapped that bundle in half.

Sophie reached into the white box one more time. "Let's try twelve."

Twelve proved to be too much. A bruised kneecap was all Deet gained from his strained attempts.

"Let's give the young man a nice round of applause." Sophie smiled and gave him a quick wink as she excused Deet. After the audience's applause died down, she beckoned again. "Is there anyone out there who thinks they can snap a dozen dowels?"

Intimidated by the Gotham woman's ploy, the crowd of usually raucous rubber workers remained silent as if a blade hovered over anyone who'd speak up. After a pause of elongated seconds, a lone voice piped up from the back. "Mike!"

"Mike!"

"Mike!" Several others called out a familiar name, stirring the entire throng into a staccato chant, "Mike! Mike! Mike! Mike!"

Massive Mike Kobenko, the Ukrainian, ambled up from the right side of the seated audience and made his way up the stage.

"I guess your name is Mike, correct?" Sophie asked with a half-smile poking one cheek to the side.

Mike nodded.

She handed him the bundle of a dozen dowels.

His hands surrounded the entire cluster, and he broke them over his knee in the blink of an eye.

"My!" Sophie's dark eyes expressed her surprise more than her voice. She went back into the cardboard box and retrieved a larger number of the dowels, counting them as she formed a new bundle. Some in this bundle, perhaps four or five, were painted black. "Twenty. Twenty dowels. They're all I have left. Willing to give it a shot, Mike?"

Again, Mike nodded. His eyes flashed on his first unsuccessful attempt. Gritted teeth and groans accompanied a succession of failures. After a half-dozen tries, he clutched the twenty dowels in one bear paw of a hand and muttered into the microphone, "Too tough to break."

After Mike walked back to his seat to the applause of the crowd, Sophie made her final pitch. "My grandmother's Iroquois knew this lesson as they formed a bad-ass confederacy of six tribes, the strongest native nation east of the Mississippi. The C.I.O. is coming to the realization that the bigger your bundle is, the tougher it will be to break."

Numerous shouts of approval broke out as Deet reconnected his hand to Lacey's.

Sophie held up five black dowels. If you didn't notice it, the last bundle included these five black dowels. At some point, men and women of the U.R.W., you will have to consider allowing Black co-workers into your body of membership."

Noticeable grumbling broke out in various parts of the audience.

"Your colored co-workers could be the arrow that makes your union's bundle unbreakable. The choice is yours," Sophie's clear voice dominated the room. "*Stand together* or be broken one by one."

"Thank you, Miss Getz," Gene Shaw said as he returned to the mic. "Now, I'd like to introduce Mister John Monroe from the C.I.O. Washington D.C. office, who'll talk a bit about precautionary measures."

Deet watched as a man, perhaps no older than thirty, walk from the area where Sophie had just seated herself. He wore a white shirt with a striped bow tie and navy-blue trousers. Black, thick-rimmed glasses dwarfed an alabaster face beneath slicked-back, wavy blond hair.

This guy's never worked a day in a factory in his life. Pansy!

Monroe stepped up to the microphone with a sheet of paper in one hand as he adjusted the angle of the mic upward. "Thank you, Mister Shaw, and greetings to members of Consolidated's U.R.W." Monroe's steady voice certainly wasn't that of a sissy, yet it didn't overpower its listeners. "I believe Miss Getz made a powerful case for standing together. The reality of your situation is that the Big C won't respect you until you are united in your cause. Furthermore, you will need all the help and goodwill you can get."

Deet noticed that Lacey seemed glued to every word that flowed from Monroe's thin lips. Yet, with all the anxiety he'd undergone in Sophie's presence this afternoon, he took comfort that it was his hand comforting Lacey's.

"If you do end up in a strike, there are several guidelines to follow." By now, Monroe glanced occasionally at notes on his paper.

"We know what we're doing!" One voice shouted from the middle of the audience.

"After what you went through two years ago, I would agree. You kept that work stoppage as peaceful as one that large could ever be." Monroe pushed his glasses up the bridge of his nose. "I commend you for it. But it doesn't hurt to review strategies that will engender goodwill with the public while maintaining peace as well. Be orderly on the picket line. Don't be provoked into violence by company cops, Akron police, or worst of all, vigilantes. The press will crucify you for it, and the company will label you as anarchists and/or communists in order to smear your good name and demands. Nothing spreads as fast as nasty rumor." He paused and energized the next sentence. "Since when is asking for a fair shake considered *un-American*?"

Deet felt Lacey's hand slip out of his as she joined the audience in giving Monroe a respectful round of applause.

"As in your '36 strike, police yourselves. Don't let the local saloons get you liquored up to the point you can't think straight. Patrol East Market Street to keep an eye out for trouble *before* it begins. You made some gains two years ago, but the Big C is still the only major rubber manufacturer that hasn't recognized our union. If you can maintain your composure in a tight situation, you will eventually turn the tide against Consolidated, *and it will have to recognize you.* Thank you."

Deet watched Lacey telegraphing a broad, toothy smile and flashing eyes toward Monroe as she enthusiastically clapped as the rest of the crowd offered polite applause at best.

"There's a man with a good head on his shoulders." Lacey told Deet as they got up to leave.

Did she pick up something between Sophie and me? The wink . . . was it the wink Sophie gave me?

Chapter 22

Akron

May 1938

Deet watched as his father deteriorated in front of him like some grand old building being brought to its knees, one arching blow at a time from a heavy steel ball swinging from a crane. The trouble was Arch Jenkins wasn't yet that old.

"I'd like to go back to Consolidated to see if I can get my job back." Arch's arms shook so much he put down the roll and butter knife and dropped one fist on the kitchen table, upending portions of all five place settings. "Damn it!"

"You want me to help you with the red cabbage, Dad," Ricky asked as Trudi buttered her husband's roll.

"D-d-don't th-think me un-gr-grateful, s-s-son," a bristly Arch picked up his fork, "but I-I'm n-not a b-baby." Half of the cabbage tumbled from the fork's tines before he managed to find his mouth.

"I heard that this new Social Security might pay some benefits if you couldn't work for some medical reason." A clean-shaven Louie devoured some scrambled eggs, his contribution of protein to the meal since Trudi pared the grocery budget.

"B-bull-sh-shit! I c-can st-still w-work." Arch struggled to pick off a strand of purple cabbage from his bare chest. Unbuttoned short-sleeved shirts and pajama bottoms were the norm most days. Except for the monthly trips to Doctor Salter, no one outside of family had seen him since he came home from the hospital.

"I've already talked to their downtown office." Trudi sipped some black coffee. "Unless you've reached sixty-five, the only ones who can get extra cash from it are children of deceased workers or blind folks."

Deet knew life hadn't been fair to his father, nor his mother, who labored each day to keep her husband comfortable while absorbing most of his contempt for his condition. Just about every dollar Deet made, and the occasional pay Ricky got from whatever Bill Mowery had him doing, went to keep the family's bills paid. Whatever plans Deet had for the future—his own vehicle being foremost—had been put on hold.

After apple strudel for dessert, Ricky and Louie helped guide Arch to the downstairs bathroom off the kitchen and then back to bed in the dining room. Meanwhile, Deet helped his mother with the dishes.

"Dad's not going to get better is he, Mom?" Deet scrubbed the cast iron frying pan in which the eggs had been prepared.

"Doctor Salter said . . ." Trudi sniffed some tears back as she placed some plates on the counter next to the sink. "He said there's no real cure for Parkinson's. He's given your father the only available medication, but even the doctor admits it will have limited effect on his tremors."

"Has he said anything about . . . about how long Dad has?" Deet whispered as he put the frying pan on the drying rack. He turned to his mother while draining the sink of the dirty water.

"The doctor has told me he may have a few years . . . five, maybe seven . . . or it could be much less." She attached her fingertips to Deet's bicep. "Please remember, Dietrich, each day with your father will be better than any other day he lives into the future." Trudi sobbed into her son's shirt sleeve.

Deet let hot water collide with powdered soap to fill the sink as he hugged his mom. He moved one hand up to stroke the dark wave of hair headed toward the bun, which had gained streaks of gray in recent months. After their embrace ended, just as he set a stack of plates into the sudsy dishwater, someone announced his presence with the tarnished, brass door knocker on the front door. Deet walked through the foyer, a drying towel in hand, and opened the door to greet none other than Detective Gerald Ragmon.

"Good evening, Deet, I wonder if I could impose on a few minutes of your family's time?" Ragmon smiled, enlarging the bags under his swollen eyelids, making them look even bigger than Deet remembered..

Deet's imagination ran wild as the cat caught his tongue.

He has a figure of a toy top, narrow at the top and bottom and overly wide in the middle.

"Yes, Detective, please come in." Coming out of the temporary bedroom, through the living room, Trudi rescued her son from an awkward moment.

"Of course, Detective," Deet finally spoke up with a surge of hope in his voice. "Come on in." He led Ragmon a few steps towards Arch's favorite chair. "You have some word about who attacked our house last fall?"

As the three stepped into the living area, they encountered Louie who'd just closed the pocket doors to the improvised bedroom. "Hello," Deet's uncle said.

"Detective Ragmon, this here is my uncle Louie Jenkins."

Open-mouthed for a few uncomfortable seconds, Ragmon shook Louie's hand. "Greetings, Mister Jenkins"

Deet repeated his question as everyone, except Ragmon, sat down. "Detective, do you have news about who attacked our house last fall?"

"No, sorry to say I don't. Is your brother home?" Ragmon looked in the direction of the staircase, where footsteps were heard thundering downward.

Just as Ragmon completed his question, Ricky bounced down into the foyer and stared at the gathering in the living room. With his eyes ready to burst from their sockets and his flushed face, Ricky's frozen figure told Deet his brother wanted to bolt out through the kitchen. For whatever reason, whether his feet froze or his heart thawed, he didn't.

"Just the man I need to see." The detective allowed a serpentine smile to cross his face.

"Ricky, please come here," Trudi said. "Detective Ragmon needs to talk to you."

"Come on in, Ricky, and have a seat." Ragmon gestured toward Arch's upholstered chair. "I won't take up much of your time. I just have a few questions."

Ricky backed into his father's favorite spot as he scanned the room to see four sets of eyes pinning him to that corner.

"Ricky," Ragmon began, "do you know Bill Mowery?"

"Yeah, sure."

"Is it true you work with him on various delivery runs?" Ragmon whipped out a pencil and small note pad from the inside of his suit jacket.

Ricky barely opened his mouth and eyes, just nodding as if drifting into a deep sleep.

"Tell me about those deliveries."

"We pick up stuff from a warehouse or shop and take it to another warehouse." Ricky snapped out of his self-imposed trance. "What's this all about anyway?"

"APD is investigating a possible theft ring." Ragmon made a point to address the three members of the Jenkins family seated on the sofa before turning back towards Ricky. "Any facts you can offer us, Ricky, can help us clear up this situation. Now, where's that drop-off warehouse?"

"Near the rail line on Crosier."

"Who sets up these deliveries?" Ragmon spoke into his notepad as he scribbled away.

"I don't know. Mowery never told me any names . . . except one time he referred to the boss as 'she'."

"So, as far as you know, your employer was a woman."

Ricky nodded again.

The dick flipped his note pad closed and put it back in his inside pocket. "One last question, Ricky, do you know a Tug McGirt?"

Deet's memory flashed to Maria in the hospital and the friendly, yet suspicious neighbor, *Toog*.

"Mowery talked about him on occasion, but I never met him."

"Thank you, Ricky." Ragmon turned to those seated on the sofa. "Thank you, folks, for allowing me to interrupt your evening." He took a step toward the foyer before stopping and turning around. "Ah, Mister Jenkins, may I see you outside for a just a moment before I leave?"

"Sure," Louie said as he escorted Ragmon onto the porch and down the concrete steps.

Deet closed the porch door before perching himself at one of the adjacent windows. He watched long enough as Ragmon offered a smoke to his uncle, and the two puffed away like a couple of old locomotives as they conversed. Then he turned his attention back to the living room, where his mother brooded over Ricky.

"Is everything alright, Richard," she said as she stood over him, still in the chair. She knotted her apron with her fingers until her knuckles turned white. "Is this where your money came from, something the police need to deal with?"

Ricky chewed on his nails.

Deet wasn't as indulging. "What the hell did I tell you about hanging around Bill Mowery! What kind of shit have you been doing?"

"Richard, have you gi-ven us d-dir-ty money?" Tears streamed from his mother's eyes.

Like a dam bursting loose, Ricky catapulted himself out of the chair. "Let me the hell alone!" He raced past a surprised Louie, who was just entering the house.

Deet ran halfway up the stairs after his brother before he heard the lock engage on the door to his brother's room.

Whatever's happened can't be undone now, not by me, not by anyone.

He walked down to the foyer where Louie and his mother stood. "What did Ragmon want?"

Louie wrapped his arms across his chest. "Betty's dead. She was murdered a week or two ago and dumped in a clay pond. Just yesterday, some cousin of hers identified her body."

"Oh, Louie." Trudi gave him a hug. "I'm so sorry."

"Do they think you had something to do with this?" Deet asked.

"No, I don't think so. I haven't seen her in almost ten years, about the same amount of time we were together. I don't necessarily feel sad. It's not like we had a great marriage. Still, someone bumped off a person who was close to me at one time." Louie lit another cigarette and inhaled some burnt tobacco. "I don't feel much of anything about it right now. When it hits, if it does, I'll bring it up in my weekly meeting."

Deet's amazement of his uncle's turnaround wouldn't let him stay silent. "Louie, you know you can talk with us, don't—"

"Trudi! Trudi! Burluk is dying! They've turned into skeletons! Come help them!"

The three marched off to bring Arch back to reality.

****

Cliff Colson mesmerized the dance hall with his relaxing clarinet as the High Notes backed him with plenty of brass and bass as they played Artie Shaw's version of *Begin the Beguine*. Deet and Lacey crept to the outer edge of the dance floor, ready to immerse themselves among the numerous couples already enjoying the bliss of close bodily movement. She surprised Deet this evening by ditching pants and wearing a mint green dress—nothing flashy but definitely suited to her curves.

"This is what you live for, isn't it?" Deet's head nuzzled close to Lacey's as one of his hands held hers up high while the other fit perfectly into the small of her back. He felt her other hand caress his side.

"Outside of sex," she whispered, "there can't be any better sense of togetherness than slow dancing the night away." She pulled her head away from him and smiled before pecking his cheek and resting her head on his chest.

Slow dances proved a conundrum for Deet. He loved feeling Lacey's form next to him. She was right, it probably was the next best thing to making whoopee. Yet, it gave his feet too much time to think. Unlike an up-tempo swing beat, where he danced by the seat of his pants, slow dancing often turned him into a dead hoofer, his feet plodding more so than gliding.

Deet felt a tap on his shoulder and turned his head.

"May I cut in?" A bespeckled John Monroe stood next to the couple in a long-sleeved white shirt, checkered pants, and a checkered bowtie.

"What the hel—" Deet's gut wanted to ram the egghead into the nearest saxophone, but Lacey cut him off.

"Sure, Deet doesn't mind, do you, Sweetie?"

Before he knew it, Deet stood on the perimeter, looking at some blond bookworm who stole his gal and showed off like Fred Astaire. The two started with both arms extended and hands clasped before stepping towards each other and then stepping back again. Then Monroe released one hand and let Lacey twirl as they switched positions, the bottom of her green dress spinning parallel to the oak floor. Then they came together for a few close order steps before beginning the entire sequence again.

He's messing with the wrong guy's doll.

Chin dipping to his chest and eyes glaring at the couple, Deet stood with his arms crossed as he watched Lacey smile through the entire number as her caboose shook every now and then as she separated herself from her substitute dance partner.

The music ended, sending Lacey and John off the floor. "Wow," Lacey said, "you sure know how to do the Beguine. You're one of the best cats to ever swing around here."

"Takes a great partner to make it work," Monroe said before turning to Deet and grabbing his hand. Thanks, pal, you've got quite the girl there. Better hang on to her tight."

Unimpressed by Monroe's soft, callous-free hand, Deet secretly wanted to deck him, but his past broke in to haunt him.

"Hi Deet!"

A hand slapped Jenkins across his back, and he turned to face Jake Carver, who was with some short-haired blonde, wearing a red bucket hat and low-cut dress.

"Hey, how ya doing, Jake?" Deet offered a cheery welcome to cover his anger more than anything. The blonde's hat tickled a memory in his mind, but he couldn't place it. A long necklace of cheap, shiny beads diving into very limited cleavage didn't ring a bell as well. "Who's your friend?"

"This here's Lilly." Jake beamed. "We met at Wiley's a couple nights ago. Lilly, this here is good union man, Deet."

Lilly tried to balance herself on the tips of the toes of one foot before stumbling. "Hel-l-l-o, De-e-et. Don't I know y-y-you from some p-place?"

Oh, shit! Sophie's hotel room!

"Excuse me," Lacey interrupted as she pointed towards Deet, "just in case this big lug forgot, I'm Lacey. *Supposedly,* I'm his girl."

"I'm sorry, Lacey, I should have introduced you." Jake apologized while keeping his arm around Lilly, probably to keep her upright.

"That's alright, Jake, it wasn't your call to make." The disgust in Lacey's voice wasn't disguised in any way.

Lilly twirled the end of her necklace around one finger as she stared at Deet. Her eyes bugged. "I-I-I re-e-emem-ber. Sophie's place." With that, she gushed vomit all over one leg of Jake's trousers.

Stiff-legged, Jake went to the men's room while Lacey accompanied Lilly to the women's bathroom. Deet, surrounded by strangers in a vacuum of his own making, stewed at the thought of what Lacey would learn from Lilly.

What the hell, the bitch is drunk as a skunk.

The dance ended earlier than expected for Deet and Lacey as she gave him the cold shoulder for the rest of the abbreviated evening. Deet drove her home but didn't bother suggesting coming up to her apartment. "Look, Lilly was drunk. How can you really believe anything she'd say . . . a perfect stranger at that." Deet peered over the steering wheel of his father's Pontiac, talking into the night.

"Sometimes, people aren't their true selves until they are plastered. She seemed to know quite a bit about you and Sophie."

"Lacey, Dollface," Deet turned toward his girl. "I met Sophie at Wiley's one evening a while back because she wanted my opinion as a regular Joe member about having Blacks in the union. We had a drink or two, and that was that. I walked her back to her hotel room. You know she'd be an easy mark for some nogoodnik."

"It wasn't just Lilly's comment tonight, Deet." Even in the darkness, Lacey's eyes flashed as her fury rose. "You acted like a complete asshole in front of John. The man politely interrupted to get a dance with me, and you couldn't handle it. I saw you standing there, brooding like a little kid forced to share his toy with someone else."

Now, it was Lacey's turn to look into the darkness beyond the windshield. "Just so you know, I really enjoyed dancing with him. He might not be a hard-nosed gummer, but the man has style. A guy who supposedly cared so much about me that he'd be upset with a guy cutting in on us on the dance floor, surely wouldn't have been catting around with Sophie, sharing her *sweets!*"

Sweets! Oh God! She knew!

Lacey pulled up on the door handle. "That guy has no style!" She opened the Pontiac's door and slammed it shut.

His fingers cemented to the wheel, Deet sat motionless in the car for minutes. Remorse boomeranged off a hardening heart, flaring into anger. The thought of storming into her apartment tempted him.

How dare she say I have no style.

He turned the ignition on and allowed the headlights to illuminate the night. Having made his decision, he shifted into reverse.

Fine! There are plenty of other broads in this town.

Chapter 23

Akron

May 1938

Aweek later on the following Thursday night, Deet walked down Laird Street on his way to work. He realized he'd alienated two of the small number of people he cared about most in the world. As far as his brother went, he knew the first shoe dropped when Detective Ragmon arrived on a fishing expedition at their house. A smell more powerful than the burnt rubber hovering over Akron lingered around Ricky's dealings with Bill Mowery, let alone Tug McGirt. Yet, Ricky clammed up, icing him out of his life. All Deet could do was wait for Ragmon to drop the other shoe.

Lacey's pain, one with a different source from his brother's but with similar results, didn't ease over the past seven days. With each passing day, he regretted his fling with Sophie even more. Earlier this evening, he called Lacey for the third time this week. With Decoration Day coming up next Monday, they had a standing date for the union picnic at Eastern Hills Park. He hoped the upcoming picnic and the intervening week would have thawed her heart and given him a second chance. She never answered the first two calls, but his heart raced when she answered this evening and didn't hang up at the sound of his voice. However, after skirting around the issue with nervous small talk, he finally asked her about the picnic. Her response nearly froze the line.

I don't think so. Click.

Plodding up Laird toward Fulton Street, Deet itemized a short list of girls he could take to the picnic on short notice. Mary Lou Schnitzenfelter had had a crush on him back at Central. A great kisser, Mary Lou's idea of having a good time was playing gin rummy with her parents. Then there was Penelope Grubinski, who lived just down the street from the Jenkins. Deet took Penelope out to the movies during his senior year and canoodled with her in the cemetery situated one street behind their house. She didn't talk much, but worst of all, her kiss was that of paper—dry and without any passion. One more name popped into his mind as he saw Fulton Street ahead—Kathy Tudsill. A petite blond, she worked as a clerk in the Consolidated offices, where Deet met her when he turned in the necessary paperwork after he was hired. He took her dancing one evening, and while she could swing her ass fairly well, boasting about her perfect, polished nails and how her goal in life was to become an assistant payroll clerk, created the majority of her exhaust. To her credit, she lived with her divorced mother who hadn't interrupted their goodbyes in the living room.

"Let's go! Let's go! Let's go!"

By the time Deet got to the intersection, where Laird and Fulton formed a seventy-five-degree angle, a crowd's chant somewhere on Market wiped away his brooding. After arriving a minute or so later when Fulton met East Market, he turned to his left to see masses of people, perhaps thousands. Like so many ants on a discarded dollop of jam on a summer's day, they milled about across from the massive Consolidated Plant One some two blocks away. With little traffic, he jaywalked across Market Street and crept toward the most outrageous scene of his life.

"Let's go! Let's go! Let's go!"

The repeated cheers came from the crowd pressed against Consolidated Hall, directly opposite the plant entrance. Along the factory side of the street, more people, some cops, and a couple patrol cars straddled the curb, with police trying to keep the plant entrance open. Every now and then, one or two cars squirted through as the crowds ebbed and flowed with no consistent current.

Deet drew closer towards his usual entry to work and scanned the horde for a friendly face. It was like walking through a mass of fans outside Cleveland Municipal Stadium before the gates opened for an Indians' Sunday doubleheader, but these folks seemed riled up. A fair portion of the people were women, and no matter the gender, all of them were agitated. The chants continued, coming from twisted faces with raised fists. Meanwhile, a thin line of granite-faced coppers, maybe a dozen or so, guarded the entrance, nightsticks tapping in their hands.

"Deet! Deet!"

Deet looked up, thinking the voice came from one of the guys hanging on to the wrought iron fencing atop the five-foot brick wall, surrounding the five-story Consolidated factory. For a moment, the five rows of illuminated rectangles, seemingly stretching toward infinity, snatched his attention. Then, a hand grabbed his shoulder and spun him around.

"Deet!" Jake Carver heaved. "Don't go in. We're on strike!"

Close enough to smell the oregano-spiced tomato sauce caked around Jake's mouth, Deet yelled his disbelief, "What?" Surrounded by the clamor of strangers, he shouted some more, "What the hell is going on? Nobody ever told me!"

Carver pulled Deet away from the street as more cars inched their way past the confusion. They ended up fifteen feet away from the police line in a pocket of unclaimed real estate, where they could flex their elbows without having someone else blow their wig. "Word got out just a couple hours ago," Jake said, placing his hands on Deet's shoulders, "that Consolidated had loaded over a dozen tractor trailers with office furniture and file cabinets. It's looking like they're expecting a strike."

"Is this all official?" Deet wriggled out from Jake's grip.

"Who knows?" Jake walked a few steps toward the brick wall and leaned against it.

"Did our union call the strike?" Deet crossed his arms over his white tee shirt, wondering if he should go into work.

"If they didn't, they've got one now."

"I've never seen these people before." Deet continued to gaze at the crowd on the opposite side of the factory from left to right. With so many women, he hoped Lacey was here, but with so many people, the faces melded together.

"Some of these guys were laid off in the last couple years," Jake said, his head on a swivel. "I did see Dixon and his pals go in, not that I blame them."

Deet nodded, knowing the union hadn't accepted Dixon's kind as of yet.

"Stay there! Stay there! Don't let 'em move you!" A guy clinging to the iron fence urged the crowd to stay close to the entrance.

"You guys are going to have to pick ten men to be at the gate, and the rest need to back off." A hoarse police captain barked orders at the throng closest to the gate as it continually shifted due to constant vehicle traffic and a packed house across the way.

"So, what do we do, stay here? Go home?" Deet questioned Jake.

Jake shrugged his shoulders and then pointed toward Plant One. "Anything, except go in there."

Deet kept looking across the street at the swarm lingering about in front of Consolidated Hall, a do-it-all, seven story building with offices, gymnasium, auditorium and classrooms. It seemed as if the loiterers were a make-shift mob, waiting for a fuse to be lit. A bubble of space appeared in the wake of a shiny, late model Cadillac, and behind the Caddie, a familiar face got Deet's attention—the guy from Duke's Billiards Hall, the one with the sunken blue eyes and the *Brigade* tattoo. A red bandana flapped about his neck as he weaved in and out of the crowd.

Pike?

"What the hell is *he* doing here?" Deet cried out to no one in particular.

"Who—" Jake never got the chance to finish his question. The burly police captain yanked him by the collar and pulled him toward the gate.

"You're one of the ten legal pickets Bub," the surly cop said.

"Alright, men, let's clear them out!" The captain shouted.

Deet felt a horizontal nightstick in his gut and sewer breath of a stone-faced policeman pushing him backward. In the melee that followed, Deet spotted Detectives Ragmon and Kelly, along with a handful of other plainclothes cops helping the single line of police, which stretched across East Market. They attempted to move the crowd westward, the direction from which the nineteen-year-old had come. Grunts and profanity spiced both sides of the undulating line.

No longer sensing pressure on his backside, Deet turned his head to notice the portion of the mob on the factory side of the street started to separate. When he looked forward again, the copper in front of him pushed off his toes, fully extended his arms, and gave a garbled shout, "Aargh!"

Like a struggle on the line of scrimmage in football, Deet held his ground for a time before falling over the body of another man, whose head and shoulders lay under the front tire of a parked car. As soon as he picked himself up, he scrambled behind the vehicle along the sidewalk. From there, his eyes caught a glimpse of the red kerchief streaming under the dark hair of Pike as he hopped over a low stone wall into an adjacent cemetery.

What is he up to?

A billy club dangling in the air midway down the police line came down on a civilian's head with a loud *thump* as if it were a watermelon.

"They asked for it, goddamn it, let's give it to 'em!" The crusty voice of a policeman signaled a full-blown assault on the ever-retreating crowd as all the nightsticks went into the vertical position and began connecting with skulls and shoulders.

Deet moved back from his relative island of safety behind the car towards the gate and the majority of the crowd. That mass of people still screamed cat calls and insults but weren't overly interested in physical confrontation. He thought the odds against a concussion lay in this direction. In short order, an ominous sign forecast an even nastier fate. At the entrance gate, Consolidated gorillas, a dozen uniformed company guards, came out into a clearing with what looked like over-sized revolvers. With a rifle-like stock and chambers the size of tin cans, these weapons didn't look good.

The guards formed a semi-circle and began shooting canisters from their weapons along East Market. As soon as the cylinders landed—some in the street, others in the middle of the crowd, and still others on store awnings across the street—a steady ribbon of smoke hissed out of them.

Tear gas!

Clouds of noxious gas streamed out of each can, casting a dense fog over a block-long stretch of the street. Deet figured he'd take his chances by evading the police on his way home rather than risking burns to his eyes, skin, and lungs. Then again, making his way west on Market wasn't going to be a walk in the park. The blue line bogged down about a hundred yards short of Fulton, Deet's jumping off point to get home. In a dark corner of the cemetery, which bordered Market Street, rioters started to launch bricks and rocks at the police.

"Take off those guns, and fight us like men," hidden voices taunted the police.

How much does Pike have to do with all this shit?

While Deet hunkered down behind a parked Ford, the salty captain directed a couple men to chase after the camouflaged stone throwers. The rest of the nightstick-flailing police continued towards Fulton, a human chain acting like a massive bulldozer. He figured the police were headed to the next major intersection with a traffic signal, less than a block west of Fulton. However, time wasn't on his side. An easterly breeze, unusual for anytime of the year, wafted the tear gas toward him.

Although the cemetery brick launchers had been ousted, the mob confronting the police line still threw occasional rocks, cracking on the pavement. As the cops beat their way past Fulton, Deet sprinted across Market, headed for safety. He heard his greatest fear as his shoe leather beat the pavement.

Crack! Thud! "Oh God, my arm!" An anguished protestor screamed.

Three-quarters of the way across Akron's main thoroughfare, a rock whizzed past Deet's head. As he reached the sidewalk, almost home free, a second stone glanced off the back of his head. He barely felt it as he raced down Fulton toward Laird in the company of a dozen or more other people, away from the gas, away from the mob, away from the cops.

Real sleep wasn't possible that night. He lay in bed, occasionally drifting off into a trance-like state but never reaching a deep sleep as his mind played a cruel tennis match, causing him to toss and turn. Images of an irate Lacey nailing his lie about Sophie interchanged with the bedlam he witnessed on Market—an angry mob, an angrier line of police, bricks, rocks, and even the realistic odor of tear gas. On the edge of one of those trances, he bolted upright at the sound of rapid-fire shotgun blasts.

Have we gone to war with each other?

Chapter 24

Akron

June 1938

The cute brunette's fingers played the chattering typewriter as if she was performing a piano solo at the local university. Deet, seated on a wooden bench, breathed in the office's aroma of old and new. The sweetness of the young woman's lilac perfume tempered the mustiness of the previous century released by the darkened varnish of the secretary's desk and the room's woodwork and the worn rug upon which everything rested. He eyed the secretary with short, bobbed curls and a button nose. It was she, Miss Neal, with whom his mother had arranged this meeting with Mister Acker.

She's cute as a bug's ear.

With his brother languishing in Akron City Jail, charged with murder among other things, now wasn't the time to pursue another romantic adventure, something which had already cost him dearly. His mother phoned Attorney Jack Acker, taking him up on his standing invitation to help if needed, breaking down on the call into a flood of tears. With his father in need of constant care, Deet offered to deliver the family's S.O.S. for legal help. Between him and his mother and the family's resources, their best hope was that Jack could offer them the name of a competent public defender. An experienced criminal attorney on the community's payroll would have a better shot of proving Ricky's innocence on the most severe charge than a rookie right out of college.

The black phone on her desk rang, and Miss Neal picked up the receiver. "Yes, sir." After a cursory nod, she placed the receiver back on its cradle. Then, she spoke to Deet in a tone as sweet as the perfume, which scented her supple skin. "Mr. Acker will see you now."

Acker's office struck Deet as a transplanted forest in downtown Akron's concrete, soot, and asphalt. The lawyer stood up to greet him behind a large desk with a glossy, reddish-brown finish and a glass top. Bookshelves of the same color wood covered two walls from floor to ceiling with intersecting fluted, vertical rails and horizontal shelves supporting dozens of law volumes. The desk faced double hung windows looking down on Main Street while a painting of a mob tar and feathering a man dominated the wall behind Acker's chair. A small caged fan on the corner of his desk provided the lawyer with a gentle breeze.

Deet couldn't take his eyes off the five-foot-wide piece of art as he shook Acker's hand.

"Impressive, isn't it?" the attorney said, brushing back his wavy blond hair as he turned toward the painting. "It's *The Whiskey Rebellion* by Kemmelmyer."

Deet vaguely remembered a reference to the event in his history class at Central. However, as he looked at the enraged faces of the mob in the painting and the burning building in its background, his thoughts turned to the riot on Market Street.

"Have a seat, Deet." Acker pulled over a finely polished Windsor chair before he stood back and admired the painting. "The Whiskey Rebellion has always taught me . . ." Once again, his rich voice flowed like warmed honey poured onto a bed of fluffy pancakes. " . . . that the law must protect the people from injustice, and if it cannot, the people are justified in holding the government's feet to the fire. That keeps me focused."

The councilman unbuttoned the middle of his gray and black herringbone suit jacket before he sat down in a plush leather chair and scooted it close to his desk. His eyes widened, and he picked up a newspaper from the corner of his large desk. "Here!" Acker moved the paper closer toward Deet and tapped his index finger on its front page as the fan from the opposite corner fluttered the sheets of the newspaper. "Here's a classic example from today. The Jewish bankers run this country with their Marxist supporters and likewise in Europe. That Hitler fellow has put a stop to them in Germany, and good people like Father Coughlin are speaking out here."

Deet edged toward the desk and glanced at the front page of *Social Justice.*

Oh, God, not another Father Coughlin lover.

"The good Father says the rich American Jews should expect to be treated worse than how Hitler's treated the German ones. But I digress." He exhaled. "Anyway, from what your mother shared with Miss Neal over the phone, you have much more pressing concerns." He pulled the newspaper back and folded it half as he kept his eyes on Deet. "Ricky's facing serious charges as you well know."

"Yeah . . . that's what I'm here for, Mister Acker. We want to get an idea of who's the best criminal lawyer among the public defenders, if we even get a choice in the matter."

"You don't." The lawyer interlocked the fingers of his hands on the top of his desk. "The law says Ricky has the right to counsel, but he doesn't get a choice of counsel if he can't afford his own. The court appoints one at *its discretion.* I could offer my services for Ricky. From what your mother related to Miss Neal, if indeed he had no idea a shooting was to take place and wasn't even in the premises when the shooting occurred, his culpability would be greatly lessened."

"Oh, Mister Acker, we couldn't afford to pay you, but thanks for the offer."

"Perhaps you could do me a favor, Deet. I have a shipment of pipe scaffolding needed for a remodeling job on one of my rental properties that will arrive in Cleveland fairly soon. My regular driver has had an eye ailment and can't drive for a while. I take it you can drive a '37 Ford Model AA box truck. Correct?"

"Oh, sure, that's just a standard three-speed." The younger man lightly bit on the tip of his tongue. "Are you sure that's all you'd want to defend Ricky?"

Acker nodded. "I've always admired your family. You're good people." The words came out a bit coarser, in a deeper tone than usual.

"When and where would you want it delivered?" Deet crossed his legs.

"You work the grave-digger shift, right?" Acker pushed his chair away from his desk.

Deet nodded.

"It's about four hours round trip, including loading and unloading. If you left around four in the afternoon, you should be done by eight in the evening . . . nine tops, well before your midnight shift begins."

Deet bobbed his head as he sensed a change in his family's luck. "Sure, I can do that. Where do I go?"

"Excellent." Acker pulled out a road map from one of the desk drawers. "Your destination will be the East Ninth Street pier, just north of downtown Cleveland. You'll take Route 21 north—"

"Mr. Acker, may I borrow a piece of paper, a ruler, and pencil?"

Acker cocked his head and curled his lip. "Surely." He took all three items out of a lower desk drawer.

"I remember directions better if I draw them out. They stick in my brain."

Over the next few minutes as the attorney explained the directions, Deet meticulously drew out his route from Laird Street to the pier on East Ninth in Cleveland and back to a warehouse on Bowery near the old Ohio Canal.

"Very good, Deet. I appreciate a young man who's big on the details. I will call you as soon as I get the word the shipment's arrived. In the meanwhile, I will meet with Ricky to plan his defense within the next twenty-four hours."

****

"Another thing we cut off at the knees," a mouthful of sandwich muted Chaw Nelson's Appalachian accent, "the company's damn plan for double standard wages." Chaw inhaled a bit while his face went pale. He stood up, and his breathing heaved before downing some milk.

"You alright, Chaw?" Deet asked.

193

"Yeah, just . . . just must have had some chew left in the back of mouth." Chaw chuckled, wiping the white coating off his moustache with the back of his hand. "Stuff ain't meant for eatin'."

"What's a double standard wage?" Deet rounded up his paper wrappings and finished his milk.

"Hog 'anure. Any farmer knows nothing stinks worse than hog 'anure. The company sets a lower wage for new hires after a certain date. It ends up dividing the work force between *haves* and *have nots*." He held one hand higher than the other. "It can break down a union's bond."

The bell rang, and Chaw left Deet nodding, thinking about what the hillbilly gummer just said. When Deet walked out of the breakroom, he encountered Dixon waiting at the door.

"I can tell you about *hog 'anure*, Jenkins." After smirking at his teen co-worker, Dixon strode off into the belly of the milling department.

Once again, Deet stood gawking, feeling like a fool for not appreciating the truth Chaw's analogy had on the milling floor.

"Deet, I need to see you upstairs," the voice of Nate Benson called out from behind the young rubber worker.

Deet turned to see the night shift plant manager standing next to Harley Kershaw. Both men offered a poker face before Benson took off to the stairway and his office.

By the time Deet tracked down Benson, the boss shot past him, heading out of his office. "Somebody needs to talk to you in there." The plant manager flicked a thumb behind him.

"Hello, Deet." G-man Burt Smith greeted him with an outstretched hand and a toothless smile.

Not again! Now what?

Deet responded with a sweaty hand and a dry mouth. "A-a-agent Smith . . . hello."

"Please, sit down." The F.B.I man opened his hand toward one of two wooden chairs positioned across from each other in front of Benson's desk. He closed the office door before sitting down across from Deet, wearing a long-sleeved white shirt topped with a broad blue and gray striped tie. "Again, I apologize for the cloak and dagger scenario of our meeting, but it's important to keep your association with me, and with the Bureau, a secret." His lips barely separated as he spoke. "The Bureau has a favor to ask of you, young man."

"M-me?" Deet could hardly produce enough saliva to release the simplest of words. He looked down at the carbon black stains on his tee shirt and oil-spotted trousers

"Yes, you." The legs of Smith's dark blue trousers remained uncrossed as he reached into his shirt pocket for a pack of smokes. "Cigarette?"

"Yeah." Deet knew he needed a crutch as he reached for Smith's offer.

Smith stepped over and lit Deet's cigarette before igniting his own. Then, he put his silver lighter back in his trouser pocket. "The Bureau would like you to attend the next meeting of the Summit County Communist Party. We've learned that, soon, Jimmy Bryant will place flyers in your breakroom as he's done on various occasions. We want you to pick one up and go to the meeting." Smith removed the cigarette from his mouth, and a river of smoke streamed from his nose.

Amazed by the casual nature of the man's voice, let alone that his words were able to sneak out between nearly closed lips, Deet was shocked how this conversation came off as an old friend seeking a favor. "Why me? I mean the other flyers Bryant's laid out said these meetings were open to the public. You can get anyone to go. Sh—, ah, crap, you could go, so why don't you?"

"A fair question." Smith blew more smoke into the room while letting the two fingers holding his cigarette bounce up and down like an orchestra leader's baton. "Leaders of the SCCP can spot me or one of our other agents with relative ease. That might change their tactics and their message. It's important, especially important for this meeting, that we get someone there who blends in. We want to get information from a meeting that isn't staged for the Bureau's benefit."

"Alright, so, again, why me?" Deet spoke through lips barely holding the cigarette, ashes about to fall.

"One of our agents spotted you coming out of Sophie Getz's hotel room some months back." The G-man inhaled more tobacco before continuing. "We've been surveilling her for a while. As a union organizer, she's a possible communist sympathizer."

"Since when is it against the law to try to get a fair deal from your boss?" Deet yanked the cigarette out of his mouth, staring into the agent's unwavering green eyes, as ashes cascaded like grayish snowflakes.

"It's not—"

"You do know she's publicly stated that capitalism is the best economic system in the world, right?" Deet took another drag and vented bluish exhaust.

Smith's tepid smile morphed into a temporary frown as he shrugged his shoulders. "People can say anything." He crushed the remnant of his cigarette into a green, glass ashtray on Benson's desk. "It's what they do when they think we aren't watching that we need to know."

"Besides, since when is it against the law to be a communist?" The mill worker inhaled one last dose of nicotine. "I thought it would only be illegal if you were actively trying to overthrow the government. Right?" Deet expelled a final trail of smoke as he reached across to bury his butt in the green glass.

"That is correct, but we need a person on the inside of the next meeting to see who's attending and what objectives are being planned. So, would you be interested in helping out your country?"

His father's deteriorating health, Ricky's serious trouble with the law, and Lacey's break up with him—squeezed out an apparent, unpatriotic reply. "No, not really. Got too much other stuff on my plate to go about playing G-man."

"I get it. At nineteen, you've got the weight of the world on you. Your father's very ill, your brother's facing murder, grand theft, and breaking and entering charges, and your girlfriend has dumped you."

Speechless, Deet's face soured as if he'd eaten the cigarette. "Wh-h-a—"

"It's my business to know these things."

"Wait a minute . . . you know everything about my life!" Deet glared at the soft-spoken G-man, who probably couldn't hold Jimmy Cagney's shoes. "What the hell do you need me for?"

Smith interlocked the fingers of his hands on his lap. "I told you. We need someone from the inside of the factory, someone the Jimmy Bryants of the local communists won't suspect."

"Nah, I can't see me doing this." The boy shook his head. "I'm no Red, but I'm not a stool pigeon either."

Agent Smith put his arms at his side, crossed his legs, and inhaled a bit. "Unfortunately, Deet, I can't cure your father, and I can't counsel your girlfriend into changing her opinion about you, and I probably can't help with your brother, but—"

"That's just fine. Jack Acker's offered to defend him for free."

Smith's mouth stopped in mid-sentence, and his eyes bore through Deet. "Jack Acker?" The G-man cocked his head to one side. "The city council president?"

Deet felt he one-upped the G-man for once and continued to spill the beans. "Yeah." Deet laid the back of his head against the office wall. "He said because he likes our family, he'd defend Ricky for free."

"*Pro bono*?" Smith's lips actually separated for the first time Deet could remember.

"Huh?" Jenkins straightened his frame against the back of the chair.

"*Pro bono* is Latin, meaning *for free*."

"Oh, yeah. All he wants is for me to make a delivery run for him to Cleveland to pick up some scaffolding for some remodeling job on one of the houses he rents."

"Really." Smith tapped an index finger and middle finger against his temple. "Your brother is sixteen—"

"Actually, seventeen." Deet lowered his head. "Over the weekend, he spent his birthday in jail."

"Of course, but he was sixteen at the time of the alleged offenses. If Mowery sticks to his story that McGirt was solely responsible for the killing of the shop owner while Ricky remained outside in the vehicle, the prosecution's case against your brother could be weak."

The more Deet heard Smith's chaplain's voice, the farther forward he leaned.

"As far as the string of burglaries goes, if Ricky cooperates with the district attorney against Mowery and whoever planned those heists, it would be easier on him." The agent leaned forward. "Deet, if you help us out by attending the upcoming meeting, we can lean on the district attorney to get the murder charges dropped or at least bumped down to accessory to murder. As for the theft charges, perhaps we can push for several years of probation."

"You could do that?" In that moment, Deet zeroed in on getting his brother out of his fix. It was all that mattered.

"I'll be up front with you, Deet." Smith sat back in his chair, but his voice remained calm. "There are no guarantees, but we've swung similar deals in the past with other prosecutors."

"If I did this for you guys, and Jack Acker defends Ricky, he might have a chance." Deet rubbed the palms of his hands over his dirty trousers. Deet bobbed his head. "Okay, I'll go to that meeting. What exactly do you want to know?

"Simple—how many people attend it? Do you recognize any of those that do? Does anything unusual happen during the meeting? Most importantly, what are they planning?"

"I can do that."

"One last thing," Smith said as he stood up. "Don't let anyone . . . *anyone* . . . know what you're doing, especially here at the plant. From what I understand, many of the folks in here don't take kindly to communists."

Deet stood up. "Alright. How do I get hold of you after I go to this meeting?"

"We'll know when that meeting takes place. I'll arrange for another meeting with you at that time . . . but it won't be here. By now, your colleagues might be wondering why the Consolidated brass are so interested in talking to you." Smith stalled at the door. "You walk home around six each morning, right?"

Deet nodded. "Market to Fulton to Laird . . . pretty routine."

"Don't be surprised if one morning a black Plymouth stops and offers you a ride. That will be me." As Smith turned the doorknob on Benson's office door, he abruptly pulled it shut and turned back to Deet. "Just one more thing, Deet . . . "

Chapter 25

Akron

June 1938

Head down, Deet meandered out of Plant One towards the main gate. Oblivious to the other gummers who surrounded him at the end of their shift, he brooded at how Agent Burt Smith bamboozled him. Spying on the commies was one thing, but snitching on a good friend was totally different.

"Hey, ash-hole!" The gruff, accented shout sounded as if it came out of a megaphone right behind Deet's ear as the teen made his way through the Market Street gate.

Before Deet could turn out of a combination of curiosity and annoyance, a massive hand clamped on his shoulder and spun him around. "I thought you weren't a Red." The pale orange of dawn funneled in between the man-made canyon between Consolidated's offices and factories along Market Street and settled on Big Mike Kobenko's frozen, blue eyes. "I should mash you now."

"Hold on, Mike!" Deet squirmed and twisted to no avail as Kobenko shoved Deet along the sidewalk beyond the gate. "What are you talking about?"

"I should beat shit out of you." Mike pushed Deet against the brick wall supporting the wrought iron fencing at the front of the plant. The Ukrainian's chest heaved a bit, but his breathing stirred the hairs of his dark mustache. "When you thought no one looking, you took one of those communist papers Jimmy Bryant put out. I stop just behind door and watch you."

Showing his teeth as if he were a rabid dog, Mike terrified Deet. He had to come up with a valid excuse fast or his chance of helping Ricky would be gone.

Ukraine!

"My d-d-dad, Mike, my d-dad." The pressure of Kobenko's hands molded the rough texture of the brick into Deet's back, separated by only the thin fabric of his tee-shirt. "I know it's strange, but my dad wanted to see one of these flyers. He's delusional at times. He—"

"Don't bull-shit me, boy!" Mike's cheeks twitched, ruffling his beard from ear to ear in a wave as he towered over Jenkins.

"No, I'm not. Honest!" Deet took a half-truth and ran with it. "My dad has Parkinson's, and he hallucinates a lot. His dad came from Ukraine, just like you. We can't explain it, but he's been having weird delusions about places in Ukraine. Burluk . . ." The name came out of the recesses of Deet's memory as if delivered by a guardian angel. "Burluk is where my grandfather grew up, and Dad sees these crazy —"

"Bur-luk? Did you say Bur-luk?" Mike's eyes softened, and he eased his hands off of Deet while they still touched the boy's shirt.

Delt felt soothing relief on his shoulders. "Yeah, it appears that was my grandfather's hometown. At least, that's what my dad and my uncle say. Anyway, during his last hallucination, the day before yesterday, he begged me to get one of those flyers that Jimmy passes out every now and then. I can't explain it, but I just wanted to get one to calm him down in case he has another one of these spells." Deet caught his breath and hoped his wits had saved him a beating.

Mike removed his hands from Deet and stood erect. His well-kempt beard no longer stood at attention. "You have time for coffee?"

"Sure." Deet counted the trickles of sweat coursing down from his armpits

"I buy. We talk about Bur-luk."

The two went to a small coffee shop off Market. Mike anted up a dime for two cups of black coffee. The coffee's heat appealed to Mike as he took a long swallow as soon as the waitress put it in front of him. "So, tell me about Bur-luk."

Deet put two spoonfuls of sugar into his java and twirled the spoon around. "Well, a couple months back, Dad gets out of bed and starts walking around in circles and talks about having to go to Burluk to rescue some kids. He's saying their grandmother is going to kill them because everyone is hungry and suffering, so she's started a fire in their hearth and closes the damper. It made no sense at all until my uncle remembered my grandfather talking about growing up in Burluk in Ukraine." Deet chuckled. "Turns out our family name was Jenkevko." He took a sip before putting down the cup and looking straight at Mike. "You're from Ukraine. Does any of that make sense?"

While swallowing more coffee, Mike nodded.

"Please explain it to me, Mike. If my dad ever mentioned Burluk before, I certainly don't remember it, but then again, my dad's really sick now."

Mike put his large paw on Deet's arm. "I'm sorry . . . for your dad, a good man. I'm sorry I get angry with you, Deet." He lifted his hand and drank more coffee. "I'm sorry for Burluk, my old home."

Deet couldn't believe his ears. "Did you grow up in Burluk?"

Kobenko nodded. "Not in town, but on farm outside of town." The big Ukrainian stared out the café's front window, where cars slowed and accelerated as they turned onto and off of Market Street. "I come here in '25, but I still get letters from family. In '32, Stalin wants wheat, all the wheat in Ukraine. He sends soldiers and goons. They kill farmers who have good farms. They take all crops and send them back to Moscow. Stalin's goons burn out farms. People starve. Communists make it illegal to eat dogs or you get shot. Millions die. My family tells me some of this in letters before the letters stop coming. The rest I read in newspaper later that year. I have not heard from any relative since '32. This is why I hate communists."

"Whoa. This explains why a grandmother would be so desperate as to kill her grandchildren. But how could my father have hallucinated about that place? He's never been outside the states."

"Maybe the ghosts of my people are trying to tell you something."

****

Sitting in the ballroom of a downtown hotel, Deet watched as various folks, mostly working-class people based upon their patched trousers, worn shirts and faded dresses, trickled into the dance room. Keen to follow Burt Smith's instructions, he took a seat toward the back of the fifteen rows of folding chairs, ten to a row. He'd at least get an accurate count. With ten minutes left before the program began, he counted forty-five heads already seated. Yet, the only person he recognized was Jimmy Bryant. Most of the people looked like those he saw across from the entrance at Plant One's gate the night of the strike.

Maybe they're unemployed and looking for answers?

He couldn't help reflecting on what happened to Mike's family in Ukraine and the F.B.I.'s obsession with communists. He looked at skinny Jimmy Bryant at the front of the room, positioning the podium and some chairs, the glare of the suspended lights bouncing off his partially bald head.

Would Jimmy conspire to starve Akronites?

Deet wondered what kind of ideas would be presented as another familiar person walked up along the right side of the formation of chairs—Pike, the tattooed guy from Duke's Billiard Hall.

If, indeed, he's a Brigade vigilante, what's he doing at a commie meeting?

The dark-haired Duke's employee moved to the far-left side of the row he entered and sat several rows in front of him. Simultaneously, Deet noted a tall middle-aged man with a long, flowing beard and an old-fashioned top hat sit down at the end of the same row as the tattooed guy just as the meeting was about to begin. With a flannel shirt patched at the elbows, the man exposed full head of salt and pepper hair once he removed his hat. A cluster of other men filed into the row behind those two within seconds of the first two, challenging the accuracy of his count.

Seventy-one, seventy-two, seventy-three people seated and five standing, including two men talking to each other behind the podium. Mostly men, fifteen women.

A frail-looking middle-aged man with a balding dome took the microphone behind the wooden podium while an elderly man to whom he had been speaking sat down in a small row of chairs behind the stand. "Good evening, ladies and gentlemen, I'm Richard Marcus, local facilitator of the Greater Summit County Communist Party, and I want to welcome you to tonight's meeting. Because of a scheduling conflict for our speaker, the review of last month's meeting will be pushed back to the second item on the agenda. Now, our guest speaker this evening is one of the leading political science scholars in northern Ohio. Professor William Grayson graduated from Harvard in 1887 and received his doctorate in political science from Columbia University in 1893. He's been a foreign relations advisor to presidents of several administrations, including William Howard Taft and Woodrow Wilson. On sabbaticals, he has taught at Oxford and Cambridge in Britain as well as the Sorbonne in Paris and Heidelberg in Germany. Without further ado, ladies and gentlemen, please welcome the University of Akron's own Professor William T. Grayson."

The audience gave the professor a warm applause, but Deet noted little, if any, clapping from Pike, the bearded man, and the row behind them.

They're here for trouble.

"Thank you Mister Marcus and to you, ladies and gentlemen, for your warm welcome." The silver-haired Grayson adjusted the microphone for his approximate six-foot frame.

To Deet, each word already escaped the man's mouth with mechanical precision—a sign either of upcoming boredom or a spell-binding speech.

"From the outset, let me be clear. I teach university students about the various political systems man has used since the beginning of recorded history. I admit to a personal bias that the American *experiment* with representative democracy has been the most successful the world has ever seen, in regards to balancing the rights of the governed with the efficiency of the government. That said, the study of all political systems offers us the insight into the benefits and pitfalls that exist in other systems."

His voice sounded deeper than Jack Acker's and wasn't as smooth, but to Deet it carried a commanding presence, with a sense of urgency about it, compelling him to listen.

"The word *Aryan* has but one meaning, but we hear it thrown about a lot in recent newsreels. In anthropology, it refers to a group of European languages derived from ancient India. If pushed, an anthropologist might lend credence to an *Aryan* as a dark-skinned Hindu praying along the banks of the Ganges." A sly smile crept to the edge of Grayson's cheeks as he looked at his audience before glancing down at his notes. At this point, he stopped, inhaled, and scanned the ballroom as if he was about to share a fantastic revelation. "However, in the scientific approach, the word should be limited to languages.

"Over in Germany, there are crackpots engaged in illicit activities for which they need a cover story." Again, the professor took a deliberate pause and stared at his audience, emphasizing his next point. "Rather, to be exact, they need an alibi."

Grayson stalked away from the sanctuary of the podium to the left side of the room. "You see, when the Nazi fascists need a whipping boy, they create a theory to legitimize the persecution of others. For them . . ." he put a forefinger into the air as his piercing gaze drew Deet's attention toward him. ". . . for them, the theory of Aryan superiority, the white, Nordic master race, is their way of committing crimes against humanity with the bare minimum of guilt, if any at all."

The well-dressed scholar returned to the lectern for a quick look at his notes. "Herr Hitler has looked to the United States for inspiration in these matters. Eugenics, the disturbed genetic experiment by which society should rid itself of *undesirables* was initiated within our shores. Meanwhile, white nationalist groups such as the Ku Klux Klan have always fostered the belief of white superiority over non-white races. The Jews believe, and I can understand their belief, that Hitler and his minions have singled them out. After all, the daily reports out of Germany have documented the demonization of the Jewish population. One can only wonder to what all this will lead."

Grayson walked toward the right side of his audience, his voice never in real need of a microphone's amplification. "Now, the truth is . . . the truth is that Jews may well be at the bottom of the Nazi pecking order, but other groups are submerged there as well—the Slavs, the Negroes, the Mongoloid races of China and Japan. Hitler even holds a special disdain for what he views as the black bastardization of the Latin race among the French and Italians. So, to be blond and blue-eyed—"

"Enough of this eggheaded bullshit!" A voice with the refinement of one of the mixing machines used to blend the ingredients needed to excrete bands of tire ply hijacked the meeting. The bearded man stood up with one fist raised in the air and the other hand outstretched, fanning toward the crowd. "You have an eager crowd wanting to know how they can get work, and you're feeding us this anti-Nazi junk that pinheads read and write about, but it doesn't put food on the table! You know what Hitler has done, Mister Professor? He's put people to work. There's no unemployment in Germany. He's making Germany great again. It's long past time for talking. It's time for action!"

Professor Grayson stood emotionless with one hand on top of the other at his waist as if he were waiting to be seated at a restaurant. "Shouting down what one doesn't wish to hear doesn't diminish the truth of the matter."

Mister Marcus sat frozen with his jaw almost touching his chest.

"Just like at the Consolidated strike a couple weeks back." The bearded man's gravelly voice took an accusatory tone as he looked around the audience. "You guys were content to stay cemented across from the main gate, and you never had the nerve to take on the police in the street as they marched west on Market. This party just blows smoke up the people's ass!"

"Hey, hey, hi, ho, FDR's got to go!" Tattooed Pike rose up, almost on cue, and started pumping his fist as well. "Hey, hey, hi, ho, FDR's got to go!"

The staccato chant filled the ballroom as the half-dozen or so men, who had seated themselves in the row behind the bearded man, stood up, thrust their fists toward the ceiling, and joined in the chorus, "Hey, hey, hi, ho, FDR's got to go! Hey, hey, hi, ho, FDR's got to go! Hey, hey, hi, ho, FDR's got to go!"

Deet observed the gnarled faces of several men in the rest of the gathering, who didn't take kindly to this interruption. "What the hell do you think you're doing?" One man grabbed the guy, who interrupted the professor, by the middle of his beard, before he delivered a haymaker to his jaw.

Soon there was a scrum with other male members of the audience pouncing into the row with the mocking rabble-rousers. The sound of knuckles on bone replaced the rhythmic verse of the protestors as most of the assembled backed away. The void they created became the melee's arena, featuring at least a half-dozen individual fist fights.

Having no dog in this fight, Deet positioned himself a safe distance away at the front entrance to the ballroom, where he chuckled to himself about what he'd report to Agent Smith. Within a few minutes, he heard the distant approach of police sirens. Apparently, so did the protestors. After pummeling a man into unconsciousness, the bloodied, bearded man stuck two fingers in his mouth and let loose with a high-pitched whistle. He and his crew bolted out a back door at the far corner of the room. By the time the police entered, some of the women were checking on minor wounds of the men, and Mister Marcus sprinted to the incoming officers. "They went out the back way! They went out the back way!"

Meanwhile, Professor Grayson spoke to an officer before calmly walking out past Deet to whatever pressing engagement awaited him.

"Good speech, Professor," Deet said.

"Don't ever underestimate the treachery of a fascist, young man." The words hung in the air as the doors swung closed in Grayson's wake.

Unscathed and somewhat amused, Deet helped reposition the chairs as the confusion settled down, and Marcus gave the details of the incident to the police. Deet felt grateful to Smith for *a night at the fights*.

Chapter 26

Cleveland

July 1938

Like bullets, rain pelted the windshield of the truck to the point the overmatched wipers couldn't keep up with the deluge. Without much traffic behind him and lightning daggers crackling over the dark expanse of Lake Erie in front of him, Deet downshifted to first gear as the box truck crawled down East Ninth Street. A sliver of bright orange on the northwestern horizon promised a dryer drive back to Acker's warehouse in Akron. However, at present, he strained to locate the designated warehouse opposite the pier through the opaque curtain of rain.

The thunderstorm's fury let up just in time for Deet to spot twin buildings to the left of the pier. He turned on a side street, which served as a concrete driveway to the warehouses. Each building featured a pitched roof at one-hundred-and-twenty degrees at its peak. In front of the first building, he got out of the truck still wearing a rain slicker as a steady rain bounced off it.

Since it wasn't six o'clock yet, Deet walked up to a service door, hoping it'd be unlocked, which it was. Inside, rows of industrial lamps hung from a metal skeleton supporting the roof which was being assaulted by a steady pounding of rain. About the size of a football field, the warehouse seemed to have a gridwork of tow motor paths in between rows of bins formed from vertical I beams and thick, horizontal, wooden boards. The bins varied in size, but most appeared to be about eight feet high and twelve feet across, stacked three bins high.

Deet saw a small office off to his left with its door open and a light on. He stuck his head into the cubby space, a broom closet in size compared with the rest of the building, but no one was there. "Hello!" He cried out to the silent statues of stored cardboard boxes, wooden crates, and lengths of fabricated metal pieces.

He walked toward the middle of the building and looked down the aisle that dissected it. "Hello! Anybody here?" A metal door slammed at the back of the warehouse. "Hello! Anybody here?"

As the roof telegraphed the easing of the rain, a distinct thud of footsteps grew louder as Deet listened. His ears told him someone was walking down the farthest aisle to the left, and he followed his ears back towards the office. "What the hell are you doing here?"

"I should be asking you that question," answered Cousin Hugo. "At least I work here."

"I'm supposed to pick up some crates of pipe scaffolding belonging to Jack Acker down in Akron."

"Pipe scaffolding?" A lone, dark brown curl dangled over Hugo's furrowed forehead, "Do you have a load out sheet?"

Deet opened several snaps on his slicker and dug a paper out of a shirt pocket. "Right here." He handed it to Hugo. "So, how long have you worked here?"

"About six months." Hugo reviewed the paper as if it were a study sheet for an upcoming examination. His face bloomed into a full smile before grinning at Deet. "Oh, I see what you need. Come, follow me."

Hugo led Deet to the far side of the building. "I started just after Christmas." Hugo stopped and turned and offered a compassionate face, one Deet had rarely experienced from his German American cousin. "That reminds me. How's your father doing?"

Deet shook his head. "Not so good. Parkinson's set in shortly after he came out of his coma. He can't get around without help, and he hallucinates off and on."

"I'm sorry to hear that, Deet. It must be tough on your whole family."

"Thanks. We're all working together to make things work at home." Deet wasn't about to share that Ricky was in jail, charged with murder. He changed the subject as gracefully as if he were walking barefoot across a path of broken glass. "You still want to go fight for Hitler?"

"Yeah, someday, I'd like that." Hugo looked up at the steel rafters for a moment before moving forward. "The communists must be stopped. I think the crates you need are in the last aisle."

Deet followed Hugo stride for stride as Geller made his way to the far side of the warehouse. Thinking about what Mike Kobenko told him of how Stalin had starved millions of Ukrainians softened his outlook of his cousin's ambition a bit, but he didn't want to talk politics. "Ever end up making time with Gertie while you were in summer camp?" he asked with half a grin.

"Unfortunately, not." Still walking, Hugo turned his head toward Deet. "She and Vogel got sent back to New York for 'unbecoming behavior'.

Deet raised his eyebrows, pursed his lips, and nodded. "I see. Got a girl friend?"

"Yeah, Betsy and I hooked up a couple months before graduation." Geller turned down the last aisle. "She works as a nurse's aide in a hospital fairly close to where my parents live."

"What's Betsy think about you going off to fight for *Herr* Hitler?"

"I haven't told her yet." Halfway down the farthest corridor, Hugo stopped, bent over, and checked some tags on a group of narrow crates, each roughly three feet wide. "This is it. Six crates."

Deet looked down where the shadows and dim lights conspired to paint the crates in a dull green color. Unable to determine how long each crate was due to the darkness in the depths of the bin, he lifted the end of one in order to pull it out. "Whoa."

"Let me help," Hugo said as the two pulled the visible end away from the bin. With the six-foot length of the crate exposed, he offered a solution. "Let's put it down. I have a better idea. I'll bring the tow motor over, and we'll put the crates on the forks. While I'm getting the tow motor, back your truck up to those large double doors up front. We'll slide them off onto your truck."

"Works for me."

In the wake of the storm's passing, resurrected daylight presented Deet with a better look at the crates as he and Hugo slid two off the steel forks. An army green, they had patches of black paint which blocked out previous lettering. "Where'd this scaffolding come from . . . the Army?" Deet joked after pushing the last crate onto the bed of the truck.

Hugo chuckled as he pulled off his work gloves. "It was probably Army surplus. I see a lot of it in here."

Just before Deet hopped off the bed of the truck, a low ray of evening sunlight hit the end of one of the crates, exposing the last numbers of a code—*903*, which through a careless error hadn't been blacked out.

As Deet stepped into the driver's seat and closed the door, Hugo grinned and leaned in through the open window. "I hope your Mister Acker enjoys his *scaffolding.*"

Deet drove off towards East Ninth Street and saw Hugo laughing behind him in the mirror. Something was definitely off about those crates, so he pulled the truck along the curb a few blocks down East Ninth. He took out a pencil and a scrap of paper he found in the glove compartment. In a matter of seconds, he rendered a decent image of the crate with the *903* left showing on the end of it. Agent Burt Smith would probably find it interesting.

****

Akron

July 1938

The creases around Agent Burt Smith's mouth barely hinted at a frown after Deet's summary of the communist meeting from the other evening. The smell of smoke overwhelmed the tangy musk of his cologne as it had already ruined the factory fresh scent of the black '38 Plymouth's interior. Grateful for having brought a clean pair of trousers to change into after his shift, Deet ran the tips of his fingers over the dark tan velour of the back seat.

"Tell me more about the younger man with the tattoo." Smith took out a pack of cigarettes from the pocket of his white shirt and offered one to Deet.

Getting enough of tobacco's effect from the air in the car's interior, Deet shook his head this time. "I saw him the first time at Duke's months ago . . . his name's Pike. That's when I noticed his Brigade tattoo on his arm. He's got a strange look about him . . . deep set blue eyes. Then, I saw him wearing a red bandana around his neck at the Consolidated riot. He was headed toward the cemetery right before the police got pelted with rocks from the same area."

"And this Pike began chanting at the communists' meeting right after the bearded man charged the communists for being too passive and not going after the police during the riot?" Smith exhaled more smoke as he looked at Deet. "Is that right?"

"Yeah, that's right."

"I'm getting the picture, slowly but surely," Smith, his fist, extended forefinger, and thumb stuck to his cheek, muttered to himself as if lost in his thoughts. "Those guys who interrupted that meeting can't be comm—"

The driver laid on his horn. "Bastard! Ass doesn't know red from green." He turned the Plymouth north on Main.

The G-man snapped out of his daydream and turned toward Deet. "Tell me about the scaffolding pickup."

"The guy who loaded me at the East Ninth Street warehouse was my cousin of all people. He's been a Hitler Heiler for the past couple years. He and his dad belong to the Bund. Anyway, after we loaded the crates, he laughed about hoping Acker would enjoy them. I thought that was really odd."

"How did you get them off the truck? Was there someone at Acker's warehouse to help you?"

"No. He'd given me a key to the front gate. I unlocked the padlock to the gate, swung it open, and drove the truck under an overhang. I put the gate and truck keys into a slot in the entrance door. Then I picked up my car, drove out beyond the gate, walked back to lock the padlock, and then I drove home."

"No one there . . .," again Smith drifted out on his own as the whirring of rubber on bricks stopped and pavement took over on the North Hill Viaduct.

Deet took a peek out the window and realized he was seemingly riding on air for over a half mile, some hundred-and-fifty feet up. He looked down at his carbon black-covered shoes and the mess he'd made on the brown carpeting.

"Anything unusual about the crates, Deet?"

Thankful for Smith's interruption, the teen dug into a pocket of his clean trousers and handed the crumpled drawing of one of the crates. "All the crates looked like this one. They appeared to be Army surplus. They were about three feet wide by six feet long and were all basically khaki-green colored wood. Except, they all had the markings painted over in black. But there was one number, or code, that was missed on the end of one box." Deet pointed to the number *903* at the end of the illustrated crate.

"Are you sure?" Smith's face lit up as never before as his voice raised an octave Deet thought impossible for the man.

"Yeah. I drew as I saw it before I left downtown Cleveland."

"If Acker ever wants you to drive a load back for him in the future, would you contact me before you go?" The agent's eyes cast a steady gaze on Deet.

"Sure, why not?"

"Here's my card." Smith handed a business card to Deet. "Make sure you call me, preferably from a phone booth. Your party line can give you away to too many gossips."

Chapter 27

Akron

August 1938

Post shift coffee shop meetings continued to surprise Deet. Of course, he was grateful Big Mike Kobenko changed his mind about *mashing* him, instead inviting him to the café off Market. Now, Dixon wanted a word with him at the same place.

"Jenkins," Dixon said after the two ordered their coffee, "there's three things I knows for sure about working at Consolidated." Dixon thrust out the first three fingers of his left hand to within a foot of the young man's face.

Wide-eyed despite the time of day, Deet fixated on the Black man's intensity.

"One," Dixon tapped one of the three fingers with the forefinger of his other hand. "It's a damn dangerous place to work, especially the milling department. Rogers, who lost the top half of three fingers last week into those rollers, won't be the last guy to get maimed unless someone does something. Two . . ." He tapped the middle of his three extended fingers with the other hand's index finger. "The union, which doesn't even give a shit about Negro workers, can't convince Consolidated to take safety seriously. Three . . ." He touched the last of three fingers inches from Deet's nose. "I can't stand by and watch it happen over and over again."

The waitress brought their coffees, and Dixon laid down a dime.

"So, what can you do about it?" Deet shoveled two teaspoons of sugar into his black coffee.

"Hopefully, work some magic." Dixon managed a toothy grin as he spiraled some cream into his cup, enjoying the momentary parfait of parallel white and black swirls before they mingled together into tan. "I knows those three things, but there's two things I'm not sure about." He took a sip of the hot java and sat back with a look of satisfaction. "H-m-m, h-m-m, h-m-m, that's good."

"What are those two things?" Deet noticed the contrast between his fingernails, still jammed with oily carbon black, and the white porcelain cup as he sipped the steamy drink.

"First, will the company take a safety suggestion from a Black man?" Dixon put down his cup, sat back, and folded his arms across his chest.

"Considering the union hasn't even taken you guys under its wing, thinking the Big C will listen to you might not be too likely." Deet leaned in as if he was sharing a major secret. "You think you can even get past Harley Kershaw? You could have the plans for the next great tire, and he'd either tear 'em up right before your eyes or present them himself to the top brass as his."

Dixon nodded and let half a smile form around his mouth. "Yeah, you're probably right about that. We're the livin', breathin', walkin', talkin' example of a double standard as the union likes the term." The half smile flipped to a full frown in a split second. "I knows you knows it."

Deet's work partner dug a folded piece of paper out of his trouser pocket. "That leads me to the other thing I don't knows for sure."

"Which is . . .?"

"Would you present this idea to Nate Benson?" Dixon unfolded the crinkled paper in front of Deet and smoothed it out with his calloused fingers.

Deet looked down at a crude drawing of a rectangle with ragged lines, some sort of hinge at each end, and what he guessed to be milling rollers behind the rectangle. Had he not worked side by side with Dixon for over a year, the elementary artwork would have been unrecognizable.

"Is this a safety guard for the milling machines?"

The graying whiskers on Dixon's face popped up with his ear-to-ear smile as he nodded.

Deet cocked his head as he widened his eyes. "Why me? I mean this is your invention, the drawing's rough, but I get the point. I think Benson would too."

"I knowed you'd wonder about that," the Negro said as he put his cup to his mouth. "First, scuttlebutt has it that you've made some pretty detailed drawings of maps and buildings and such. You certainly can do something with this kin-de-garden drawing. I will get you the exact measurements. Second, you seem to have Benson's ear. You're always being called up there to gab with him. You and your drawing of my idea might just swing it."

Deet thought about Smith picking him up in a car instead of more meetings in Benson's office. Dixon just gave him the milling department's take on his relationship with Benson. "Hey, I've been up there twice—once Benson wanted to express his concern over my dad, and the other time Detective Ragmon filled me in on some trouble my brother got into. Trust me, I don't have Benson's ear."

Dixon drained the last of his coffee. "Whether you do or don't, will you do it?"

"Draw the design of the guard? Sure, no problem." The younger man flipped open the palms of his hands.

"And?"

Deet stared into his empty cup, void of coffee just like he'd become absent of excuses. "Alright. After you get me the specs, I'll work up a design and present it to Benson when I think the time's right. It won't be this week or next."

Dixon inhaled and exhaled with a short smile on his face. "Good. Take your time, but don't take too long. I don't want any more men mangled on those rollers."

****

Deet took no satisfaction from his sterling performance in the last American Legion game of his career. He pitched a two-hitter but still lost a 2-1 decision to a team of hayseeds from Millersburg. He pined for something more than to play another game in the days ahead. Every time he walked off the mound after each inning, he scoured the bleachers behind home plate and the chicken wire fence, searching for the face who wouldn't be there. Lacey hadn't come to any of his games this summer, and he cursed himself for thinking with his groin in order to be seduced by the beauty and maturity of an older woman.

Oh sure, he tried to make a go of it with Kathy Tudsill, the aspiring assistant payroll clerk at Consolidated. They'd gone out a couple of times, and he convinced her to come to one of his games. Yet, he knew not much was to come of it, especially after the game she attended. He talked about a crucial double play his team executed in the sixth inning, and her reaction was, "Double play? I thought that was the name of some sort of cocktail."

The final straw with Kathy came at the end of their second date. With her mother obligingly upstairs, out of sight and earshot, the two of them engaged in passionate necking. No amateur on the couch, Deet read the signals and attempted to reach second base by loosening a button on her blouse, working his hand through in order to cup her bra and maybe more.

"Hands off, Deet!" Kathy protested as she pulled back from him. "There's not goin' be any squeezing of the goods."

Deet said his farewell and never looked back. He couldn't say the same about Lacey. He yearned to be back in her arms, to hear her analysis of the game he'd just played, to play billiards again with a worthy opponent for whom he cared, and to enjoy a movie with meaningful conversation about it afterward. In all honesty, contorting their bodies in writhing pleasure also crossed his mind.

What the hell? The worst that could happen is to have her shut the door in my face.

In his dusty, grass-stained uniform, he drove over to her apartment building, walked up the stairs, and knocked on her door. The butterflies in his stomach fluttered halfway up his throat. He hadn't experienced such anxiety since his first at-bat in high school as a freshman versus a senior flame thrower. He didn't want the humiliation of another swing and a miss of that nature, but his desperation to correct the biggest mistake of his life overruled everything else.

"Deet . . . hi." Lacey's one hand rested on the doorknob while the other clenched into a loose fist.

Deet continued to lift his head upwards, reading his former girlfriend as he crawled out of a grave of shame. Her mouth opened just enough for the tip of her tongue to show between glistening teeth. Her soft brown eyes weren't glaring, rather with a tilt of her head they expressed wonder . . . maybe confusion. He wasn't sure, except there wasn't the disgust of several months ago.

"You . . . wan-na come in?" The bite and rage in Lacey's voice, which Deet carried in his head daily from their last face-to-face meeting, had vanished. She sounded almost as he felt.

"Thank you." Deet walked into a dark apartment in which the only light was furnished by the late evening August sun seeping its way through pulled curtains. He sat down on the far end of the sofa as Lacey eased into the burgundy upholstered chair.

"What brings you over, Deet?" She spoke just above a whisper with her fingers interlocked over one knee.

"We just ended our Legion season with a loss, and . . ." Deet sensed his mouth getting dry as he, too, used a librarian's voice. His gaze drifted from the wave of her light brown hair to an old, brass pole lamp, which she just turned on. Its light cast an inviting sheen on her head, and he yearned to bring her swooping strands close to him.

"And?"

"And I pitched a two-hitter, complete game." He turned his attention back to Lacey.

"Very nice." In this game of romantic poker, Lacey's face didn't surrender her hand.

"But that's not what brought me here. Every time I walked off the mound between innings, knowing this might be my final game, I . . . I . . ." Deet's hands rubbed his thighs as he inhaled and exhaled.

"You what?"

"I couldn't help looking up in the stands, wishing you were there." In this critical moment of unconditional surrender, he looked squarely in her eyes, ready to accept the consequences. "I really miss you, Lacey. I know I was all wet by pitching woo with Sophie, but I'm still dizzy for you, Lace."

Deet's gaze remained steady as she leaned toward him on her chair, her reaction a closely guarded secret worthy of Agent Smith.

"Tell me, Deet, shortly after your fling with Sophie, did you feel like the fool?" Lacey's head was askew, her lips pursed, but most importantly, her eyes remained soft, almost inviting.

It might have been a mirage, or a baited trap to put a finishing dagger into his heart, but Deet thought her eyes might be welling a tear or two. "Oh, brother, did I ever. Right after, she sent me on my way as if I was a glass of spoiled milk poured down the drain." Now, his eyes moistened. "Lace, I was a twit."

She got out of her chair, and glided to the middle of the couch, sitting sideways facing Deet. With her athletic shorts exposing smooth lower thighs, her legs bent backwards underneath her. No other girl Deet dated would be so bold to wear shorts . . . ever. Her hair bounced once before settling on the top of her shoulders.

"I know I was pissed that night in the car when you brought me home. *Hurt* and pissed to be exact. It's taken a while, but I can understand you better now. You know what they say, 'people in glass houses shouldn't throw stones'."

She understands me . . . better?

"Am I missing something here?" As he turned to face her, he rested an arm on the top of the sofa. Feeling hopeful, his voice gained some confidence. "Right now, I'm doing my best to eat crow and ask for your forgiveness. If there's a chance for us to get back together, I'll take it any way you hand it out."

"You know how I said John Monroe had style?" She blinked once, broke eye contact, and inhaled.

Deet nodded, wondering why she brought up his name.

"Well, he asked me out, and I said yes." Lacey took another deep breath and pressed her fist against her lips and nose, leaving a pale impression on it.

Deet's jaw dropped a fraction of an inch.

"We went out a couple of times before . . . before I slept with him." With closed eyes, she dropped her head.

The young gummer's heart stopped while he gulped for a breath. His imagination ran wild at the disgusting thought. Good girls *never* did that. "Why?" The simple question squeaked out of Deet's deflated chest cavity.

"Part of it was he was handsome, and he did have style." She inhaled, opened her eyes, and her jaw stiffened. "He was charming, . . . but I was also vindictive." Her tone wavered between compassion and bitterness like the spinning of a double-sided coin, not knowing which side would land face up. "I wanted to punish you, even if you never knew about it. But it came back to bite me in the ass."

Deet caught his breath and mulled his response. He could walk out right now—girls weren't supposed to be sleeping around. Guys could get away with it—hell, they were almost expected to cat around —at least until they were married.

Then again, she sounded like she wanted him back as much as he had wanted her. This was no time for a knee-jerk reaction. "What happened?"

She leaned in toward him a bit and ran her tongue across her upper lip. "I went to his hotel room just for a surprise visit. I knocked on his door, but no one answered. As I was about to leave, another union official, who was leaving his own room, told me John had to leave suddenly for Washington, D.C. His wife called, and his child was pretty sick." Whatever faint light existed in the room flickered in the moisture in and around her brown eyes.

"Oh-h-h." Deet took a deep, long breath and of all things, Dixon's face showed up as if the two mill workers were seated across from each other at the coffee shop.

We're the livin', breathin', walkin', talkin' example of a double standard.

Now, Lacey's eyes dripped tears. "Deet, I was such an idiot. I felt cheap, dirty, and above all, guilty." She broke into a soaking cry as she fell forward into his arms. "All I could imagine," she inhaled as she sobbed, "was lying in bed with him . . . as his wife, his wife . . . walked into the hotel room, yelling at me that I was a two-dollar whore . . . and, and—" She convulsed onto his shoulder, soaking it with her tears. "She'd have been so, so right."

Give her the cold shoulder like he did to Betty Fingerhoffen?

A faint voice squealed for revenge, but whether it was his earlier conversation with Dixon or the months of self-berating his own foolish choice, he ignored it. He had her back in his arms, and he wasn't going to let petty male peevishness loosen their bond this time. "Oh, Dollface, don't think of yourself that way." His arms wrapped around her heaving body, exhilarated by their need to be one for each other.

"You made a mistake." He pulled back just enough to gently prop up her chin with the tips of his fingers as their eyes met. "Remember, this just happened because I was the twit to begin with." He couldn't stop the welling of his eyes while he parted some wisps of light brown hair off of her cheeks. "I came here tonight to ask your forgiveness for being an ass. Will you forgive me?"

She whimpered as she nodded. "Can you forgive me?"

"With all my heart." He pulled close to her and kissed her as their upper limbs became a fleshy web binding them together.

After their make-up canoodling dried out his mouth, Deet broke their embrace. "Lace, one thing I've come to appreciate in the past couple months is that you're one of a kind, and . . . I love you."

Horizontal on the sofa, the two melted into one.

Chapter 28

Akron

September 1938

Arch's head lay on a compact white pillow, with his hands folded over his lap. Dressed in his only suit, he was surrounded by the interior white cloth lining of a six-sided, *toe-pincher* coffin. Shaved, with his gray-streaked, blond hair combed back and with just the right amount of make-up pasted upon his face, Arch could have passed for the living at a single glance.

However, Deet hovered over his late father, knowing full well that he wasn't alive and would never come back. Once the funeral director closed the pine box, all he'd have left would be the memories of learning to play ball, his first 3.2 beer, working on a car, bowling, and witnessing the legacy of his father as he stood up to a bunch of company thugs. A gentle touch to his bicep and a whiff of lilac interrupted his thoughts.

"Are you alright?" Lacey stood close enough for them to be attached from the hips to the shoulders. In a dark green dress with her tawny hair curled in waves which would make the ocean blush, she blended seamlessly into the reverent gathering for Arch Jenkins.

"Yeah," Deet said as he took Lacey's hand, an unintelligible buzz of conversation around them. "Just remembering the good times with Pop."

"Keep the memories of those who've passed close but be sure to keep the living closer." She whispered in his ear before kissing him on the cheek.

Deet's fingers coursed the edge of the coffin and felt the flimsy lining, which was no thicker than one of his tattered work shirts. Even though his father had left a small life insurance policy of a couple hundred dollars and something called Social Security offered a few dollars, splurging on the dead when the living had to scrape by eating overloaded slugburgers didn't seem to make sense. A hand rubbed the back of his shoulder.

"So sorry for your loss, Deet."

Deet turned and looked down on Nate Benson. "Oh, thank you, Mister Benson for showing up. That's very kind of you."

"The least I could do, Deet." Wearing a black suit, Benson held a fedora in his hand, pointing it toward the wall where a framed photo of Arch hung next to a floral wreath. "The company sent that wreath for your father's graveside."

For the first time, the young man noticed the circular group of red roses propped up on some sort of tripod. "That was very thoughtful of Consolidated."

"Deet," Benson stared into his eyes, "your father and I often had different ideas on how the plant should be run, but as God is my witness, I want to leave you with two things that I never questioned. First, Arch was a helluva tiremaker, one of the best I've ever known. Second, he didn't pull wild ideas out of his ass just because he wanted to cause trouble." Benson shook his head. "No, sir. Everything he did was designed to advocate for the workers in the plant." He grabbed onto Deet's arm as he started to step away. "I just wanted you to know that."

At first, Deet resented that Benson would clamp onto his arm like a crotchety Sunday school teacher. However, as he stared down into his chief supervisor's face, he blinked several times as his own eyes softened when confronted with Benson's compassionate expression. "Thank you, Mister Benson, that means a lot."

"Oh, one more thing." Benson raised an open hand. "That roller guard idea . . . I like it and passed it along to the top brass across Market. Don't be surprised if it takes a while before they spit out a decision."

"Thank you, thank you very much. I'll let Dixon know." Comforted by a superior's recognition, Deet scanned the viewing room awash with neighbors and fellow workers. A few he didn't recognize while others stood out—Chaw Nelson, Jake Carver, Mike Kobenko, Cass Miller, Maria Rossi, even Old Lady Dingus.

His mother sat with the Lutheran pastor, presumably speaking about the graveside service which would follow. Louie, who seemed to have turned his life around, cracked a smile as he spoke with a wide-eyed Ricky, perhaps the biggest surprise guest at his father's funeral.

Deet reconnected with Lacey, and the two drifted toward his uncle and brother. "What's got you smiling, Louie?"

"Oh, I was just telling Ricky about your grandfather's wake when you were a baby and Ricky wasn't even born." The well-kempt Louie's eyes swelled behind his glasses as he retold his story. "Back in those days, your grandpa's coffin was laid across some sawhorses in the middle of his living room, and the folks came to the house to offer their respects. Well, things got so tight, someone accidentally kicked the leg of one of the sawhorses, and Pops tumbled out onto the floor."

"Holy sh—!" Lacey caught herself just in time and covered her mouth with her hands while Deet chuckled as he hooked his arm around her waist and pulled her close to him.

Louie's face almost froze with an ear-to-ear grin. "Except for the war, it was the strangest thing I ever saw."

Deet's smile waned as he released his hold on Lacey and turned his attention to Ricky. "I'm so glad to have you back, Brother."

Ricky's frame straightened and he inhaled. "I'm so grateful to be back."

"We owe a lot of gratitude to Jack Acker," Deet said. "You wouldn't be here without him. It would have been nearly impossible for us to round up five hundred dollars in bail money."

Although it took a while, Jack Acker had come through. At first, he succeeded in getting Ricky's murder charge reduced to accessory to murder. After McGirt's murder trial, in which Bill Mowery testified to the impromptu nature of the killing, Acker convinced the judge to lean on the prosecutor to drop the charge against Ricky, because he couldn't have been an accessory since he had no idea the murder would take place. Furthermore, once it did, he didn't furnish McGirt with a car, nor did he drive him. He just happened to be there.

"Here's something Acker told me," Ricky whispered in confidence to the other three. "McGirt will certainly get the chair, if not for the pawn shop killing, then for the murder of Aunt Betty."

"Really?" Eyes narrowed, Uncle Louie leaned in toward his youngest nephew. "Explain that one."

"The bullet that killed Aunt Betty came out of McGirt's pistol. Ballistics tests proved it."

"Why would he have killed *her*?" Deet asked.

"Police figured out all the places I helped move stuff out of with Bill were on her mail delivery route. She was planning the heists. Somewhere along the line, she had teamed with McGirt, who furnished the warehouse to store the goods. Police think that when McGirt saw how much was being stored, he wanted more money from Betty. She refused, and he shot her."

"Speak of the devil, or in this case, an angel, look who just walked in." Deet was gobsmacked by the arrival of Jack Acker, outfitted in a dark, pin-striped suit, black patent leather shoes, and a black fedora.

Louie, standing between both brothers, pulled them close to him with an arm around each of their waists. "Whatever may have happened to Betty and whatever you may have done wrong, Ricky, from this point forward, let's all work together to help your mother. You know she's going to need it."

With his eyes on Acker, who was now speaking to his mother, Deet nodded his head. "You're right, Uncle Louie. Funny thing though . . ."

"What's funny?" Louie asked.

"Mom brought up the idea of finding work again now that she doesn't have Dad to care for anymore." Deet's vision moved from Acker to Ricky and Louie before landing on Lacey.

"She can always apply in the flipper department. I can put in a good word for her." Lacey smiled.

"Well, if she persists with that idea, I'll let her know," Deet said. "I got a notion things are going to be tough on her for a while. Excuse me." Deet saw Acker start to back away from his mother, and he headed in his direction.

Before he made more than three steps, he got sidetracked by Chaw Nelson. "Oh, Deet, pardon me, but I just wanted you to know that I gave your mother an envelope with a little collection we took in the milling department. It ain't much, but we wanted to help youin's in this tough time."

Deet looked into Chaw's rounded, stubbled face on one of the few occasions when it wasn't stuffed with chew. "Thank you, Chaw." Deet grabbed the gummer's hand and shook it. "I'm sure whatever it is, it *will* help."

He turned away from Nelson and almost knocked heads with Jack Acker. "Oh, excuse me, Mister Acker."

"That's quite alright, Deet," the lawyer said with a closed smile. "Why don't we migrate to a less congested area." Acker headed toward the funeral home's foyer, which happened to be void of guests at the moment.

Deet took hold of the councilman's hand with both of his and started pumping his arm. "I just wanted to thank you so much for all you've done for Ricky . . . for us. To think that Ricky was able to be here tonight, after over three months in jail. I don't know where to begin in thanking you for that generosity and for getting the murder charge dropped." He sensed his eyes welling and inhaled, hoping not to break into tears.

"Not to worry, Deet," Acker spoke in his soothing baritone voice. "I know I'll get my bail money back, because there's no way Ricky will be a flight risk. As far as his legal representation, I pride myself in giving back to worthy members of the community. I do so every so often throughout the course of a year."

Deet finally let go of the man's hand and nodded with approval and gratitude.

"There is one small favor I might ask of you again, Deet." Acker looked down at the fedora in his hands.

"Name it."

"Could you pick up another load of scaffolding for me in Cleveland?"

"Sure, just say when," Deet gushed.

"Would you be available this Friday evening around four?"

Jenkins cocked his head and closed one eye, giving it a thought. "Yeah, I'm available."

"Good." Acker's lineless face glowed with confidence. "The same arrangement as last time. You know the warehouse off East Ninth, right? You'll be back at my warehouse around eight. Just leave everything on the truck and put the keys through the slot in the door, just like last time . . . okay?"

"No problem." Deet bobbed his head. "Pick up the truck around four and return with the scaffolding around eight."

"Very good." Acker topped his blond head with the hat. "Well, I must be off. Again, my condolences to you and your family."

Deet returned to the viewing parlor, where the buzz of the conversations had diminished into whispers. While his back had been turned, speaking to Jack Acker, his milling station partner, Dixon, walked in and now stood next to Arch's coffin.

"You know, I've been working with you for well over a year, and I still don't know your first name." Deet walked up next to the Black man.

"You never ask me." Dixon smiled. "It's Theo."

"Well, Theo, thank you for coming. Let me introduce you to my family and my girlfriend."

****

Cleveland

September 1938

A glum-faced older man sat in the warehouse office off East Ninth Street when Deet arrived. Wearing a dirtied flat cap, he removed a burning cigarette from his mouth. "Yeah, what'd'ya need?"

"I'm supposed to pick up a couple crates of scaffolding for Mister Jack Acker, down in Akron." Deet handed the man the paper order.

As the older man scanned the paperwork, his exposed wrists below his partially rolled sleeves drew Deet's attention. On his right arm was the distinct tattoo—*Brigade*—with two crossed lightning bolts underneath the lettering. "Where's Hugo tonight?"

"Don't know the guy." The man put down the paperwork and stood up. "Never heard of him."

"Just asking since he was here about a month ago."

"Follow me." The man left the small office with a noticeable limp. "Guys come and go through here. I don't even pretend to get to know their names."

The two went the far aisle, just as Deet had done with Hugo. The man struggled to pull out the first crate, which sat on the concrete floor.

"Let me help," Deet offered.

"Get away!" The bent over man swept his left arm behind him. "I can do my job! Go, get your truck and back it up to the big door up front."

Deet couldn't wait to follow the grouch's order just to escape his presence, and by the time he'd positioned the truck, the door opened. The tow motor forks lifted two of the six olive drab crates to the level of the truck's bed, where Deet pulled them off. The routine was repeated a second time, but the final load came with a surprise.

Deet watched as the one of the last two crates teetered on the front of the tow motor's tines. He hopped off the truck and waved his arms in the air. "Hey, hold—!"

The crate at the front edge of the tines tumbled off the forks with one end busting open.

Deet gawked at a dozen rifle butts at the opened end of the long, wooden box.

"Shit!" The man hobbled back toward his office and returned with a claw hammer and crowbar, which he used to pull and straighten nails before pounding the splintered fragments of the cracked end cap back into place. "You never saw nothin' but scaffolding, kid, right?" The man glowered with a cold stare.

Deet nodded and hopped back onto the truck. He couldn't wait to contact Agent Smith.

Dear God, let me get home in one piece tonight.

Chapter 29

Akron

September 1938

On an overcast evening, Deet couldn't help but notice lights on inside Acker's Bowery Street warehouse. In fact, a man stood by an opened garage door, waving Deet to drive into the facility. It wasn't until the teen stepped out of the truck that he recognized the bearded man with the crinkled top hat, the one who had interrupted the communist meeting.

At first, Deet's eyes glanced upward at the trusses which held up the roof. Numerous smaller triangles supported each three-sided truss. However, his admiration for the structure's geometry disappeared as he observed the scowl on the bearded fellow's face. "I thought I was to just park the truck outside, just like I did on my first delivery." Deet strained to keep secret the back flips in his stomach.

"Things changed, kid," the surly-looking man, said in a sandpaper voice as the large garage door slowly closed behind them somewhat quieting the clatter of a passing train.

"Hey, what is this!" Deet shouted as the man pointed a pistol at him.

"Let's just say that you seeing those rifles wasn't part of the plan," the man said with an emotionless face as he wagged the weapon back and forth.

"What plan?" Deet turned to the sound of footsteps on concrete behind him to see Pike, the tattooed employee of Duke's Billiard Parlor. Sweat dripped from his arm pits.

"The one you're not going to know about . . . ever." A glint of light bounced off the blue eyes in the darkened recessed sockets of Pike. "What do we do with him for now, Phineas?"

"Bring the extra chair in the office, the wooden one, over here with some rope."

Deet watched the younger man walk towards the office, where a clock was easily seen through an observation window.

Ten minutes 'til eight.

"So, you've got a stash of Army surplus rifles?" Deet's stomach continued to roil as he desperately played the role of indifferent bystander even though his breathing quickened. "What's the big deal?"

"We'll let the boss decide on how big a deal it is." Phineas pointed to the chair with his gun. "Sit down."

"Put your hands behind the chair," Pike barked. "You're going to take a dive from the viaduct tonight." He convulsed in laughter, which could have been confused for a cough.

"Pike, shut the hell up, and get him tied up!" Phineas barked as he yanked off his hat in frustration. "You don't know what the boss has in mind."

Deet didn't react, but his heart raced as the bile within his stomach started to rise up into his throat. Just about convinced he would vomit, the service door opened, and the deliberate beat of leather-soled shoes came up from behind him.

Phineas joined Pike and whoever had just entered the warehouse in a muted conversation.

Deet decided to make his case. "Hey! I just did what Mister Acker told me to do—deliver these six crates to his warehouse. I can't help the guy up in Cleveland botched the last load on his tow motor."

"Right you are, Deet, right you are." The unmistakable, sophisticated voice of Jack Acker ambushed Deet from the rear.

"Too bad for you that damn cripple couldn't load those last two crates correctly." Acker walked into Deet's peripheral vision on the left. "We wouldn't be in this awkward position."

"Mister Acker, what's going on?" Deet's voice weakened under the stress of envisioning his last moments on earth.

"A revolution, my boy, a revolution." Acker, in a long-sleeved white shirt and navy-blue pants, turned his back to Deet and spoke to the several rows of crated material. He dug a cigarette out of his shirt pocket and lit it with a silver lighter. "Jefferson wrote that 'a little revolution now and then is a good thing'."

Acker took a drag on his smoke before vanishing between the aisles of steel and wood shelving with only his resonating voice to indicate his presence. "Democracy has proven too complicated and slow in dealing with the myriad of society's problems. The Jews, the communists, the foreign *melting pot*, and yes, even your unions— they've all gummed up the works. We've even elected a communist president. What bullshit! It's time to cleanse our shores of this vermin." Acker came out of the shadows with his sleeves rolled up, holding a rifle.

Shocked, Deet thought his hero rabid as he eyed the *Brigade* tattoo on his lower left arm. "You're . . . part of . . . the *Brigade*?"

"Commander of the Summit County cell." Acker flicked away the remnant of his smoldering cigarette. "Truth be told, we're just a small cog in a nationwide series of gears that will rise up on *Der Tag*." He held up the rifle. "This is what's going to help us do it—1903 Springfield, thirty caliber . . . standard Army issue until recently."

"*Der Tag*?" Deet squirmed on the wood chair not knowing which was worse—the rope cutting into his wrists or a man he'd admired sounding like his Uncle .

"It means *The Day*. We're part of numerous, loosely connected cells collectively known as the Silver Shirts. On *The Day*, we will rise up with our stored weaponry and render an all-out assault on the nation's cities, creating such chaos that the government will crack into pieces, leaving us to take over and restore the white man's supreme place in our society."

Deet shook his head to fling a drop of sweat from running into his eye when he remembered something Acker told him in his office earlier in the summer. *The good Father says the rich American Jews should expect to be treated worse than how Hitler's treated the German ones.* "Damn, you sound like Hitler."

"Close." Acker pulled back the rifle bolt and then pushed it forward as if it had ejected a spent cartridge and reloaded another. "*Herr* Hitler has done wonders with the German economy . . . things we could only dream of here in the states." He raised the rifle, keeping it snug to his shoulder, and aimed it at the depths of the warehouse as if he were on the front lines. "By ending the German flirtation with democracy, he's restored German pride and put Jews, communists, and foreigners in their place."

From the rope burn to the ache in his shoulder sockets to Jack Acker's stunning revelation and the expectation of his own death, every part of Deet's being was on the verge of implosion. Visions of helping his mother in the kitchen, his uncle at his garage, going on a double date with his brother, and kissing Lacey flashed through his mind like a 1920's Buster Keaton silent movie.

"How . . ." Deet choked up. "How can you be such a caring man to help us out in a time of great trouble and need . . ." His voice rose as it quivered, " . . . and th-then t-t-turn into a r-r-raving son-of-a-bitch?"

"Simple. The hunter never lets the hunted know he's on to him." A slow, but steady, smug grin crossed Acker's movie star face.

Deet frowned, and he felt his skin from the forehead down shrivel like a grape turned into a raisin.

"Democracy is the most inefficient and ineffective form of government. To destroy it, you can't start by going around with soldiers goosestepping. That comes later. First, you must have something to offer the masses, even if all your offering is lies and fear of those around you."

"Later?"

"Yes. First you must spread chaos, which the Silver Shirt Legion will do on *Der Tag*. Then we will take control and implement our ideas, similar to what *Herr* Hitler has done—order through efficient autocratic means. No more bureaucracy and needless delays as the various branches of the present government play a game of hot potato on so many issues."

"What about the Constitution?" A spark of hope flared within Deet as he remembered his call to Agent Smith. He wondered if the G-man had any intention of coming here.

Keep talking.

"A worthless scrap of paper. One supreme leader, unencumbered by the restraints of a democratic façade will rule without question." Acker leaned the rifle against a metal rack. "As of yet the sheep of democracy aren't even aware that the wolf is stalking them. It's unfortunate you won't be around to witness it."

Seemingly having second thoughts, Acker picked up the rifle in one hand and walked back toward the entrance, out of Deet's vision. Jenkins knew he had to think of something fast before his life was snuffed out. "Any explanation of my death will lead straight back to you, Jack! People know what I was doing tonight, and the questions will grow." He wanted to scream out loud *The F.B.I. knows about you, and your time's over!*

"You really think I haven't planned for that? The truck you drove will be doused with gasoline and burned. Once police find your body at the bottom of the viaduct, they'll conclude a criminal gang hijacked the load after you drove it into my lot, burned the truck, and did away with you. Of course, you can be assured I'll send flowers to your funeral.

"Your time to worry about such things is over." Acker's voice hung over top of Deet.

A sharp blow to his head sent Deet into total darkness.

Deet awoke to be seated at his kitchen table across from his father with an elderly couple seated on either side of him.

"Hey, Deet, it's too early for you." His father, seemingly free of the aftereffects of his illness, got up to get another cup and saucer. "You can't follow so closely on my heels. You've got the world to beat over the next forty, fifty years." Arch poured some coffee into the cup and handed it to his son.

Stunned and speechless, Deet took the coffee from his father, actually feeling the turtle shell complexion of his hand.

"Say hi to your Deede and Baba." A smiling Arch pointed first to the stout, old man to Deet's left before extending his arm to his son's right.

The emigrant from Burluk in Ukraine offered a hidden smile behind his full salt and pepper moustache. Short and muscular, with a mop of gray hair and a weathered face, his Deede spoke with a distinct accent. "I never expect to see you so soon, Dietrich. Then again, the last time, you were but a baby."

"What happened, my grandson?" Slight of build with kind, green eyes, and a double bun of silvery hair, his grandmother still held the outline of her youthful beauty, at least what Deet had seen in old photographs.

"I'm not quite sure. The last thing I remember I was in Jack Acker's warehouse when—"

"That son-of-a-bitch skunk." Arch's face hardened. "Always looking for ways to stab the union guys in the back."

"I know that now, Pop, but he seemed so genuine . . . I mean he helped Ricky a lot."

"That's another story. In trying to do good for the family, your brother screwed up by getting caught up in the wrong crowd. Acker just used his situation to make his cover even better."

Deet's grandfather, who'd been slurping his coffee as he stared at his grandson, finally spoke up. "You've grown into strong, young man, Dietrich."

"Your Lacey," his grandmother interjected, "she will miss you something terribly if you do not return to her. She cares a lot for you. Her world turns around you."

"I know, Baba. I've learned that my world turns around her as well."

"Say good-bye to your grandparents, for now." Arch stood up and walked around the table to take his son's hand and shake it. "You're not ready to join us on this journey, yet."

****

Deet stirred, wiggling his fingers, as fog shrouded the inside of his head as well as what little he could see about him with the limited light which seeped into his eyes.

Am I dead at the bottom of the viaduct?

Sensations told him differently. Something soft cushioned his back and his head, highly unlikely for the shallow, rocky bed of the Little Cuyahoga. Then again, his head ached as if someone had used it for batting practice with two by fours.

The pain inside his skull forced his eyes open, but he still languished in a cloud while inconsistent pattering along with an occasional, muffled *Thump* stretched the limit of his hearing. For all he knew, minutes interchanged with hours, but gradually shapes formed out of the mist which surrounded him. The single clue to consciousness continued to be the excruciating pain in his head. He struggled to bring his right arm up to his face, where he allowed his fingertips to explore his face and head. He found nothing abnormal about his face, but a coarse wrap covered most of his head like some sort of Arabian turban.

By now, with the assistance of his toes, he recognized the tubular foot rail at the end of a bed, even though it remained blurred. Appearing in duplicate, an individual in a white coat—man or woman, he didn't know nor care—bent over him, clueing him to these all-too-familiar surroundings. "My head . . . feels like . . . a cracked . . . . walnut. Can you . . . give me . . . something . . . anything?"

A response sounded as if the person spoke underwater. However, a few minutes later, someone handed him a pill and a paper cup of water.

****

A doctor greeted him as Deet awoke a second time. "How are you feeling, young man?" The white-coated physician wore dark-rimmed glasses, which exaggerated his egg-shaped bald head, fringed with a bit of dark hair around its base. He pulled a pen light out of a breast pocket.

Before he could answer, his stomach grumbled. "Hungry, I guess. At least my head's not splitting open like it did a little bit ago."

"A *little bit* ago?" The doctor bent down and aimed the light into Deet's eyes. "What day is it?" His breath reeked of tobacco.

"Must be Saturday." Except for his lips, Deet froze as the doc inspected his eyes.

"Do you know what happened to you?" The doctor popped back up, his entire body board stiff and perpendicular to the floor.

"I got clubbed by something, not quite sure."

"I have it from a *reliable source* that a rifle butt dented your skull." The physician's speech slowed a bit as he took the clipboard from the end of the bed and jotted a few notes on it. "You were in a coma for about eighteen hours, until yesterday afternoon. You awoke briefly, but you did gain consciousness, which was fantastic." He attached the clipboard back on its hanger. "And you've slept for the past eighteen hours." He let an obligatory smile dent his cheeks.

"No wonder my head felt so bad." The nineteen-year-old brought a hand up to his head, still feeling the gauze wrap.

"Here's the deal." The doctor stood stiff, peering down his nose at his patient while wagging a forefinger. "You've had a severe concussion. You'll stay in the hospital for observation for another day or two. If all's well, we'll send you home, where you'll be on bed rest for at least two weeks."

"Two weeks." Too weak to whine too loud, Deet's reaction to the doctor's orders alerted him to the dryness of his mouth and the stabbing pain of recent memories.

"That's standard—"

"I've got a job. My family needs the money. You don't understand my dad died recently, and I'm the breadwinner."

"H-m-m." The physician put a finger on his lips. "Your short-term memory doesn't seem to have been affected. That's a good sign, but I still must impose bed rest." He retreated to the end of Deet's bed.

"I'm sorry young man, but you are very lucky you're still alive. Bed rest is prescribed so your brain can heal itself. No physical or mental exertion—no work, no play, no reading, no writing. Now, I will see about getting you some soup or broth, nothing heavy to start out with. By the way, that *reliable source* I mentioned, I think he'd like a word with you . . . but not too many words, sir."

"Hello, Deet." As the doctor exited, F.B.I. Agent Burt Smith walked in, dressed in his usual suit with hat in hand. "I've dropped by to check on how you're doing and to apologize."

"I feel a helluva lot better than I did when I woke up the first time yesterday. What do you mean *apologize*?"

Smith pulled up a chair next to Deet's bed and offered his best impression of a smile, a tight lipped one that barely creased his cheeks. "Based on your call after Acker wanted you to make a second delivery, we posted one agent in a car to surveille the warehouse starting around 7:30 Friday evening. As soon as you arrived, he radioed to me that there were other men there. That's when we figured you might be in trouble. We didn't arrive until shortly after eight, just in time to see one of Acker's goons bust your head with the butt of one of those Springfield's. Well, we rounded up those three. Akron's a tough town, but with the help of Acker's secretary—"

"You mean Miss Neal?"

"Yes, Miss Neale. We raided Acker's office yesterday and found a batch of incriminating letters and documents linking him directly to the Silver Shirts and others bent on conspiring against the United States government. If it hadn't been for information from you and Miss Neal, Acker might have given us the slip and caused all sorts of problems."

"How did Miss Neal help?" Deet's face dropped as he looked over toward the G-man. He couldn't help but remember the sweet dish but couldn't imagine her as a threat to anyone, let alone her boss.

"She was the first to realize what Acker was up to when, during the course of her duties, she misfiled some papers and accidentally came across some of those incriminating letters. She called and gave us the tip, and when you told us about his wanting you to deliver *scaffolding* from Cleveland, that gave us the opening we really needed."

"Well, I'm glad you came when you did, or I'd been dumped off the viaduct."

"Your country owes you a great debt of gratitude." Smith got up from the chair. "For one, don't concern yourself with your medical bills. We've already instructed the hospital to bill the bureau for all your care." He carried the chair back to its original spot before turning back toward Deet. "As far as Ricky goes, under these circumstances, I do believe we'll be able to convince the judge to side with probation. I also understand you'll be off work for some time. I will see what accommodations the bureau can procure to assist your family and—"

A gaggle of voices and rushing footsteps obscured the rest of Smith's words as he melted into the background as Trudi, Ricky, Louie, and Lacey surged into the small room.

"Dietrich, *meine* Dietrich!" Trudi, nearly collapsing on her oldest son, planted kisses on his cheeks and forehead.

His mother relented just long enough for Deet to see Uncle Louie shake Agent Smith's hand and hear him thanking the lawman for rescuing his nephew. Meanwhile, Ricky patted his left shoulder and beamed down upon him. "Smooth deal, Deet, really smooth."

As his mother bent down for a second round of smothering, he felt the softest touch envelop his right hand as the edge of his bed along his leg stirred, counteracting the weight of his mother at his shoulder. When Trudi declared a truce to her embraces, Deet focused on Lacey seated on the side of his bed.

She didn't waste the opportunity, sliding through a temporary gap between Trudi and Deet. "It's so good to have you back. I love you." Her personal whisper transitioned into a deep kiss.

In that instant, everything was right in Deet's world, at least until the return of the doctor moments later.

"I'm sorry, but all these people must vacate this area at once. This is in complete violation of all medical protocol. This young man must have complete and utter rest for the next two weeks. No physical, mental, or *emotional* exertion of any kind. Do you understand, young lady?"

Epilogue

Akron

April 1939

“ Whatever it is, I hopes it don't take long.” Sweat dripped off Theo Dixon's face as he trudged up the steps toward Plant One's second floor. “It's Saturday morning, and I's got places to go and things to do.”

“Me, too,” Deet said as he followed Dixon's shadow. “I'm supposed to have breakfast with my girl's father. I'm going to ask his permission to marry her.”

Dixon stopped and turned around. “Jenkins, you *do* have big plans. We need to make this short for sure.”

“Not too short.” The two continued up the staircase. “I'm hoping this is about Consolidated wanting your design for a roller guard.”

A smiling Nate Benson walked through his office doorway and welcomed both workers with an offer of coffee and doughnuts. “Have some java and a doughnut before you sit down, men.”

Dixon and Deet gave each other the side eye as they each poured a cup from a pot on a burner, which sat on a small side table against the wall of the overcrowded office. Jenkins couldn't help but think that mill workers don't usually get invited to such a wing ding, even if the party was in the space of a closet.

“You've probably guessed the purpose of my wanting to talk to you.” Benson ran his fingers over the part of his brownish hair as he took his coffee behind his desk. He sat down, erect with his hands interlocked on his desk. “Simply put, Consolidated is very interested in the roller guard idea.”

Dixon stopped chewing on his doughnut and grinned.

Deet swallowed his coffee and smiled. “That's great.”

"Now, Theo, I just want to be clear on this since it's been since last summer that you gentlemen brought this idea to the company's attention." Benson sipped some coffee. "Theo, this *is your* idea . . . that is, you created the concept of the roller guard, correct?"

Dixon bobbed his head. "Yes, sir . . . yes, sir. Too many men gettin' hurt."

Benson nodded once. "Alright, and Deet, you were responsible for drawing the actual design which was handed over to the company for review. Right?"

Deet looked over at Theo, whose brow furrowed and whose grin had vanished, replaced by a look of caution. "Yeah, I drew up plans, but the specs came from Theo." His last bite of doughnut stuck halfway down to his stomach. "I mean I just drew what Theo created."

"Good." Benson nodded again. "Just wanted to make it all crystal clear. Well, Theo, most of what the company has directed me to offer is directed toward you."

Dixon inhaled, put down his cup, and wiped his mouth with the sleeve of his work shirt.

"The company is prepared to offer you five hundred dollars for the rights to patent the roller guard." Benson exhaled and held up a hand. "If you accept that offer, you relinquish ownership of the roller guard to the company."

"Five hundred is a chunk of money." Dixon looked at Benson before making eye contact with Deet. "How long before the guards are put in place?"

"The brass thinks they can produce them while the patent process is ongoing. Their guess would be late summer or early fall."

Dixon scratched the grayish stubble on his chin. "If I's don't agree?"

"You are welcome to get the guard manufactured by yourself through some other firm as well as working on the patent process yourself."

"That's a half years pay." The bristles on his chin straightened as Dixon slid his hand over them, muttering to himself before looking at Deet for guidance.

With the fingers of his hands entwined, Deet leaned toward Dixon. "It's a good bit of dough."

"There is one more thing," Benson interrupted their pondering. "Theo, the company would also promote you to tire builder."

Theo Dixon's eyes welled as he looked at Deet, who nodded with a friendly smile. "When do I start?"

"Midnight shift, Monday."

"Deal." Theo shook Benson's hand.

Deet stood up in anticipation of leaving for his breakfast rendezvous with Gene Frazier, Lacey's dad.

"There's just one more item," Benson said as he sat back down, "and it concerns you, Deet."

"Me?" Deet sat down again. The portion of doughnut, which was earlier stuck in his throat, squirmed in his stomach.

"The brass was impressed by the detail and quality of your rendering of the guard's design. Would you be interested in becoming a draftsman's apprentice? You'd be working across Market on the second floor, and even as an apprentice over there, you'd be making more than in your present position."

"Th-h-hat . . . be s-s-well." The words came out of a saucer-eyed Deet's mouth like a slow leak from a punctured tire as he shook his superior's hand.

"Well, great, it's all settled. Deet, Mister McArdle will be expecting you in the Drafting Department on the second floor of the building across the street on Monday morning at eight. You'll be working a regular eight-hour day."

As Dixon walked alongside Jenkins down the steps toward the first floor and a side exit, he carried a five-hundred-dollar voucher, which he'd get cashed across Market in the company's cashier office, as well as his signed copy of the roller guard's transfer of rights of ownership. Walking out toward the sidewalk on Market Street, he turned to Deet with an outstretched hand. "I guess this be good-bye."

Deet grabbed his hand while placing his other hand on Theo's shoulder. "For now, yes, but we'll be bound to run into each other sooner than later."

Just as their clutch broke, Dixon hesitated with a forefinger in the air. "You know what?"

Deet offered a blank stare while his head shook.

"We both be *Travelers* now." Dixon roared with laughter.

It was the first time Deet had ever heard Theo laugh with abandon.

****

Aboard the Swedish freighter "First Star" in the Atlantic

Late August 1939

The higher Hugo Geller climbed the ladder out of the bilge, the less noxious the air became. As assistant to Sven, the ship's engineer, Hugo helped clean out the bottom of the ship of the accumulated solution of salt water, petroleum, diesel fuel, and any other liquid, which escaped its containment system. Most importantly, he carried Sven's tools which the engineer used to maintain the bilge pump. The pump vacuumed the bilge's bottom and funneled the toxic mix out into the ocean. Hugo would mop up the residue.

Having finished just such a detail, he returned to the galley for a midday meal of boiled potatoes and cabbage along with some milk. As a stowaway, he felt fortunate to have found a position on the ship. As soon as the Statue of Liberty vanished on the horizon, he came out from underneath the canvass shell of one of the lifeboats. When confronted by the captain, Hugo stood at attention and told a convincing story of how he'd received word his mother was on her deathbed and that he had no other means of returning to Germany, the port of Bremen being the ship's destination.

The truth was that at nineteen, Hugo became a runaway. With the German American Bund in disrepute and collapse, he'd viewed the Silver Shirts as their likely successor. His relative anonymity at their warehouse as a part-time employee allowed him to escape the dragnet after Jack Acker's arrest in Akron. With war imminent, his desperation to help Hitler against the Bolsheviks led him to hop a freight train to New York and head toward its harbor. His parents were left to console themselves, given his understood goal of fighting communists for the *Der Fuehrer.*

Some of the twenty men on board spoke a bit of German, while others knew some English. When he wasn't in the bilge, he swabbed decks, cleaned toilets, and peeled vegetables for the chief cook, a surly Russian whom he despised. For a ten-day journey, it was a small price to pay in order to join the Nazi assault on communism.

A three-day-old copy of the *New York Times*, crumpled and fringed with dirt and grime, lay abandoned on the table. Hugo glanced at the headline just as the Russian cook dropped a bowl of steaming potato chunks and cabbage in front of him.

Germany and Russia Sign 10-Year Non-Aggression Pact

With the cook's breath on his neck, Hugo expelled the only word he could with the air sucked out of him. "What?"

"*Da,* that Hitler schmart. He no poke the bear." The cook cackled as he walked into the ship's pantry.

"*Scheise! Scheise! Scheise!*" Hugo beat his forehead with balled fists.

Author's Note

Divisions in American society are no secret. Conservative/liberal, far right/far left, religious/secular, straight/gay . . . the stark contrasts abound. When politicians seek to exploit those divisions, they risk deepening the chasm for their own short-term gain. Because of their inherent constitutional freedoms, American citizens have often agitated against each other throughout the nation's history.

As an author, I've enjoyed researching and writing historical fiction novels in which an older teen protagonist comes of age in a divisive era, one in which difficult decisions are foisted upon him. In *Hobbadehoy Rising*, an orphan must learn to trust during the turbulent antebellum period of the 1850's. In some ways, *American Brush-Off* could be considered the follow-up to *Working the Angles*, as it's set during World War II, where fear and innuendo combine to intern legal German aliens and German Americans.

The intent of *Working the Angles* is to engage the reader with another era in American history with its society torn by different ideologies. It was never designed to disparage any particular business, and with that in mind, the names of all the rubber companies mentioned within it were fictionalized, as were the characters. Yet, the framework of this novel is built on the historical record. Not unique to any one company, all rubber factories shared dangerous, dirty conditions. Those accidents mentioned within the story came from documented accounts. The 1930's was an important decade for the growth of unions, especially after the Wagner Act (1935) recognized the right of workers to unionize and engage in collective bargaining. The German American Bund (representing a small fraction of ethnic Germans in America) made a great deal of noise lauding Adolph Hitler and attempting to cast him as a German George Washington in order to take advantage of the public's wariness of communism. Various domestic political groups hated democracy and looked to reign over its hopeful demise. The 1938 riot/strike on Market Street did happen, and, at best, race relations were tense. Black rubber workers, like Theo Dixon, were kept out of the URW until the World War II era. Finally, although not known by its very recognizable name at the time, Alcoholics Anonymous was, indeed, started in Akron in 1935.

For a list of sources I used in writing this novel, please visit my website, www.maxwilli.com and click under *Resources*. Scroll down to the listing for *Working the Angles*.

If you enjoyed *Working the Angles,* your positive review on Amazon or Goodreads would be greatly appreciated.

Other Books by Max Willi Fischer

Hobbadehoy Rising

American Brush-Off

Revelations from the Dead:
Chronicles of the Night Waster

The Reformation of Nate Adare

www.historiumpress.com

www.historiumpress.com/max-willi-fischer